Novel Hearts

A special Edition

Write More Publications

Valentine's Day Anthology

I0618856

Featured Authors:

Rebecca Boucher, Molly Bryant,

Stephanie Greenhalgh, Theresa Oliver,

Jennifer Paquette, Amber White,

Elaine White and J.S. Wilsoncroft

Write More Publications
Kissimmee, Florida

Authors tell stories every day. Oftentimes, our characters come alive, taking on personas of their own. Our characters live not only on the pages of our books, but within the pages of our hearts, as well.

We, the authors of Write More Publications, came together and decided that we wanted to create stories to share the characters of our books with our readers, as we just couldn't let them go. All of the books within which these characters reside are published by or coming soon from Write More Publications, unless otherwise stated.

May these characters come alive for you as they have for us, and give a message of love to all who read them. This book is dedicated to our readers, whom our characters live for.

The stories that you will read within these pages are from many genres—fantasy, paranormal, romance and horror—creating a Valentine's Day anthology that steps out of the box. We hope you enjoy reading …

Novel Hearts

Table of Contents

The River Liffey
By: Rebecca Boucher

For Dad

The characters in this story are based on the book

Hunting the Moon

By: Rebecca Boucher

I remember a Celtic legend my mom used to tell me in my youth. It was a favorite story she would pull out every Valentine's Day, becoming her way of showing that gifts were not always monetary. It also reminded her of how she met my dad.

Dad never was a favorite of Grandma. It was a story of two lovers determined to be together, but held apart. The lovers were from warring villages. One was a druid, but Mom sometimes changed the villages from year to year; however, the gist of the story was the same. The lovers had to meet under the cover of darkness in the forest or by the sea to exchange words of love and small gifts. The two were inseparable, but fate was cruel. One night their love was discovered by a priestess from one of the villages. Their punishment was fierce. Under penalty of death, they were warned never to see each other again, but the couple could not be deterred. They refused and fled together to the edge of the sea.

In Celtic times families were identified by the color of their village painted on a rock and engraved with their name or family symbol. The rock was meant to follow the person wherever they traveled, and when they died, it was to be cast in the sea. The name on the stone was their identity for eternity. The young lovers rejected their stones, leaving them behind. Instead, they created a new one, a single stone with both of their names engraved upon it as a symbol of their love. Fearful that they would be caught, the young lovers cast themselves into the sea with their stone, saying these words, "May we ever be united in love and hidden as long as this stone hides in deep waters."

My mother was always careful to point out that the young lovers were never seen again and neither was the stone. By the time I was in high school, I had heard it so many times I began to roll my eyes and flee the room whenever Mom started telling it again. It was always the one time her Irish borough came out. But now, as I sat in a airplane bound for Dublin with my husband of two years by my side and two urns of ashes under my seat, I began to finally realize what Mom was trying to tell me.

"Do you realize we will be in Dublin for Valentine's Day?" The soothing voice of my husband, Daemon, brought me from my thoughts. "Which, coincidently, is three weeks before your due date. I really hope we make it back to the states before the baby is born."

Instinctively, I placed my hand on my large belly as the plane banked to the right. So far, the flight had been uneventful, but this last leg over the English Channel was filled with turbulence. "You worry too much, Daemon. The doctor said I had plenty of time, and that I could go. Besides, I'm traveling with my own personal doctor anyway." I reached over and placed my hand on his leg, giving him a reassuring squeeze.

"I have almost one more year of residency to go and then this doctor is all yours, but in the meantime, I'm still questioning my sanity in letting me be talked into this trip. I mean we could have held on to the ashes for a while, it's not like they will ever know." I lifted my hand and swatted him on the arm. "Oww, what the hell was that for?"

I pursed my lips into a pout. "That's for speaking ill of the deceased. I made a promise and I intend to keep it." Just then, the baby kicked me in the ribs and I jumped a little.

"I saw that. See? Even baby thinks it was wrong for you to hit me," he said with a sly smile.

I smiled at Daemon and rested my head on his shoulder. I never got tired of being close to this man. "Well, it's not like Dublin is known for its romance or anything. I mean the inn we are staying at prides itself as being 'close to the action and the night scene'," I replied, doing my best to impersonate my mother's Irish borough.

Daemon laughed. "Oh, I beg to differ, my sweet. I was just reading that the relics of St. Valentine are buried under the Whitefriar Street Church. Did you know that Valentine's Day was originally the pagan festival of fertility?" he asked, as he leaned over and kissed my belly. "And you, my sweet, are very fertile these days."

I had to laugh. "Very fertile? What am I, soil?"

He nuzzled my belly again. "Nice way to change the subject by the way. I still think it was risky to take this trip, but I know what the promise means to you." I closed my eyes and snuggled deep into the crook of Daemon's neck. Of all the things we faced together—homicidal fairies, revenge minded ghosts, shape shifters and lost friends—there never was any doubt in my mind that he was on my side.

Then, a thought occurred to me. "We never took a honeymoon, Daemon. We can use this as an opportunity to be young lover's. Does it say anything in your guide book about Valentine's Day festivities and all that goopy, sappy stuff?" A large yawn punctuated the end of my question.

Daemon laughed. "Why don't you take a little snooze before the plane lands."

~ 7 ~

I nodded at his suggestion and closed my eyes, taking in one last, sweet smell of all that is Daemon.

When the plane landed in Dublin, we are greeted by gray skies and frozen drizzle. We easily cleared customs. As Daemon carried our bags, I held the woven tote that housed the urns. Actually, I was surprised that they weren't heavier. Until now, I felt a strange kind of detachment from the whole adventure, but as my feet touched the ground outside the airport, and I admired Dublin, I felt a lump in my throat. In my hands I held all that was left of my greatest friend, who was also my greatest adversary. My quest was clear; to cast her and her lover deep into the ocean.

"You ok, sweet?" I was brought out of my reverie by Daemon's voice and worried eyes.

I gave him a weak smile, then replied, "Yeah, just jetlag and the baby's kicking up a storm. I'll be better once we're settled in the hotel."

"Ok, let's call a cab and get this show on the road." Daemon raised his hand to wave down the next cab he saw. It stopped quickly and he settled me in before placing our bags in the trunk, but I clutched the tote in my lap. I instantly fall in love with the cranky old man behind the wheel.

He was stereotypical Irish and very opinionated. "Once your lass is settled, I think there's plenty of room for her satchel in the back." I saw his ice blue eyes watch me intently in the rear view mirror the whole time Daemon was placing our bags in the trunk.

"No, I'm holding on to this one. I'm fine … really."

He gave me one more look over. "Are you sure? In your condition, I don't want the baby being born in my cab."

I look to Daemon for help. "She's fine, sir. We're headed to the Castle Hotel. Do you know it?"

The kind old man slid the car into drive and pulled away from the curb, fighting the airport traffic. "Aye, I do, sir. It's a bit rundown, but comfortable enough to suit your needs. Clean and orderly. Can't ask for much more, can ya?"

Daemon hid a chuckle. "No sir."

The old man moved cautiously down the narrow streets. "What are you two doing in Dublin during such a cranky weather time? You must be planning on visiting Whitefriar Street Church and the whole St. Valentine's hoop la, aren't ya?"

I shifted the tote bag to the seat between Daemon and I. "Actually we came here to fulfill a promise, but we just saw that in the guide book. Is it worth it?"

The cabdriver absently rubbed the stubble on his chin and screwed up his eyes. "If you are in for that romantic babble. At my age, I have no use for it. There are far better things to do in the Temple Bar area with the pubs and even the art galleries, but there are always the pubs, mind ya," he said, punctuating the last bit of information with a deep throaty laugh, giving the impression that it was some private joke we weren't in on.

I looked out the window through the fog and gloom and made note of the river beside the road. "Does that river go through the whole city?"

"Aye, it does. That is the River Liffey. It cuts Dublin in half, separating the Southside from the north. If you are looking for the Whitefriar Church and the Temple Bar area, that's the south side. The Halfpenny Bridge is a good pedestrian bridge close to your hotel. Walking would be the way to go."

I reached for Daemon's hand and continued to stare at the river, as my mother's legend ran through my head. "And it flows all the way to the ocean?"

The old man gave me a weird look. "Don't most rivers lass?"

"Yeah, I suppose they do," Daemon cut in. "It looks kind of dingy."

"Well, sir, they have cleaned it up the last couple decades, but it's the peat bogs, mind ya. The river originated from the bogs. That there is what gives Guniess its trademark taste … water from the Liffey … but I don't suppose the lass will be sampling much of that now, will she?"

I shook my head and closed my eyes. The cab ride was taking much too long for my taste. Bless my husband's soul as he tried to change the subject again. "Do you get much snow in Dublin?"

"Nah, we mainly get cold, icy winters. Snow won't last long here. You don't see too much snow on the Liffey. Ahh here's you hotel."

I was relieved when the cab finally came to a stop. A moment later, I was standing on the curb, watching silently as Dameon paid the fare. My mind was focused on the river, thinking that it might be just the place to lay them to rest, to sprinkle their ashes from the bridge and let them float peacefully down the Liffey. Maybe I could find a stone to cast into the river with them. "You ready, sweet? Let's get you inside to rest. I really don't like all this traveling for you," Daemon's voice brought me from my revive.

"Yeah, I'm ready when you are."

With that, he took our bags and the tote from my hand and carried them toward the front doors of the hotel. We entered the hotel shaking the cold mist from our hair.

True to the old man's word, the hotel was rundown, but comfortable. I couldn't find anything wrong with our room, and I was happy to see that our windows looked out over the Liffey. Sometime later, I stood watching the cold rain fall, when suddenly I felt Daemon's arms around me and his lips on my neck. He loved my pregnant body and his hands roamed over it under the warm terrycloth of my bathrobe. I was lost in the moment, content to stay here forever … lost in the cold rain and welcoming warmth of Dublin, and lost in the arms of my husband. Since we arrived early this morning we were in our room, making love and sleeping, lost in a fairy tale moment, savoring every caress.

"We should eat," I finally said, unable to ignore the hunger pangs. I turned to face him and buried my face into his chest. "Must we? I don't want to leave this cocoon of happiness you have spun me."

"Oh man, you are so sappy. It must be the pregnancy ..." Damian said, chuckling.

"Or the company. Can you get food and bring it back?" I asked.

He turned to face me, sliding his naked body next to mine, pulling me into his arms. "But then I would have to get dressed, Lilly."

I laughed at his theatrics as I got up and threw his pants at him. "Hurry. The baby's hungry."

"Yes, my bonnie lass. Your food will grace the table sooner than you can say Blarney Stone."

Rolling my eyes at his horrible accent, I crossed the room and adjust the tote for the tenth time, checking the contents, then stowed them safely back inside. I jumped when I felt Daemon's arms surround me. "Maybe we should take care of that tomorrow," he whispered gently into my ear, referring to the urns. "Then we can spend the rest of the week touring Dublin without the weight of the "fae" hanging over us." I nodded as he continued. "And I was thinking we could go to the ceremony at the Whitefriar Church and renew our vows in the classic Celtic tradition in front of St. Valentine."

Tying the robe around me, I walked back to the window. "I was thinking that the Liffey would be perfect. We could find that bridge the cab driver was telling us about and sprinkle the ashes from there."

Daemon nodded, kissing me on the cheek. "Sounds perfect. You know, I admire what you're doing. It takes a big person to forgive and then fly halfway around the world to forget."

"I'm not forgetting, Daemon. I could never forget either of them. Their actions led us to each other. What I'm trying to do now is close the chapter; to make peace before the baby is born." I cleared my throat and brushed a single tear from my eye before he could see it. "Now, where is that food you promised me?"

He released my waist and pulled his wool coat over a t-shirt, laughing at me. He was still is the most gorgeous man I had ever seen, especially with his golden brown hair tousled from our day in bed. "Be right back. You sure you'll be fine here alone?" he asked, then ran out the door as I tossed a pillow at him. Instead, it hit the closed door and slid to the floor.

Sometime after midnight, I woke up. I'm uncomfortable and whatever dream was screaming in my head spooked me. I looked over at Daemon, but he was sleeping so peacefully that I didn't want to wake him, for fear he would think I was in labor. So, I rose from the bed and walked across the room to sit in a chair by the window overlooking the quaint street. In spite of the late hour, sporadic crowds walked down the street, chanting and singing, followed by quiet couples lost in their own little worlds of love. I smiled and wrapped my hands around my belly, softly humming to the baby. A faint whisper brought me from my thoughts. "Penny for your thoughts."

I looked over at the bed and Daemon was still sleeping. "Who said that?"

A petite woman stepped from the shadows dressed in early fifties finery. "I did. I'm Deirdre and you are Lilly. Correct?"

"Crap! Why do they always find me?" I asked, as she stepped toward me.

"Did you say something?"

"Not really. Do I know you?" I asked. Her skin was so translucent that I could see through her, but she was beautiful in a classic Irish way, as if she stepped out of one of the paintings in the Gallery. She almost reminded me of Kat.

"To quote you, not really, but I heard of you. I was told you could see our kind; that you are sympathetic. I was sent to watch over your … cargo … shall we call it?" She stopped next to my chair and lowered herself to the floor and wrapped her arms around her knees. Then, she leaned her chin down onto them.

"So, do you guys have some kind of otherworldly telephone system?" I asked, curious.

Her laugh reminded me of church bells. "No, I wouldn't say that, but we have some friends in common among the angels. Rita knew you were making the trip."

"And by 'cargo' I assume you mean the ashes. Why are you interested in them?" After I asked, I looked over at the bed. Daemon hadn't stirred.

She followed my gaze. "Let's not wake him. Well, Lilly, you see, we among the angels have a vested interest in those ashes. Kat had fae blood, not enough to make her immortal, but enough to make her soul valuable. If those ashes do not rest at the bottom of the sea, Morgana might be able to gather them. She is still searching for power."

The baby suddenly kicked me, a gentle reminder of why I made this trip. "But what we don't understand, Lilly, is why you brought the other ashes."

I rub my belly with one hand to sooth the baby and ran the other through my hair. "Why am I lucky enough to see you guys everywhere I go? The other ashes ... well ... are just something I need to do. I understand now why Kat did what she did and I'm grateful. That's why I agreed to do this. It only seemed fitting to send her off for eternity with the only man she ever truly loved."

Deirdre rested her cold hand on mine. Once again I was struck with the realization that I could feel her. What boggled our minds when Daemon and I struggled with Aaron's ghost was that they were substance, mixed with an angelic glow. "Then you are certainly living up to all I was told. Your forgiveness knows no limits. Your compassion is unequal in other mortal beings."

I scoff. "Well, I don't know about that, but I do know we were once friends. And I can certainly do this final act for her. Will the Liffey be acceptable?"

Deirdre stood and walked toward the door. "I think the Liffey will be perfect. It flows to the sea and what better way to honor Kat's Irish roots and fae blood?" Then, she turned as her light grew faint. "Be well, dear Lilly. Bless the child in your womb, and harm none." With that, she walked into the shadows from which she came.

The baby nudged me with a swift kick to the ribs. "I get it you want to go back to bed." Leave it to me to be followed by ghosts. I didn't know the whole story of Kat and the fae, but I was promised answers when I needed them. The whole encounter left me feeling strangely melancholy and reflective. Before I crossed the room to go back to bed, I glanced out the window and made a note of the light snow that was falling. "I thought it didn't snow in Dublin."

We woke the next morning and the street outside the hotel was covered by slightly more snow than a dusting. Icy rain fell softly onto the ground, giving everything the appearance of being covered by diamonds. The street was eerily quiet compared to the jovial pedestrians I saw last night. As I lay in the bed with Daemon's warm arms wrapped around me, I recounted the conversation I had with my midnight visitor last night. "She was calm and beautiful. At least three out of our four ghosts have been helpful," I said with a shrug. He chuckled into my neck, leisurely stroking my back. "But she didn't shed much light on things. Actually, she was kind of cryptic if you ask me. We got more info out of the craggy cab driver." Then I thought of the ashes, knowing what we had to do. "Let's do it today. Let's go on over to the Halfpenny Bridge and release their ashes into the Liffey. Then we can spend the rest of the day in a quiet pub and go to the church tomorrow and renew our vows." I spoke fast, wanting to get my plan out of my head before Daemon asked me the same question Deirdre had. Why had I brought Aaron's ashes too?

"Wow. You said that with such conviction, but there's one problem with your plan, fair lady," Daemon replied.

I rolled my eyes since he can't see my face. "And what is that?"

"When I went down to get our breakfast earlier, the front desk clerk was telling another guest that almost everything was closed for the day. Her exact words were 'good luck finding a cab.'" He kissed the nape of my neck. "So, it looks like I get another day relaxing in bed with my Bonnie Lass."

I shook my head. "So, let's walk instead. We're hardy New Englanders. Don't tell me you're afraid of a little snow. The bridge is only about three blocks from here."

I felt his body stiffen before he turned me within his arms. "Lilly, you're three weeks away from delivering and you're in a foreign country. You think I'm going to let you walk in an ice storm? Besides, what's the hurry?"

A single tear rolled silently down my cheek. "I need to release them, Daemon. I need to let them both go before this baby gets here, before we go see the relics of St. Valentine. I have to make my peace with my friend."

He stares at me long and hard. "But why Aaron's ashes?"

I thought for what seemed like an eternity, then replied, "He was the only man she ever truly loved. I saw it in her eyes when he died, only I didn't realize it until later … when she hated me for betraying him. But how can you betray someone who's dead? Really, she was the one who betrayed him and herself when she walked away from what they could have had. So, I think the only way to give him his final peace and hers to escape the fae is to set them free … together. Let me do this, Daemon. In a sense, he set me free to find you when he died. I want to do the same for them."

Daemon looked at me in silence, but his eyes were as wet as mine. We both jumped, as the baby kicked so hard that my stomach lurched. The outline of his little foot appeared on the skin of my belly. "Well, I guess baby agrees with you, but Lilly, if I see you slip or getting cold we're turning right back around and coming back to this hotel." I grinned from ear to ear and jumped out of bed. "Where are you going, my sweet?"

I laughed at him as I pulled on my robe. "To shower and dress. Let's get this show on the road."

Forty minutes later, we were walking in the deserted Temple Bar area. Its cobblestone streets were a mixture of old and new architecture packed closely together. A few other couples are out, as well, braving the cold wind. The covering of snow mixed with the freezing drizzle gave the area a surreal feel. The buildings became brownstone ice castles. I took note of the patrons in the pubs laughing over their pints and wished I was in one, holding a steaming cup of Earl Gray. It didn't take long until I saw it, spanning the gray Liffey connecting the south and north sides of Dublin. The Halfpenny Bridge was a beautiful structure of cold steel gently arched over the water beneath. Graceful Victorian light fixtures were evenly spaced on either side of the bridge, topped with glowing orbs of white. It certainly was a pedestrian bridge, with a walkway barely five feet across on either side. It didn't look like it could accommodate a large tour group. Daemon wrapped his arm around my waist as we start up the incline.

"It doesn't seem overly slippery, but I'm not taking any chances. Go slowly, Lilly."

I smiled at him. It was nice to have someone watch over me. I missed this closeness with the endless hours he was spending in his residency. "Do you know how much this trip was worth it?" I stopped about seven feet into our climb.

"Yes, you told me at least a hundred times," Daemon replied, staring into my eyes as he kissed my forehead.

"And not just for that," I said, gesturing at the tote holding the ashes, "but for this … for us. Having you all to myself, spending the day in your arms and the night wrapped up in sheets, and for being in this classic city with the man who saved me from myself."

He leaned in and pressed his lips to mine, encircling me within both of his arms as he threaded his gloved hand into my hair, knocking my hat off into the snow. I took in every breath of his kiss, not caring about the cold gray sky that surrounded us, then he took a step back. "Well, then, let's finish this up and get our asses back to that hotel."

As we continued to the middle of the bridge, I saw another person walking toward us from the north side. His gate was slower than ours and he walked close to the railing, holding on. As we drew closer, I recognized him. "Daemon, I think that's the cab driver."

He squinted into the mist that seemed to be slowing down. "I think your right. That's weird."

"Well, hopefully we can get this done and be respectful without having to engage in idle chit chat." I take the tote from his hands and set it down next to the railing, as Daemon's hand rested on my shoulder. "I would give you your privacy and wait over there, but I really don't like how slippery this bridge is."

"Your such a worry wart. It's okay; I need you here." My mind wondered back to that autumn night in the cemetery and how glad I was that he followed me. His presence always gave me comfort. I reached into the tote and took out Kat's urn. The cold waters of the Liffey swirled beneath us, dark and deep, promising an eternity at the bottom of its reaches. Then, I twisted off the lid, trying not to glance at the contents, racking my brain for one of my mother's Gaelic blessings and, surprisingly, remember one. *"Ar dheas Dego raibh a anam.* May her soul be on God's right hand." I tipped the urn and watched as the ashes streamed down into the Liffey and were swallowed up immediately by the churning water. I was surprised that the stiff wind didn't catch any of the ashes and blow them wayward. "And please don't be one of the ghosts who comes back to see us," I added. Daemon gave me a wink. "What?" I asked, feigning innocence. "Don't you think we've had enough of them?" I reached back into the tote and lifted out Aaron's ashes. "Here I am, letting you go once again. Hopefully, this time you'll rest in peace and finish your journey." Tears were streaming down my face, mixed with the sleet that had returned. I methodically took the cover off the urn and tipped the contents over the side of the bridge to follow Kat's down into the abyss. "May you see her in heaven." With that, the last of his ashes drift down. Then, Daemon took the urn from my hand and returned it to the tote, as we watched the water swirl below.

Suddenly, a rough voice brought us out of our reverie. "Are you not the young couple from my cab? What brings you to stand on the Halfpenny Bridge on such a God forsaken day?" the old man asked.

I was sure that he witnessed what had just transpired, but I could detect the tone of someone fishing for more information. Thank God Daemon took the lead. "Just fulfilling someone's last wishes," Daemon said, stepping closer to me to wrap me in his arms.

The old man cleared his throat roughly. "Tristan Callaghan's the name. Don't think I introduced myself the other day." Then he glanced at the bag containing the urns. "Anyone I know?" He really was too curious.

"No, just some friends," Daemon replied cautiously.

The old man was dressed like he just came from a formal affair, except for his hat, which was well worn and thread bare. It was the kind of hat that you see cabbies wear in old movies. I found myself trying to guess his age, but years of hard living and drinking seemed to have marred his face. Acne scars covered his face and his rosy cheeks were that of an alcoholic. His slight frame looked strong, though, as he stood tall and stiff. He took a flask from his pocket, twisted off the cap and took a long sip. Afterward, he silently held the bottle up to Daemon, who shook his head no. "Really? You two made the trip from America to deposit friends in the Liffey? Everyone should be as lucky to have such friends. *Is maith an scathan suil charad,* a friend's eye is a good mirror. I see you two are very loyal." He punctuates this with another sip from his flask. I am sure my face betrayed what I was feeling. I'm so easy to read.

"Actually, one was my first husband, and the other was my best friend who I found out was in love with him. It goes beyond loyalty."

Daemon pressed his face into my hair and whispered, "Why are you telling him this Lilly?"

But I wave him off, feeling conviction in me from some unknown force. The words rush out of me before I could stop myself. Something inside told me this old man was a kindred spirit. "Do you know anything about fairies?" Daemon grunted and dropped his head.

The old man nodded, taking a step closer. "I dropped the ashes of my own dear wife, God rest her soul, from this very same bridge nearly twenty years ago. She was a believer; a true Celtic lady of old. She kept in close communion with the fae. Some of those little devils were beasts, to say the least. Lost many a cat to them." Then, he took a well worn locket from his pocket and opened it and studied it closely before he handed it to me. "That's my lass." I looked into the locket and a beautiful young woman was staring back at me. I tried to remember where I saw her face before, but I shrugged it off, closed the locket and caught the inscription on the back, *Not all who wander are lost,* before handing the it back to him. "She was beautiful."

He laughed as he tucked the watch safely back into his pocket. "Beautiful, but a spitfire. I lost count of how many times the priest tried to cure her of consorting with magic. Everyone in the neighborhood came to her when they needed to be rid of some aliment or needed some potion. She learned all she could from the fae." He studied me for a long moment, as the rain started to fall heavily and the wind blew with more force. I could feel something in my bones.

Daemon leaned in and whispered into my ear, "We really should be going." But I shot him a look that asked for one more second.

The old man looked at me intently. "Tell me, lass, you believe in the fae folk? Have you seen them?"

I looked into the old man's earnest eyes, wondering how much I should admit. But then I took a deep breath and replied, "I was told last night that my friend might have had some fae in her, if that's possible, but my experience is more with ghosts."

He looked out over the river. "I was just wondering if they were over in the states. You know, it was St. Valentine's Day twenty years tomorrow that I set my Deirdre free here. I just hope someone sends me to meet her someday. if I had friends like you."

Suddenly, my stomach felt as if it had been poked with a hot iron. "Did you say Deirdre?" I took a step away from Daemon closer to the old man.

"Yes, that was my good wife's name. A stronger woman you will never meet."

I cautiously placed my gloved hand on his arm, ignoring the concern on my own husband's face. "I have met her. Last night she told me I needed to do this soon to keep my friend's remains safe from the fae. Her ghost came to me." No wonder the picture in the watch looked so familiar to me.

His face softened as a cold tear slid slowly down his cheek mingling with the wind driven rain. "You can see her, too? You can see ghosts? Then, I'm not crazy?"

I tightened my grip on his arm. "No, Tristan, you're not. The coincidence is unfathomable, but she must have had other reasons for me to come to the bridge today. I can't explain it all, but my first husband was a ghost also. He almost lost his soul to the evil fae goddess Morgana." My voice trailed off. Choked by tears, I could not go on.

Daemon took my hand. "We really should go, my sweet. It was a pleasure to meet you Mr. Callaghan."

But as we turned to go, Tristan Callaghan reached out his hand and grabbed my arm. "Wait, I'd like you to have this." He reached into his pocket and placed a locket into my gloved hand.

I tried to give it back to him. "I can't."

He shook his head. "You must ... please ... Deirdre would want you to have it, for the wee one. It was blessed by the pontiff. She hid her own magic in it. It must be why she wanted you to come." I took the locket, nodding my thanks and turned to go. Then, I heard his rough voice call out one final blessing to us as we made our way back across the Liffey, *"Nar laga Diathu,* may God never weaken you."

I sleep soundly that night, as dreams flood my mind ... beautiful dreams filled with color and light, and castles nestled in green fields filled with wild flowers. Among the fields walked a beautiful child, her dress was flowing gossamer and lace, her hands were filled with wild daisies. The child reached out to me and I swept her into my arms. Laughing, we fell onto the green grass and I noticed a locket hanging around her neck. It was Deirdre's locket on a thin thread of gold. But behind the castle walls lurked a pair of intent eyes, watching our every move. Although I knew we were protected by the power around us, I was still uneasy.

The next morning, I woke and my hand reached across the bed for Daemon, only to find cool empty sheets. I sat up drenched in a cold sweat. Even though the room was warm, I shivered. Then, my stomach lurched and a slight pain grabbed my back along with a twinge of a cramp, but the moment it came, it was gone. Hearing the water running in the shower, I knew where Daemon was. My mind wondered to the place I really don't want it to go. That wasn't a labor pain, was it? *Please, not today of all days,* I thought to myself. After all, we were going to the church to renew our vows, then Friday we would be back on a plane to the states. I sat quietly, watching the clock. By the time Daemon came out of the bathroom, I had no other pain, so I decided that it was better not to tell him.

"Well, hello, sleepy head. If we want to make it to that mass, then you'd better get a move on it," he said, as he walked over to the bed and placed a soft kiss on my cheek, but he knew something was wrong. "Are you okay?"

I stifled a cough and glanced up at him. "Never better, why?"

He raised an eyebrow at me. "You feel clammy and you're a little pale. Maybe we should stay here today and check on an
early flight?"

I swatted his arm away and swung my legs off the bed. "Nonsense. It's just a little hot in here. Look the sun finally came out."

He eyes me suspiciously. "Yes, barely."

"But it's the first time we've seen the sun since we've been in Ireland and I don't want to waste it," I replied.

"You sure your okay?" he asked, ignoring my enthusiasm.

I skipped a little toward the bathroom and grinned, ignoring the pain in my lower back. "Yep, and I hope you're ready by the time I'm out of the shower."

When we pulled up in front of the Whitefriar Street Church, I'm a little taken aback by how it looks. It could easily be mistaken for a school or business block, and the gray concrete did nothing to help it stand out from the other buildings around it. The only thing that denoted it as a house of worship was the golden statues and stained glass that grace the entrance. One of the stone columns by the door read, *Refuge of sinners, pray for us.* It certainly didn't prepare visitors for the beautiful opulence that greeted them when they walk in. We were greeted in the great vestibule by a young Carmelite Nun dressed in traditional robes. She handed us a program and directed us to the chapel of St. Valentine, where the blessings and mass were taking place, but Daemon took his time looking at a display of wedding pictures and a collage of portraits. "

Those are some of the couples blessed here over the years," the sister informed us in a thick Irish borough. "Like you, they came from near and far to see the relics of St. Valentine. It is a draw of old Dublin."

Daemon called out to me. "Lilly, look at this! It couldn't be him, could it?"

I walked across the room to stand next to him. He was pointing to a picture of a middle aged couple, prominently displayed in the middle of the collage. It was unmistakably them. "It's him, and that's Deirdre. There's no mistaking her. She looks just the same as she did when she came to me the other night."

The nun stepped closer. "You knew the Callaghans?"

I turned to face her. "Not really. Mr. Callaghan was our cab driver when we arrived. Then, we ran into him again on the Halfpenny Bridge yesterday and he told us about his wife."

Her face went pale. "That's impossible. Mr. Callaghan passed on two nights ago. He was a huge benefactor of the church. I never met his wife, as she passed on some time ago." Just then, another contraction hit me. The pain radiated across my lower belly and I stifled a sharp intake of breath.

Daemon jumped a mile. "Are you ok? What the hell was that? Oh, sorry sister."

I shot a sheepish look to the nun, then back at Daemon. "I'm fine; I just need to sit down. Let's go to the chapel, hon," I said, pulling him away, leaving the stunned nun standing in the hallway.

"Lilly, please tell me you just didn't have a contraction," he asked, concerned.

I stopped and lowered myself down into the nearest pew, suddenly very tired. "Well, I might have, but it was a quick one."

Daemon ran his hand through his hair and sat next to me in the pew. "And how many have you had?" he asked, going into his doctor mode.

I steadied myself for the scolding I knew he would give me. "This is only the second one. The first one was when I was in bed, so that was like two hours ago. I mean, there's nothing to worry about, right?" I asked. As I leaned back against the pew and closed my eyes, another round of pain gripped my belly and lower back. Even though I tried my best to hide it, Daemon knew what was going on.

He took my hand in both of his before he spoke. "Lilly, my sweet, please tell me that was not a contraction."

I opened my eyes and smiled at him the best I could. "Nope, no contraction here." The organ started to play and I smelled the incense as the altar boys lit the candles on the altar. The sudden surge of spicy sweet smell caused my stomach to lurch and I placed my hand over my mouth. *Please God, don't let me be sick in a church.*

Daemon took one look at my face and stood up. "That's it! We are getting out of here and high tailing it to the nearest hospital." He put his arm around my waist and helped me stand. I tried to protest, but was afraid that if I spoke, I would lose it as my stomach lurched.

As he led me from the chapel, we ran into the nun who met us in the foyer. "Sir, I beg your pardon, but the mass will be starting and his holiest the monsignor will ..."

"My wife is going into labor. I need to know the nearest hospital," Daemon said, cutting her off.

The sister took one look at my face and turned pale herself. "Rotunda Hospital is back across the Liffey. You'll need a cab. Please, sit down and I'll call one for you." She pointed to a bench and I gratefully lowered myself onto it.

"Daemon, can you please find me some water?"

He took one look at me and tried not to laugh. "Cab first, then water. That was two contractions in ten minutes. Are you sure you didn't have any others?" I tried to think back, and I didn't think so. Just then, another contraction hit, but this time my water broke right in the sacristy of the eighteenth century church in front of the poor unsuspecting nun.

I tried to answer him through my gritted teeth. "We have plenty of time for a first baby, right?"

Daemon tossed off his coat. I screamed out loud as another contraction hit me, and several things started to happen at once. The young nun produced a cell phone and called for an ambulance, and then her mother superior suddenly appeared, another couple entering the church stopped and made a makeshift wall around me, two other nuns came down and said that they were nurses, and the contractions wouldn't stop coming. It was then that I realized that my baby would be born in Ireland in the Whitefriar Street Church.

A lot of things started running through my mind. *What will my baby look like? Will the pain ever stop? Wow, I hope people don't remember how loud I'm screaming,* I thought. But I also had the feeling that someone was watching over me, besides the people clustered around me. It felt like a gentle hand was hovering just above me, whispering encouragement into my ear. I barely remembered the ambulance arriving, or the jarring ride through Dublin's narrow streets, but I do remember the soft voice singing. I remembered Daemon's feather soft kisses on my cheek, and I remembered the clouds parting and the sun shining on a cold February day in Ireland. And as my baby girl was laid on my chest and my husband held my hand, I saw my best friend Kat walk into the sun kissed part in the clouds, hand in hand, along with the last regrets of my past.

A few weeks later, we sat in the plane waiting for takeoff. My hand rested on Daemon's leg as he cradled little

Deirdre Katherine in his arms. It was a little disconcerting flying with a three week old infant, but we stayed in Dublin as long as we could. The sister's from the church were amazing, arranging for her baptism before we left and taking us under their wings. We had plenty of baby clothes and formula for the long trip home stashed in the tote under my seat. Deirdre's locket rested around my neck, waiting until she was old enough to wear it. Late the night before, I took one last walk across the Halfpenny Bridge and reflected next to the river Liffey. The bittersweet act of closure that had brought me to Dublin was nothing compared to the gift I was leaving with. As the cold water swirled below me, I said my final goodbyes to Kat and Aaron. Their own name stone was firmly planted at the bottom of that deep sea, as Daemon and I had placed it there.

Daemon's voice brought me back to the present. "Are you sad to be leaving?"

I felt the plane lift into the air and saw Dublin fade away beneath me. "No, I'm happy. Everything is as it should be."

The Twistedly True Nightmare of Ruby Hood
By: Stephanie Greenhalgh

The characters in this story are based on the book:

The Twistedly True Tale of Ruby Hood

By: Stephanie Greenhalgh

The young woman pursed her lips and wrinkled her nose as she stared at her reflection in the mirror. She stood behind an antique wooden vanity in her new room at her grandmother's house. The white cotton linen curtains bustled in the warm, September breeze, distracting her. Lost in thought, her eyes wandered, surveying her surroundings in the mirror. It was a little too pink and pretty for her taste. The girlieness of the room instinctually curled her lip, Elvis style. She caught the reflection of her grimace and laughed out loud before returning to her morning routine.

She pulled her long sun-streaked mane up into a ponytail, scowled, then let it down again. She ran her fingers through her blonde tresses to smooth them out. Finally, she pushed the sides behind her ears and scrutinized her own reflection. Her almond eyes focused on her scar. Most days she barely even noticed the slight scar under her left eye, but it caught her attention today. Was it her imagination or had her scar become more prominent since her arrival in Woodsville? She had been told it was a silly accident, but since returning home, things seemed off. Like all the stories she'd been told, this one held only a ring of truth, but she didn't have time to think about this now. She needed to get ready for the first day of her senior year at Woodsville High.

She noticed that she had her father's eyes, deep and dark, as she highlighted them expertly with a coat of mascara. Then, with a swoosh of the brush, she swept some bronzer across her high cheek bones, the perfect touch to compliment her chiseled face and narrow chin. She pouted her plump lips and colored them a deep red. Her name was Ruby, after all.

It had been over eight years since she had been in Woodsville. She barely remembered her life here. When she lived here, she'd had a mom. Since her mom died, it was just her and her dad. After the gruesome death of her mother, Ruby and Tyler Hood fled Woodsville, but Ruby's grandmother was here and that had been the reason for the return. Her father wanted to mend fences with his mother before it was too late. Eight years was too long to harbor resentment. Ruby had no idea what the turmoil revolved around, but she had a sneaking suspicion it had been her mother's death. She didn't even know much about the death of her mom. Ruby didn't like surprises and her father was suspiciously closed lipped about what happened in Woodsville eight years ago, so she did a little research before they got here.

According to the articles in the Woodsville Word—the local newspaper—only pieces of her mom had been found. After a police investigation headed up by Detective Kevin Wolf, it was concluded that a satanic biker gang that had been passing through town was responsible for the death of Kristine Hood. In fact, they were responsible for four deaths right around the same time. With the full force of the police and the community, Woodsville had banned together to avenge the deaths of the innocents. The majority of the female and children members of the gang had been run out of town. Most of them had put up a fight and a few had been arrested and incarcerated. Detective Wolf had quickly moved up the ranks in Woodsville, and still held the honor of serving as Police Chief.

Ruby's head twitched slightly. She brought her hand up to her nose, which wrinkled as an unusual scent wafted to her nostrils, as a slight breeze ruffled the cotton white curtains behind her. There was something familiar about the smell, and she couldn't help but follow it. For some reason, she found herself drawn to the window. She sat gracefully on the window sill and pushed the linen curtains out of the way, but still hid behind them. She gazed out and when she did, he turned around and their eyes locked. Ruby gasped as his name escaped her lips in a whisper, "Kent." She pulled away from the window, out of his sight, continuing to watch from the window as memories muddled her brain. She tried to make sense of them, but they were just too convoluted. Ruby peeked cautiously through a sliver in the curtain. The boy looked up, his eyebrows drawn together after finding the window empty. After a few moments, he shrugged, turned away and continued walking.

"Ruby, breakfast is ready," her grandmother's voice called from downstairs.

"Yeah, yeah, yeah," Ruby muttered to herself as she grabbed her bag off the chaise lounge, slid her sunglasses atop her head and hurried down the winding staircase. The graceful young woman lifted herself easily onto a wrought iron barstool at the breakfast nook off the counter of the kitchen, depositing her things on the stool next to her. She picked up a slice of bacon and began to munch.

"Good morning," said Grams, a short, white-haired lady with Ruby's eyes.

"Morning, Grams," Ruby said softly between chews. "Where's Dad?"

"He left early. He wanted to see some old friends about some work," Grams said, shuffling through the kitchen to place more bacon in the sizzling pan.

Ruby narrowed her eyes and stared at her grandmother until the elder woman's gaze met hers. "I want to know, Grams," Ruby said in a steely voice.

"Dear, you don't know what you're talking about. It was a tragic accident, nothing more. Don't listen to your father's conspiracy theories," the elder woman pleaded.

Ruby sat back, thinking about this new information. "Hmmm, that's interesting. Dad barely says boo about Mom … ever. I've always had a feeling there was something off about that, about why we left Woodsville and, most importantly, why we're back," Ruby said evenly. Grams staggered back slightly and steadied herself, grabbing the countertop.

"Look, I can hold my own. I know my father is hiding shit from me. At the very least, he's not being honest. I'll find out the truth. I've heard the stories about you, Grams," Ruby said mockingly. She hopped off the chair, smirking at the old woman.

Grams' hands fell from her mouth and her eyes hardened. In an instant, she grabbed Ruby by the wrist across the counter and held her granddaughter's gaze. "Ruby, I'm warning you to stay out of it. Enjoy being a teenager and don't get yourself wrapped up in old vengeance. No good will come of it."

Ruby stiffened briefly at the warning then she broke into a throaty laugh, tossing her head back. She grabbed her gear and stalked out of the kitchen. "You'd be surprised about what I've seen, Grams. Like I said, I can hold my own. Have a good day," Ruby said, pulling her large, round sunglasses over her dancing eyes, chuckling to herself. Maybe Woodsville wouldn't be so lame after all.

***

Ruby surveyed her new school, as a sea of students milled around in the large parking lot in the center of the sprawling campus. Three large, brick buildings surrounded the parking lot, or 'the pit' as the kids called it. Ruby sauntered into the office of the largest building and walked into the office. Flashing a sweet childlike smile at the woman behind the counter, Ruby spoke softly, "Good Morning. My name is Ruby Hood. I believe my father enrolled me on Friday. Unfortunately, he misplaced my schedule over the weekend. The house is a mess with the move."

"That's completely understandable," the receptionist responded. "I'd be happy to print you another. Welcome to Woodsville High, Miss Hood." The plump, little receptionist clicked a few things on a computer in front of her, then the printer beeped and spit out a piece of paper. The squat woman jumped up happily, grabbed the documents and smiled at Ruby.

"Thanks so much." She said genuinely. Ruby might be tough and a little bit wicked, but her father taught her manners. She leaned in while the woman explained the documents.

"Here is your schedule and a map of the campus. And here is your enrollment form. Please show this to each teacher, since you aren't on the roster yet." Then, a bell chimed from every speaker in the school. Ruby marveled as the school instantly jumped to attention. Doors opened, noise levels increased, students and staff hustled and bustled to and fro as the day officially began.

"If you hurry, you can make it before the tardy bell rings. Head right out of this door. Exit the building and head across the quad. Your first class is in Building B, room 104. Good luck," the woman replied.

"Thank you. Have a good day." Ruby smiled, then turned to follow the directions the receptionist gave her. As kids scuttled through the hallway, Ruby walked casually and made a detour into the bathroom, needing to check her appearance and buy herself some time. Ruby stared at herself in the full length mirror in the girls' room. Some random girls' looked her over critically, but she barely noticed. She checked out her waifish figure in the mirror. Her skinny jeans and ballet flats showed off her lean legs, a red tank peeked out from underneath a black, off-the-shoulder sheer blouse. She freshened up her red lips, smoothed her blond streaks, then tucked her hair behind her ears.

The last bell chimed just as Ruby exited the building to walk across the quad. She was officially late, but that was all part of the plan. Fading into the background was never an option. She liked people to know right up front where they stood. To do that, one had to draw attention to oneself and exude confidence from the get go. Confidence was not something Ruby had in short supply.

She pulled the door open to her classroom. The room froze and all eyes turned to face her, just the way she wanted. "Excuse me, I'm so sorry to interrupt. My name is Ruby Hood. I'm new and I got lost on the way to class," Ruby lied, meeting the teacher's gaze, holding out her enrollment form.

Mrs. Armstrong pushed her glasses up her nose and reached out to grab the form. "Welcome, Ruby. Please find a seat."

Ruby scanned the room. Right in front of her sat a beautiful young woman, with mesmerizing gray eyes and a long, black mane of gorgeous hair. She smiled genuinely to Ruby and nodded to the empty chair next to her. Ruby faked a smile toward the overzealous young woman, but walked right past her to the back. She slid into a seat across from a girl with her nose buried in a book. Ruby was surprised that the girl hadn't even glanced up.

Ruby leaned across, held out her hand and whispered, "Hey, I'm Ruby. Nice to meet you."

The girl looked up and glared at the rude blonde through her rectangular, yet quite hip purple glasses. She ran her fingers through her thick curly hair and gave Ruby the once over. "Lilly," She said, shaking Ruby's hand, then turned back to her book.

"What are you reading?" Ruby asked with a smile. She liked this girl.

Lilly looked up again, narrowed her eyes and closed the book, then pointed to the cover to show the title.

"Gone With the Wind. Impressive. It's one of my faves," Ruby said, then turned to pay attention to the teacher, but caught Lilly's amused grin in her peripheral vision. Ruby decided she and Lilly would be friends, but now she wanted to see what Ms. Armstrong was all about. Literature was her favorite class. Ruby hated to brag, but she was somewhat of a literary genius and a huge book worm.

***

Ruby walked up the five stone steps of the front porch and

paused. Of course, she could walk right into her Grams' large, two-story brick house, but she didn't. After all, it was her home, too ... for now. Instead, she leaned toward the door with her hand on the handle and listened. They were arguing. She could hear their muffled voices through the door, then suddenly everything went silent. Ruby leaned in closer and pressed her ear to the door, straining to hear. The door flung open and Ruby almost tumbled into the living room, but caught herself with animal-like precision.

There stood her dad, grinning. Tyler Hood looked nothing like his daughter except for the eyes. They both had the same deep, onyx Hood eyes. Mr. Hood was short and stocky and kept his gray-flecked, short hair neatly styled. His large, Roman nose didn't really compliment his round face, but his wide chin with a slight cleft pulled it all together. His eyes danced like a teenager. "Eat anyone alive today?" her father joked.

Ruby returned his wicked grin and sauntered into the living room. "Not today, but tomorrow's another day."

Walking into the living room, she took a moment to check out the scene in front of her. Her father had two TVs going full blast, an ear bud stuck in his ear and the newspaper sprawled out on a large, beige sectional that took up most of the room. A wooden rocking chair creaked in the corner where Grams sat knitting something with red yarn.

"Does one of you want to tell me what's going on?" Ruby asked evenly, trying to catch the eyes of either Grams or her father. Her father just shrugged. Ruby saw right through his feeble attempt to feign innocence, and Grams didn't even bother to look up. "I'm not sure what you two are up to, but I'm not a kid anymore, and there's a good chance I'll figure it out. Then, you two will have to deal with me."

Tyler laughed and paced around the room. "Aw, Rube, your active imagination and your flare for the dramatic make you one of a kind." Somewhat absently he leaned in and kissed his daughter on the forehead, "Sit down and tell me about your day, doll. Did you meet anyone interesting today?"

"I did, actually. I met many people," Ruby said coyly, not quite sure where to begin. She'd met quite a few interesting characters, but she wasn't entirely sure she wanted to share anything with two people who were obviously keeping things from her. She decided to keep a few secrets of her own, so she told her them about her new friend, Lilly.

Glossing right over some of the more interesting encounters, Ruby chronicled the mundane details of the day, but kept a few things to herself.

The more she talked the more her father fidgeted, unable to stay seated for long. When his cell phone buzzed, he jumped off the couch and it tumbled out of his hands. Grams stopped knitting and her brow furrowed. Ruby paused midsentence and watched the scene unfold in slow motion, not even closing her mouth. Her father scrambled to his knees and chased his buzzing phone across the perfectly waxed wooden floors.

Finally, he got a hold of it. "Yeah?" he barked into the phone, abruptly composing himself. He turned to the women in the room, then stalked to the porch, slamming the door on his way out.

Ruby growled, narrowing her eyes, and turned to Grams. "Well? You want to tell me what's going on?"

Grams folded her knitting tools in her lap. "Ruby, please stay out of this. You have a bright future. Don't be foolish enough to get lost in your father's silly conspiracy. Your mother died at the hands of some very bad people. In fact, several people died, but the people who did it have paid. There was no 'frame job' or 'cover-up'. Sometimes bad things happened to good people in a good town. Period. End of story." Her grandmother sighed wearily.

Ruby plopped down on the couch and looked at Grams. "Will you tell me about it? What about the *others*? The stuff I can't find in the papers?" Ruby asked.

Ruby knew this went so much deeper. Her family was a part of a unique culture called Otherly Naturals, or Otherlys. This culture is compiled of many forms of interesting creatures, most of which aren't quite human. Different and non-human didn't necessarily mean they were all bad. In fact, just like humans, there was both good and bad, and they came in many different forms. The Hoods were wolves— werewolves—even though Ruby hated that term. She knew anything related to her culture would never be spoken about in the local newspaper.

"The man killed after your mother was the resident Guardian. He was killed by the same people," Grams softly said. After all, her granddaughter deserved to know.

"No way," Ruby said slowly. Not many people, human or non-human, dared to harm a Guardian. They were leaders with a certain magical presence. Killing one was not an easy task. "Tell me."

"The first two that were killed were human—most Otherlys didn't pay any attention. We just figured it was humans killing other humans, but then your mom …"

Ruby waited patiently.

"Jarred Hunter was the Guardian at the time of her death. He had recently arrived to Woodsville, and several Otherlys had traveled here to see what the newest Guardian was like. It happens every time the title is passed. There's always an influx of undesirables," Grams explained.

Fascinated, Ruby urged Grams along with frantic hand motions, wanting as much information as she could get before her dad returned. This was the most anyone had ever spoken to her about her mother's death.

"Jarred was a good man. He was friends with your parents. It was an odd pairing of friends—wolves and a Guardian—but they all bonded. When your mom … died … the men were frantic, beside themselves with grief and wanted justice. Someone had to pay for taking your mom away, so they teamed up with a recently relocated family of Huntsmen—the Wolfs."

Ruby burst out laughing. "Sorry, Grams, but this town has a band of Huntsmen with the last name Wolf. That's irony at its finest right there!"

"Well, Detective Kevin Wolf and his brother, Officer Ken Wolf, found irrefutable evidence that this degenerate biker family of coyotes, the Coys, were behind the killings. Jarred, being the brave and heroic man that he was, lead the charge to arrest the suspects. He was shot right in the heart by the head of the Coy family. Afterward, gunfire and a bevy of Otherly Naturalness ensued. Thankfully, the Wolf brothers were there to take care of the rest of the clan. Most of the women and children fled the day before. If Jarred hadn't been so full of hatred and grief, he might still be here today. Maybe he should have taken your father with him. I think

Tyler blamed himself for his friend's death. Jarred was survived by a son, Dylan. He's your age."

"Whoa …" Ruby said, exhaling deeply as she leaned back onto the couch. Grams' story was the same as the newspaper reports, but at least now she knew the true identities of all the players.

"I don't want to have to make demands, Ruby, but stay out of this. Be a teenager and enjoy it. Date a boy, go to a party, and get asked to a dance. Woodsville is a good place to live." Grams' eyes flashed golden and she snarled ever so slightly. Ruby flinched and sat back. Then, Gram stood and patted her granddaughter gently on the shoulder. "You hear me?"

"Yes, ma'am. Nite, Grams," Ruby whispered. She stood, but kept her eyes low as a show of respect. Turning, she walked up the stairs.

"Nite, Girl," Grams whispered.

Ruby smiled and enjoyed the awe of her Grams. She had no idea the old woman still had it. If Grams wanted things a certain way in her town, all visitors must abide by her wishes. That was the Hood way and had been that way for centuries, and Ruby wasn't going to let her father create unnecessary problems by getting mixed up with hateful, old feelings.

She knew her dad had gotten into some shady stuff from time to time. Hell, she'd found herself in numerous, too-close-for-comfort situations … it came with being a wolf. There were things about the world most seventeen year old girls never even thought about, but Ruby knew all about them first hand. She'd shaken down a biker for cash. She'd broken into homes to "borrow" certain items that she intended to return. She was also quite capable of hot wiring an automobile for a quick getaway. But there was the nagging voice that she shouldn't know the kinds of things she knew, as she thought again about her Grams' advice to stay out of it.

After some thought, Ruby decided she'd start with getting to know the resident Guardian. It sounded like they had at least one thing in common. She had seen him today, which was one of the things she chose not to share. Their gaze locked as she was walking through the hall with her new friend, Lilly. It would have looked odd if Ruby had stopped and introduced herself. Otherlys weren't keen on letting the human race in on their secrets, but she nodded respectfully in his direction. She knew he was the Guardian, as they come with a certain presence. His nod and smile in return, but the look in his eyes told her he knew she was a wolf. She remembered liking his emerald eyes. It had been a meaningful moment. Meeting the new guardian moved to the top of her priority list tomorrow. Idly she wondered what he knew about her. She bit her lip and grinned mischievously, giggled and silently vowed not to cause any more problems for her Grams.

Later that night, Ruby heard the car door slam. She never slept well until her dad was home. She heard him bound up the steps and saw his shadow underneath the door. Then, she closed her eyes and pretended to sleep, as she wasn't ready for one of their father-daughter all night talks. The door opened slightly and Tyler Hood gently crept toward his daughter. He knelt over her and kissed her lightly on the top of the head, and Ruby immediately drifted off to a hard, dreamless sleep.

***

"Ruby," her dad whispered as he opened the door and knocked softly at the same time the next morning.

"Hey," she croaked, rubbing her eyes.

"Hey, I gotta run early. Sorry about running out on you yesterday, but I got a job. I'll tell ya all about it tonight. You gonna be around?" he asked with childlike pleading as she smiled.

"Sure, Dad. I'll ask Grams if she'll make dinner. Maybe we can eat together like a family," Ruby offered hesitantly. The thought of a real family dinner sounded heavenly.

"Of course, doll. If that's what you'd like."

"I would," she said, hopping out of bed and wrapped her long blonde hair into a messy bun. Her long, graceful strides put her right in front of her father. She stood on her tip-toes and kissed the cleft on his chin. "Thanks," she said, grinning from ear to ear as she brushed past him and headed into her walk-in closet.

"See you tonight!" he father called after her.

"Can't wait."

He chuckled silently, shaking his head at his daughter. She never ceased to amaze him. Pulling his cap firmly over his eyes, he headed down the steps and out the front door.

Ruby got ready with crazy quickness, as she wanted to go downstairs and talk to Grams. She felt they reached an understanding last night and she was excited to springboard off that. As she pulled on her signature skinny jeans, layered top combo, she briefly entertained the idea of a real family, like eat-dinner-and-celebrate-the-holidays-together kind of dinner. The idea of settling down was growing on her, quickly. She applied minimal make-up, then opted for red lip gloss today, thinking she might ease off of the tough, hard ass image. She smelled something yummy coming from downstairs as she grabbed her favorite black jacket and her bag before closing the door on her way out.

"Morning, Grams," Ruby greeted her. She was enjoying the change in the environment with her Grams.

"Morning, girl. Are you hungry?" Grams asked with a slight smile.

"Yes," Ruby scooted onto the bar stool at the breakfast bar. Grams set a plate in front Ruby filled with whole wheat waffles smothered in butter and syrup, fresh, ripe fruit and crispy bacon.

Ruby shoved a huge forkful of the delicious waffles into

her mouth and sighed slightly while she chewed. After she swallowed the first bite, she couldn't wait to share her news with Grams. "So, I've decided to introduce myself to the Guardian today," Ruby said proudly. "Can you give me any pointers? I only know what I know from research. I'd love a firsthand account of what he's like," Ruby said making conversation before shoving another large forkful of waffles into her mouth.

"He's a bright boy. Some call him strict, but fair. I find him to be a tad immature, but he's only eighteen. There hasn't been a killing here since he became Guardian. He has a very low tolerance for BS, plus he leaves me alone and he's handsome," Grams replied with a grin.

Ruby's juice almost shot out her nose and she blushed. "Graaammms!"

"What?" Grams shrugged playfully, "and I never heard of him treating anyone unfairly. Now, there's minimal violence, so he does a decent job, especially being so young. I've lived under better Guardians and I've lived under worse. The family of Huntsmen he hired had a lot to do with the low violence part. Dylan was so young he didn't really understand what was going on, so he hired them. He had just lost his father and his best friend."

"Who was his best friend, Grams? What happened to him?" Ruby muffled over a mouthful of waffles and bacon.

"You were, Ruby."

"SHUT. The. Front. Door!" Ruby exclaimed as a piece of waffle fell from her gaping jaw.

Grams smiled like the cat that ate the canary. "Yes, and I'll tell you more about Dylan, but I'd really like to hear your impression of him as a person. I'd rather tell you more about the family of Huntsmen, since they've made themselves an intricate part of this town: The Wolfs. Eight years ago, they took care of all the unfortunate riff raff that found their way to an area protected by a child Guardian. The Wolfs have been on the Guardians payroll ever since. Kevin Wolf is the police chief and Ken Wolf, formerly Officer Wolf, is the principal at Woodville High. His wife, Kassandra, owns a children's clothing store and volunteers at many charitable events. They have two children, Kent and Kayla. Kayla is adopted, but you'd never know. She's the spitting image of the rest of them. Dylan is Kent's best friend and together, they have big plans to run this city. They all have quite a future ahead of them," Grams said.

Ruby thought for a moment. Her eyes went wide as she whispered, "Grams, do you think …"

"Don't even utter thoughts like that Ruby. The Wolfs are highly revered in this town. Doubting their sincerity and devotion will cause too many problems," Grams said hastily as she grabbed Ruby's unfinished plate setting before her.

Ruby opened her mouth to protest on many different levels, but Grams cut her off again.

"Shhhh, Ruby, I'm warning you, girl. The Wolfs didn't have anything to do with the deaths that took place eight years ago. There hasn't been a single death since. To even utter words like that would put a target on your back, your father's back and mine," Grams whispered. "Now get on to school, girl. Be home by super time and I'll have something nice prepared."

"Yes, ma'am," Ruby obliged as she hopped off the bar stool and headed to the door. She couldn't even look back at her Grams. She walked out into the sunlight lost in her own thoughts. Surely, her mother's death and the death of Jarred Hunter had been investigated, and if not one single murder had taken place for eight years, then the Wolfs couldn't have been a part of it. One was a police chief and the other, a principal. The bad guys usually didn't have jobs like that, she rationalized … usually.

"Well, if it isn't Ruby Hood!" A nasty voice spewed forth as a lean figure stepped out from behind a large oak tree and directly into her path. Ruby stopped, eyeing the creature in front of her carefully.

"Well, now, you seem to have me at a disadvantage. You obviously know who I am, yet you haven't bothered to introduce yourself. Tsk, Tsk … not very neighborly. However, if I had to guess, I'd say you are the young Huntsman, Kent Wolf," Ruby leered, holding out her hand.

Kent's eyes grew wide. Ruby was tickled to have unnerved him. "I'd like to be friends, at least until we get to know each other. Who knows? We may end up hating each other," Ruby sneered, biting her lip. Then, she leaned toward him and whispered into his ear, "Plus, I don't bite … hard."

Kent gulped, jumped back and hissed at her. Ruby couldn't help but laugh. "He's the class president, editor of the school paper and the Guardian's best friend and he hisses. That's cute." She covered her mouth and tried to control herself. Why was Grams or anyone afraid of this guy? Ruby had a hard time picturing him as any kind of Huntsmen.

"Kent, I've got this, go," a deep voice spoke, as the hairs on the back of Ruby's neck stood up. She silenced herself instantly. Then, she took a deep breath and turned to face the newest person to ambush her on her way to school.

"Mr. Hunter, nice to meet you formally," the blonde wolf curtsied slightly and flashed one of her brilliant smiles. "I hoped we would cross paths today, and to my surprise it was sooner rather than later."

"Well, Miss Hood, it sure is lovely to meet you. You're quite breathtaking," Dylan Hunter, Guardian of the Wood, said appreciatively as he looked her over from head to toe. "What brings you to Woodville?" he asked, all business.

"Family. My father and I haven't been in town since we lost my mom. I hear we lost her about the same time that you lost your father," Ruby said carefully. Dylan flinched slightly, and out of the corner of her eye, she thought she saw Kent flinch even more. "I'm very sorry for your loss," Ruby said sincerely. She honestly wouldn't wish the loss of a parent so young on anyone. Then, she gently rested her hand on his shoulder.

Dylan turned to face her and studied her intently. "And I am sorry for yours," he replied softly, filled with regret. Her dark eyes met his gleaming emerald eyes. It was the first chance she's had to take in his features, and she couldn't help but notice how handsome he was. His solid, lean frame reminded her that he was some big shot on the football team. His chiseled features and long, narrow face had premature lines and wrinkles, probably from the early childhood trauma of losing his father and becoming a Guardian at the age of ten.

"How long are you in town … you and your father?" he asked, as Kent stiffened and sneered off to the side.

Ruby recoiled inwardly, not about to let these two get to her. Plus, the way Dylan mentioned her father and Kent's reaction put her on alert. There was still bad blood. Determined to smooth things over, Ruby composed herself and responded nonchalantly, "I'm not sure yet. It all depends on whether my father and Grams can sort out their differences."

Hunter nodded, satisfied with her answer. "Your grandmother is a good woman. I hope they find common ground. It might be nice to have you around for a while."

"I hope so," Ruby replied. "From what I hear, we have a lot of catching up to do. Apparently, you and I were very good friends many moons ago."

"That's what I've been told, too," the Guardian said softly, holding Ruby's dark seductive gaze. It was her eyes. They had that effect on boys.

Ruby wasn't quite sure where this was going, but she seemed to have diverted some of the attention off her father. She smiled brightly, feeling Kent's eyes burning a hole in her back. "I don't suppose you'd walk me to school, so we could catch up?" she asked. When she sensed Dylan's hesitation, she added, "Also, I was hoping you'd tell me a bit about Grams. She comes off like this sweet little old lady, but I have a sneaking suspicion she's a force to be reckoned with."

She laughed as she slid her arm through his, guiding him along the sidewalk. Dylan, obviously enamored with Ruby, laughed and told her a story about Grams climbing a tree just last year at 79 to save a cat. Ruby smiled up at the Guardian, but she was painfully aware they would need to pass by his friend. The tension between her and Kent was palpable. She hoped Dylan didn't notice. Ruby laughed and nodded every time is was expected. As they got closer to Kent, she stuck her tongue out at him so Dylan couldn't see as they passed so, then smiled sweetly. She knew it was childish, but she didn't care. As he grimaced, she turned to listen intently to Dylan's animated account of the story about Grams without missing a beat.

***

Ruby never experienced anything like the phenomenon that took place shortly after meeting Dylan. A whirlwind romance ensued like something straight from a romantic comedy. The lovely Miss Hood was the talk of both the school and the town. First, the students were amazed that Dylan had latched on to the new girl so quickly. They called it a fluke and made bets about when it would end and if he would ruin her. He had quite the reputation as a lady killer. The rumor mill at the high school was nothing compared to the trash the townsfolk spoke in Woodsville … especially the Otherly Naturals. No one seemed comfortable with the Guardian dating a wolf. The murders from eight years ago even surfaced in certain circles, and the fact that two of the victims were the parents of the young couple, unnerved some.

Regardless of what others said, Ruby and Dylan were completely enamored with each other. The differences in their culture didn't seem to be a problem. They spent hours staring into each other's eyes with their fingers laced; smiling … completely oblivious of the rest of the world. Puppy love, many people called it. Even though no one stated it outright, many hoped it would be over soon, but no one more than Kent Wolf. The hatred between the Huntsman and the wolf seemed to increase with each day. Ruby refused to spend any more time than necessary with Kent ... and he felt the same way about her. They were natural enemies and neither of them had any desire to change that.

While most people—except Kent—thought Ruby was a charming young girl, many people in the town worried about her father, remembering the loose cannon that went off half cocked after losing his wife. They didn't seem to remember the outstanding man, husband and father he had been before grief took over. These days, Tyler Hood seemed off to most people, but no one could quite put their finger on it. He showed up for work every day on time and he went straight home after work to spend time with his family. He appeared to have let go of the events eight years ago and the idea that a conspiracy surrounded the death of Ruby's mother. He smiled as he waved to neighbors and was congenial to all he came across—except Police Chief Kevin Wolf. The two had yet to cross paths, that was, until the bomb was left on the front door of the high school.

Ruby wasn't exactly sure what day it was when she thought about it later, but she knew it was a week or so before the highly anticipated Valentine's Day Dance. She was returning some items to the chemistry lab for Mr. Walters, the head of the science department. It was her free period and she chose to spend it as a teacher's assistant for the science department, as she enjoyed spending time with inventors and scientists. She especially enjoyed watching— or even participating in—any experiments they might perform. Since the timeline for the Woodsville Science Fair had just begun, Ruby spent most of her free periods unpacking and delivering needed materials to teachers and classrooms. When the first announcement came over the speaker she froze, "Woodsville High, we are under a lockdown. Woodsville High, we are under a lockdown."

Ruby didn't move for a whole five seconds racking her brain about everything she was supposed to do, but couldn't remember. For all the previous drills, she was in a class. Now, she was alone in the tiny storage room of the chemistry lab on the fourth floor of the main building, in the most remote location on campus. She wasn't sure she wanted to be stuck here by herself for an undermined amount of time. "Out the door, dummy," she said to herself. "Get out of here before you get locked in."

So, Ruby walked quickly to the door. She reached for the handle, but the door flew open toward her, cracking her in the nose, sending her tumbling to the ground. Then, a flustered boy crashed through the door and plowed right into Ruby. By the time, she gathered herself together and stood upright again, the door locked automatically. The boy stood by the window and strained to look through the slits in the bars, while Ruby pulled on the door and cursed.

"*OUCH,* man! I wanted out! What's going on out there? Are we sure we want to be trapped in this room? Is this a drill or what?" Ruby shouted at the boy.

"It's a bomb threat," the boy said, but didn't turn around, peeking through the slit in the window as the SWAT team and bomb squads arrived. "A bomb was delivered to the school this morning."

"What? How do you know that? What?!" Ruby paced and began to panic.

"A little bird told me," the boy said.

"Why weren't we evacuated then?" Ruby demanded, trying to rationalize the situation.

"Not sure. My guess is that the box was sent to one of the other buildings. That building was evacuated, but the other two buildings were locked down. We're probably safer here than out there. At least until they can determine the scope of the bomb."

"That makes sense, I guess," Ruby exhaled and sat down. She reached into her back pocket to retrieve her cell phone.

"No service. Even if there was, they've blocked it by now … to be on the safe side," he warned. "It's just you and me, wolfie."

Ruby looked up and her eyes narrowed. She studied the figure in front of her as she stared out the window and rolled her eyes. "Oh shit."

"Believe me, sister, I'm just as excited," Kent Wolf turned and stared at Ruby Hood.

Ruby sucked in a breath. Why hadn't she noticed how attractive her archenemy was? He leaned his muscular body lazily against the lab tables. His square jaw line was speckled with light stubble and his chiseled features only enhanced his steel blue eyes.

"Just some alone time with my favorite gal," he said, leering at Ruby as if she were prey.

"You and me both," Ruby huffed. Annoyed, she stood up and paced again as her mind raced a mile a minute. Stuck here with him? For how long? *UGH!!!* Finally, her annoyance slowed and rational thought took over. "Why did you come in here anyway?" she asked cautiously.

"It's the safest room at the school. It's been structurally enhanced to protect against certain threats," he said, peering out the window.

"Really?" Ruby asked, inching closer to Kent. She was dying to see what he found so intriguing.

"No, but there's a stash of food in the back room and a fairly decent view of the parking lot," he replied, matter of fact.

Ruby couldn't help but laugh out loud. He spun around and stared at he; her laughter was infectious. He couldn't help but smile at her as he scooted to the side, allowing her a peek out the window.

"So seriously … what do we know?" Ruby asked, standing on her tippy toes to see the ruckus outside. Hordes of police cars, some government vehicles, and a SWAT van pulled up as people in hazmat suits with dogs roamed the area, as other men in suits and sunglass swarmed the area.

"Not a whole lot. A package was dropped off outside the office of the Annex building. No one seems to know how it got there, but there's a bunch of wires and a timer. I suppose the bomb squad is checking its authenticity now. If it's a fake, we should be out any time. If it's real, hopefully they can disarm it and get us out of here soon." Kent paused to look at Ruby. "I'm going to hunt for food. You stay here and keep watch." Kent grinned somewhat lopsidedly.

Ruby chuckled, rolled her eyes and turned back to watch the scene unfold. *Nothing like fear of the unknown to bring two enemies together,* Ruby mused to herself. She hoped this was the start of something good and positive. If she and Kent could be friends—or at least friendly—it would make her life much easier. She loved being near Dylan, but she hated the animosity Kent provided, and he was around all the time. She was shaken from her thoughts when a box fell from up high and crashed to the ground. Ruby heard Kent groan while he was rummaging through the back of the science room.

"You okay?" She called, worried.

"Jackpot!" he shouted back.

"Anything good?" she asked.

Silence.

"Kent? What's going on? Are you okay?" She stood up and walked back to the small storage room, and was met with more silence.

Kent stumbled from the room recklessly with a blue face and bulging eyes, trying to breathe, pointing to his throat.

"Oh shit!" Ruby said, rushing to his side. Without thinking, she grasped her hands right underneath his rib cage and balled her fists. "Hang on. You're going to be fine," she said coolly, then thrust her hands back into his stomach, performing the Heimlich maneuver. Suddenly, a large chuck of granola flew from Kent's mouth. He gasped for breath and laughed to keep from panicking. Ruby patted his back, reaching for one of the bottles of water setting on the table. She picked one up and handed it to him. "You okay?"

"Uh ... huh ... thanks to you ..." he moaned as the water hit his throat.

"It was nothing; I took a CPR class last summer. I had to be certified to work at the children's summer camp last year. No biggie." Ruby looked at him and shrugged, then hesitantly turned and walked back to the window.

He grabbed her by the arm and flung her around to face him. "Yes, it is a big deal. You just saved my life. A wolf just saved the life of a Huntsman. Not the norm. It *is* a big deal, Ruby Hood. It's a game changer, at least for me. I owe you my life."

She studied him hard and opened her mouth to respond, but was interrupted by the loud speaker. "This is the ALL CLEAR, Woodsville. Repeat, this is the ALL CLEAR. All students, staff and personnel, please make your way to the quad."

"You don't owe me anything. We'd better go. We wouldn't want to add to the confusion," Ruby said, taking her arm out of his grip, then stalked to the door. She flung it open and moved through the corridor with great speed.

"This isn't over, Hood," Kent shouted after her. He grabbed
an unopened granola bar, tore it open, brought it to his mouth, then stopped. He stared at the bar, chuckled uncomfortably and threw it in the trash, grabbed a bottle of water and headed toward the quad.

***

A barrage of people hustled and bustled about the quad. Ruby found Dylan and his football cronies in the center of the quad, handing out water and helping to check people in. Once the students had checked in, they were allowed to leave. Many parents were loitering around frantically in search of their children.

"Dylan!" Ruby called, speeding up the closer she got to him. He turned and grinned broadly. She jumped into his arms, squealing loudly as he swung her around.

"Ah, Ruby! I'm so glad you're okay! Where were you?" Dylan asked, smiling.

"I was in the science lab. It was my free period and I was returning some stuff for Mr. Walters when the threat came over the intercom.

"We survived, thankfully," a voice rang out from behind Ruby.

She cringed slightly at the sound of his voice. She didn't know why, but suddenly she didn't want Dylan to know she had saved Kent's life only moments before.

"I'm glad, my man," Dylan said happily, holding out his hand to shake Kent's. "You guys were locked in there together?" Dylan laughed loudly. "I'm surprised you didn't rip each other's throats out."

"Nah, man. The exact opposite, actually," Kent said, looking into Ruby's onyx eyes.

She stared intently back, silently willing him not to tell Dylan. She had no idea why, but she had a terrible feeling about what might come from it.

Dylan turned around momentarily to check in a scared young freshman, handing her a bottle of water. Then, he paused, looking from Ruby to Kent. "Huh? What exactly happened in there?"

"Ah, nothing. We had plenty of food and water. In fact, we could've survived the apocalypse in that room," Kent joked, slapping his buddy on the back. "Hey, look, I'll catch you guys later. I need to find Kayla and see if she's had some sort of dramatic girl breakdown.

"Catch ya later, man. Peace." The two boys said in unison before they did some sort of elaborate handshake.

Ruby stared vacantly at them with a smile plastered on her face, wondering why she didn't want Dylan to know what happened, but she knew the answer. Because it was against ancient wolf law to save a Huntsman. Period. End of story. But at the time, she hadn't been thinking about Kent being a Huntsman; all she saw was a boy choking to death. Her survival instinct took over. She had just saved her boyfriend's best friend. Of course, a wolf and a Guardian being together was strictly taboo, too. She had just exhibited heroic behavior for a human, but she wasn't a human; she was an Otherly Natural. Ruby suddenly stood at attention, shaken from her inner turmoil by a commotion in the center of the quad, and one of the voices seemed oddly familiar.

"Dad?" she yelled, running toward the uproar, pushing her way through the crowd.

"I know you had something to do with it, Hood!" the police chief shouted.

"You are still as delusional as you've always been, Wolf! My daughter was in one of those buildings. What on earth makes you think I would even joke about blowing up a building that my daughter might be in? Not to mention the other 3,000 innocent children."

"Dad?" Ruby asked, trying to grasp the whole situation.

"Uncle Kevin?" Kent said in disbelief. The two kids looked at each other in total bewilderment and shrugged.

"That's enough, men!" Principal Wolf shouted, pushing his way through the crowd followed closely by Dylan Hunter. "I know a crisis can cause us all to overreact, but this isn't the time or the place for either of you to air your personal dirty laundry. Mr. Hunter and Kent, kindly guide the chief of police to some coffee and I'll speak with Mr. Hood," Ken Wolf said with ease. Ever the politician, Principal Wolf flashed his congenial smile that comforted the entire crowd.

"Go on about your business, folks. It's nothing but two men worried about our young people."

"Thanks, Ken," Mr. Hood said with his hand outstretched to thank the principal for his graciousness.

"Put your hand away, Hood. There is no way I or any other member of my family, will ever side with wolves. We don't belong in the same town. You don't belong here. You should have stayed away," the principal seethed through his clenched jaw.

"Might I remind you the Hoods were here long before the Wolfs?" Tyler Hood's eyes flashed, glowing momentarily before letting out a low, menacing growl. The hairs on Ruby's neck stood at attention.

"Hey!" Ruby demanded, pushing her way between the two men "What did my dad ever do to you?"

"Ah, little Ruby Hood, obviously just as naïve as your mother was," Ken Wolf mocked. Ruby's eyes flashed and glowed as Ken laughed. "See? This is exactly why your kind doesn't belong here. You're too primal and uncivilized. You shouldn't have come back. Watch your step, Hoods," Ken threatened quietly, then flashed a good-natured smile and went back to the crisis at hand.

"Dad?!" Ruby demanded, barely audibly.

"Shhhh … not here, Ruby. You've been checked in since the lockdown. I don't want to worry your Grandma. We should be safe in the Wood … at least for now …" Tyler Hood rambled as he glanced over his shoulders, twitching slightly.

Ruby regarded him carefully and she wasn't nearly as concerned as he obviously was. After all, she just saved the young huntsman's life. It was frowned upon amongst her people, but the Wolf family owed the Hood family regardless of their cultural differences. In hindsight, not telling Dylan was a mistake, but she hoped she could figure a way out of that. She had an ace in the hole and it should be enough to get her and her father out of town with the promise never to return. Ruby was used to life with her father. She enjoyed the several months she had here, but deep down she knew it would come to an end. She almost laughed out loud at the lunacy of a pair of wolves taking up residence in a town run by Huntsman. She wasn't entirely sure what motivated her father to bring them back here, but she got the message loud and clear: it was time for them to move on!

"Let's go," Ruby said, glancing cautiously over her shoulder. They crossed the quad and hopped onto the back of her father's Harley parked in front of the parking attendant's shack. Within moments, they were speeding off, away from the ruckus caused by the bomb. But neither Hood noticed that Kent Wolf had pulled out behind them in his brown four-door sedan.

***

"Ruby, you have to listen to me. I don't know what you sort of bargaining chip you think up have, but these men will kill and think nothing of it. Eight years ago, they killed four innocent people: two humans, your mother and Jarred Hunter, who was our friend and your boyfriend's father. They didn't think anything of taking those lives to get what they wanted. The Wolf family manipulated everything to suit their needs. We have to stand up to them, now, Ruby. If we don't take them down, they won't think twice about hurting us or your grandmother," he said, grabbing her by the shoulders, pleading with her to understand the severity of the situation.

"I think you're overreacting, Dad. Dylan will listen to us and he'll help. He knows we mean no harm. Come on, Dad. This is the Twenty-First Century. Surely we can all be civil," Ruby stated with great naivety.

"Ruby, you don't understand. They don't want us here. They won't stop until we are gone." Wringing his hands together, he began to pace. "I'm pretty sure they are going to frame me for that alleged bomb threat today."

"Shut. The. Front. Door! You can't be serious! Why?"

"I'm not sure. Maybe they view me as a threat. Maybe it's you and Dylan. I don't know, Rube, but we're in the crosshairs of the Wolf brothers and that, my dear, is a dangerous place to be."

"Now, I would advise getting all your facts straight, Mr. Hood, before you go spouting ill wills about decent, hardworking citizens of Woodsville," Kent Wolf said, stepping out from behind a large oak.

Tyler Wolf snarled low and Kent gently smoothed his thumb back and forth over his crossbow. Ruby stepped up and stood between her father and the crossbow. "Whoa! I have no idea what's going on here, but this is getting out of control. First, off," she wagged her finger in Kent's direction, "my father had nothing to do with that bomb! Secondly, I just saved your life, Kent, so back off."

"Ruby, I'm warning you guys. You need to go … now. They'll be here any moment. They won't think twice about killing you right here and now in the Wood. It'd be a piece of cake for them to dispose of your bodies. As far as the city is concerned, Tyler Hood is unstable and needs to be dealt with. The rumblings are already making their way through the local watering holes and rumor mill. Go *now*!" Kent whispered while ushering Ruby and her father off to the north end of the Wood. The father and daughter moved quickly to the shelter of the tree and disrobed before they shifted into more comfortable skin. Ruby turned into a gorgeous, tiny blonde wolf with eyes the color of coal. Tyler morphed into a stocky brown wolf, with gray flecks around his muzzle. The brown wolf licked his daughters muzzle before they split apart to put distance between the Huntsmen and themselves.

Ruby tore through the Wood headed west and her father went east. Her senses were definitely keener on all fours. She ran with one purpose: to scatter her scent so she could double back and eavesdrop. Huntsmen could smell a wolf if they tried. She wanted to make sure that they smelled her, but the vastness of her scent should make it impossible for them to detect her ten feet away. She made multiple figure eights and found her way back to the edge of the clearing in a tangle of bushes and grass that had grown together for centuries.

Ruby listened intently and could hear their footsteps in the distance, not entirely sure what to expect. She didn't even know who would be attending the meeting. Creatures of the night scurried past her as the Wolf brothers entered the Wood. Ruby wondered what kind of Huntsmen these were.

Ruby heard their voices and made out their conversation. She listened to Kevin and Ken joke about the name of the Wood, slurring their words as they trampled through the Wood. The pair laughed and broke through the other side of the clearing. A low, guttural growl escaped Ruby. She couldn't help it.

"Over here, Dad," Kent said, as he stepped into the clearing. He looked at the men and nodded in compliance. Then, he turned his head, looked straight at Ruby and scolded her with one swift movement of his head. Ruby took a step back.

"Kent! My boy! Good to see you. Did you take care of our little problem?" Ken swayed from side to side.

"I'm working on it, Dad. I think it'd be better if we ran them off. Another murder would stir the pot with the Guardian," Kent replied.

"'It would stir the pot with the Guardian' … do you hear this nonsense, brother? We need to eliminate Tyler Hood … now. We should have done it eight years ago. Too bad it wasn't him instead of the wife that wondered in the wrong direction that night.   He needs to go, dear nephew, and it's long overdue," Kevin Wolf sneered.

"Well, you two asked me here for a reason and I'm giving you my two cents worth, regardless of whether or not you want it. We should let this sleeping dog lie, so to speak.

I'm sure I can convince the Hoods to go within a week and never return. We leave the grandmother alone and the Guardian never needs to know you're responsible for killing his father," Kent said, squaring his broad shoulders, standing up to his uncle. His father's eyes widened.

"You don't have the balls, boy," Kevin said, laughing, spitting in his nephew's face.

"Doesn't have the balls? I don't know. I've known this kid a long time and I've never seen him back down. A little family spat?" Dylan Hunter replied, stepping into the clearing, clapping both men on the back. Immediately, the tension in the area dissipated. "Now, would someone please explain to me why my chief of police is spitting in the face of my best friend?"

Kevin laughed nervously first, then Ken joined in. "Aww, we were just busting his chops over tonight's target practice. Nothing but a little family rivalry. It seems the young guy has some secret shots he pulled out all of a sudden. I underestimated him, that's all," Kevin Wolf laughed menacingly.

"What can I say, I learned from the best, uncle," Kent said through gritted teeth.

"Everything all good?" Dylan asked, skeptical.

As if on cue, the quarrelling Huntsmen broke out into a twisted smirk and shook hands just a touch too hard.

Still in her wolf form, Ruby watched as the two older Wolf brothers went off in one direction, and the high school friends went off in the other. Thankfully, neither party came in her direction. She realized she had been holding her breath as they passed. She quickly inhaled and exhaled several times, waiting until they were gone. Eventually, she found her way back to the spot where she had transformed. Then, she shifted back into the cute blonde human version of Ruby Hood. She dressed quickly and decided to take the scenic route home, knowing that she had a lot to think about.

***

After a particularly sleepless night, Ruby continued to replay the meeting she witnessed in her head, trying to rationalize the situation while she hastily got ready for school. Deep down, Ruby knew she and her father needed to get out of Woodsville as fast as possible or her father would most likely be "accidentally" killed by the Wolf brothers. She was also pretty sure she couldn't tell her father about what she witnessed the night before. He had a short fuse. Ruby was certain he would go off half cocked and probably make things worse. She entertained the idea of telling Dylan. From what she saw last night, Dylan had no idea what the Wolf brother's had done to his father. *He should know,* Ruby thought. Not to mention that they killed her mother. They should most certainly pay for what they did. Anger pulsed through her and she growled as she brought the mascara wand to her eyelashes, but Ruby stopped short. She wasn't concocting a plan to save Dylan and seek revenge. She was trying to get herself and her father out of town alive. She shook her head and got her mind back on track as she applied her red lip gloss. She pulled her long golden locks into a careless bun, grabbed her gear and jetted down the stairs.

Then, she walked into the kitchen and froze. She wasn't entirely sure what caused her to pause, but an idea passed through her mind quickly. She couldn't quite get a handle on it and it slithered in and out of her consciousness.

"Ruby!" Grams shouted, obviously not for the first time. "What's with you, girl? I've been calling you for the last five minutes." Grams eyed her carefully as she spooned some home fries onto her plate. "Are you okay?"

"Huh?" Ruby responded absently, then smiled. "Oh, Grams, I'm just thinking about the Valentine's Day Dance this Saturday. I found a dress last week. It's black, but it's supposed to be freezing and I don't have anything to wear over it, so you know I'm totally stressing about my wardrobe. Typical girl stuff."

"Hmmm, I'm not buying it, but I might be able to help you with your wardrobe issue," Grams said as she walked to the hall closet.

When Grams turned around, a velvety crimson swooshed around her. Ruby eased herself off the breakfast nook barstool and oohhhed and ahhhed as she walked toward her grandmother. "What is that? It's absolutely gorgeous!"

"It's cloak, Ruby. It's been in the family for generations. If you'd like, I'll have it dry cleaned and you may wear it to the dance. I'd say the red is quite fitting for both Valentine's Day and Ruby," Grams said, winking at her granddaughter while she held open the cloak for Ruby to try on.

Ruby squealed with delight as she slipped her arms through the large, billowing sleeves. "Oh, my goodness, it's so luxurious," she murmured as she pulled the crimson hooded cloak around her. Golden flecks were embedded in the delicate floral pattern of the deep red cloak. It was lined with honey satin and felt soft against her skin. As Ruby fastened the three flaxen buttons down the front, it cinched and outlined her slim waist. She twirled and the cloak rippled around her, encompassing her frame. She giggled in true teenage girl fashion and ran to hug her Grams.

"It's perfect, Grams," Ruby said with affection.

"Well, then it's all set. I'll take it to the dry cleaners today. I'm sure my friend Ida can have it ready by the weekend," Grams said somewhat distractedly as she helped Ruby out of the cloak and laid it over her forearm. The women looked at each other and were about to go in for a rare Hood hug when there was a knock at the door. Confused by who could possibly be calling at this hour, the women stared at each other for a moment, shrugged and decided to ignore the knock.

Ruby teetered on the verge of confiding everything about her father and the Wolf brothers to her Grams, when

Grams sighed deeply. Ruby realized a frail, old woman would be of no help. The young woman smiled feebly and reached over to give her Grams a quick hug. "Thanks, Grams."

"Any time, girl." Grams returned the hug.

Laughing, Ruby steadied herself. Maybe Grams wasn't so frail after all.

"Hey! Everything okay in here? I knocked about five times." Dylan said as he cautiously stuck his head in the front door.

"Come in, Dylan," the women sang in unison, smiling at each other.

He walked in and stopped to stare. "What's so funny?"

"Nothing," Ruby said happily, standing on her tip toes to kiss her sexy boyfriend, and for a brief moment in time, nothing was wrong. "Sorry for ignoring your knock. We were just having a little girl bonding episode."

"No worries," Dylan said, shoveling bacon into his mouth. "Ready, Rue?"

"Yep," the stunning blonde responded. Maybe Dylan was her ticket out of this mess. After all, he seemed to really care for her. She wondered if he would help her get out of town. No, she realized. He wouldn't let her run away without an explanation. But once he learned about the Wolfs' involvement in his father's death, Ruby envisioned that he would be feeling hate, death, destruction and vengeance. Telling him about his father wouldn't make anything better and it might get Dylan killed.

"You okay?" the Guardian asked.

Ruby forced a smile, "Yeah, fine. Let's go."

***

Walking in a daze for the better part of the day, Ruby tried desperately to find a way to escape that didn't resulted in death. She was about to throw in the towel and just tell her father everything, when an unlikely ally approached her. She balanced the box she was carrying as she unlocked the science lab door. She couldn't reach the lights with the box in her arms, but she shuffled forward until she came to one of the lab tables, then set the box down carefully and turned to flip on the lights.

"Leave them off."

"Huh? What? Who's there?"

"Ruby, relax it's only me," Kent Wolf replied, stepping out of the shadows.

"Holy Crap! You totally freaked me out!" Ruby exclaimed, placing her hand over her heart to calm its rapid beating. "Why are you in here? In the dark?"

"I've been here all day waiting for you. I need to talk to you, but I also couldn't risk anyone seeing us together. Ruby, I think I can help you and your father."

Ruby eyed him seriously, "I'm listening. You have fifteen minutes. Get to the point and hurry."

***

Tonight was do or die … literally. Ruby exhaled deeply, cocked her head and stared at herself in the mirror. She was ready for the dance … well … she looked ready, anyway. A gorgeous jeweled French braid elegantly held back her long, blonde tresses. She had dark, smoky eyes with light lip gloss brushed across her lips and a touch of blush on her cheeks. Her form-fitting, black strapless dress complimented everything about her waifish frame. Lastly, she flung the red Hood cloak over her shoulders; it completed the ensemble perfectly.

Starring in the mirror, she fiddled with her hair jewels and went over the plan again in her head. She was going to drug her father, kidnap him and get out of town tonight. Kent actually helped concoct the plan. She thought back to their conversation in the science lab only days before.

"Why are you helping me? Why do you even care what happens to us, you're a Wolf." Ruby asked. They were after all of their natural enemies, but then again, nothing about this situation was natural.

"Look, Ruby, you saved my life in this very room just days ago. The way I see it, I'm paying off a debt. Plus, I like you. You're a good person. I misjudged you at first. It's just that I've never known anyone like you. I've never known a wolf like you … well," Kent paused thinking, "actually, I know one wolf like you … your Grams."

Ruby swelled with pride when Kent compared her to her Grams. She listened and together they had agreed this was the best possible scenario.

She gently pulled her gorgeous, crimson cloak tightly around her. In just a few moments Ruby would drug her dad. She had already crushed the pills, in a package inside the pocket of her cloak. Now, she only needed to empty the contents into whatever he was drinking at dinner tonight. According to the plan, he would pass out on the couch. After the dance, she would say goodnight—and goodbye to Dylan. Kent would then emerge from somewhere and help her load her father into the backseat of Ruby's car. Then Ruby would drive through the night, headed to Kingman, Arizona. Apparently, there was a large and very accepting wolf population there. Ruby hoped by the time her father woke up, they would be halfway there and she could convince him this was best.

In the other secret pocket of her cloak, Ruby felt the corners of the letter she had written to say good-bye to her grandmother. She gently crept into Grams' bedroom, kissed the letter and tucked in under her Grams' pillow.

Ruby stood at the top of the long, winding staircase. Her breath caught in her throat as she gazed below. Eyeing her at the top of the staircase, Dylan Hunter gaped at her wide-eyed, then let out a low sultry whistle. Her father grinned like a buffoon with his phone on video, as Grams smiled with her rosy cheeks and kerchief, holding an old fashioned digital camera. Tossing her head back, Ruby laughed. Another perfect moment. She knew it wouldn't last, but at least she was having more of them. Descending gracefully down the winding staircase, Ruby ran her fingers along the rail, enjoying the moment.

"Wait here, Dylan. I have your boutonniere in the fridge," Ruby said. The cloak billowed around her as she floated across the gleaming, wooden floors. Reaching into the fridge, Ruby grabbed the small plastic box, and dumped the drugs into the glass of sweet tea sitting in front of her father's dinner plate. Secretly pleased with her stealth, she turned around, coming face to face with Grams. Her eyes widened and her smile faded.

"I think I know what you're trying to do, girl," Grams said quietly, and Ruby knew better than to open her mouth. "Ever since your mom, he's been missing part of him. I'd hoped by coming back he'd be able to fill that missing piece, but it seems to have become bigger instead. Too bad, though," Grams laughed ironically, "you seem to fit in real nice here, Ruby." A tear tumbled down Grams' cheek as she looked into her granddaughter's eyes. "But I understand you need to go, for both of your sakes." Grams took out her kerchief and blew her nose. "Does he need to drink that?" she asked, pointing to the drugged glass of sweet tea.

"Uh, huh," Ruby mumbled, then nodded, confirming Grams suspicion.

"I'll see that he finishes it, and I'll pack you guys a nice basket of goodies to get you through," she said, blowing her nose again.

"I love you, Grams," Ruby said, then grabbed Grams in a huge bear hug. She resisted the urge to cry, swallowing several times to contain the lump in her throat.

"Maybe you can join us once we get settled," Ruby said, wiping a tear from her cheek.

"Ah shucks, girl, Woodsville's my home. I'm not going anywhere." Grams sniffled.

"No one is going anywhere except to a dance. Another sentimental girl moment?" Dylan asked playfully, entering the kitchen.

"Something like that," Ruby said with a smile, giving Grams one last hug before the stunning couple said their good-byes and left for the dance.

***

The music blared and the colorful lights twirled around Ruby. Smiling, she swayed along to the beat and enjoyed what was left of her perfect evening. By her calculations, she still had a few hours left.

"Where's Dylan?" Kent whispered, but she heard him perfectly, even though she hadn't noticed him sidle up next to her.

Ruby shrugged, "I don't know. I thought he was in the back getting ready for the Valentine, Cupid, King, whatever ceremony." She raised her hands absently. She had never paid much attention to high school politics. Of course, Dylan was nominated to be king of the dance and was expected to win. The other nominations were just for show. "Why aren't you there,
too?" she asked.

Kent grabbed her shoulder and turned her to face him.

She furrowed her brow. "What's wrong?"

"Dylan's gone," Kent whispered.

Ruby laughed, "What do you mean he's gone? He's about to be crowned king of something or another. Why would he leave?" Then, Ruby's phone buzzed in her cloak. She reached in and read the text message. "Shit!"

"What?!"

"Dad's gone. He never finished the tea. He got a phone call and ran out. He took a huge gulp of the tea and then took off!" Ruby cursed again. An impaired Tyler Hood on the loose was not a part of the plan.

Kent's phone buzzed next. "Shit is right! I've been called to a Huntsmen meeting in the Wood." Kent shoved a picture of Ruby's dad wide-eyed and bound to a tree under her nose. Without speaking they turned and pushed their way through the crowd of milling kids and ran to the parking lot.

"That must be where Dylan went," Ruby rationalized as they sped along over the river and through the Wood in Kent's brown four door sedan. "Maybe he's not dead yet."

"Who? Dylan or your dad?"

"Neither … both … no one … I don't want anyone to die," Ruby stammered.

"No one's dead yet, Ruby. First, I don't think they're out to harm Dylan. They've got it pretty good under his rule. Second, they need the approval of the Guardian to kill your father, if they are following protocol."

"Right! Like they're at all concerned with following protocol!" Ruby interjected.

"Plus, they'll wait for me," Kent finished sadly.

Ruby grimaced as he shrugged. "You've never been invited to a family killing?" he asked.

"Touché," she said. "I've been invited to more than I can count. I've never gone, though. My mom always said I should've been born a Guardian. She said I didn't have the stomach to eat wolf food." Ruby smiled at the memory.

Kent looked at her and respect flickered across his face. He parked and looked at her. "We're here. The meeting will be at a clearing farther in than we were last night. If a killing takes place, they'll need the cloak of the Wood."

Ruby pulled her own cloak around her. She had a terrible feeling about the new direction the plan had taken. She and Kent crept through the Wood, stepping together to mask Ruby's presence. When Ruby heard voices, she froze.

Kent brought his finger to his lips and pointed in the opposite direction. As he left Ruby, he called out and made a ruckus.

If they were listening to him, they weren't listening for me, Ruby thought. She shed her cloak and dress and stuck them deep in a hole in a large oak. Stretching and contorting her body, Ruby turned into her golden alter ego as her dark eyes lit up. Her dad howled several feet away in the clearing. She didn't dare return the call. He knew she was there. Under his howl, Ruby could move somewhat freely through the Wood to a better location. She got as close as she dared and waited.

"Well, he speaks," Kevin Wolf taunted, shoving a hot poker into Tyler Hood's chest.

"Kev, careful, we really want the Guardian on our side for this one. I'd like to keep it neat. We worked hard to frame this guy. If we do something stupid, it'll negate all our efforts. Plus, I have my political career to think about," Ken Wolf rationalized calmly.

"Guardian, smardian … I'm smarter than him. He's just a kid," Kevin mocked.

"Apparently, you learned nothing about underestimating your opponent, dear uncle," Kent said in a condescending tone. Then, Kevin rushed his nephew, bringing the hot poker to his nephew's throat. Ken Wolf stepped forward hesitantly.

"Man, this family has some issues! This is the second time this week I've seen you two at each other's throats," Dylan grumbled. "Someone, please explain to me why I was called away from the dance and my stunning date moments before coronation." Dylan held up his hand to indicate he wasn't done, "and not one of you had better make a single crack about my wolf girlfriend or I will snap your neck." Dylan looked pointedly at Kevin. No one spoke. "I assume you called this meeting, Chief?"

Kevin nodded to the bound man. The pain from the hot poker to the chest had knocked him unconscious, as his head slumped forward. "Is this what required my urgent attention?" Dylan asked, walking closer, then pulled the man's head up as an angry bellow escaped his lips. "Are you kidding me?! You've dragged me away from my evening to bring me the tortured, bound, and unconscious body of my girlfriend's father? What were guys thinking? You have to let this go! The Hoods are staying. They are *FINE!*" Dylan's voice boomed through the Wood as many critters scurried. *"DID YOU KNOW ABOUT THIS?!"* he screamed into Kent's face.

Ruby jumped at Dylan's tirade. Without flinching, Kent looked into the eyes of his best friend. "I wanted a peaceful resolution to this problem."

"Look, Guardian ..." Kevin sneered as he caressed his holster and moved in closer behind Dylan.

"I've had about enough of you, Chief," Dylan said, cutting him off. Then, he turned and sent a blue ball of power into the police chief's chest, which sent him flying into a nearby tree. Dylan walked over slowly to the crumpled Huntsmen. Wide eyed, the other two Wolf family members took two steps back. "I warned you to let this go, old man. You're forcing my hand and I don't think you're going to like the way it turns out," Dylan snarled. His face contorted menacingly as he turned to deal with the other two Huntsmen.

Ruby watched in horror as Kevin Wolf staggered to his feet. His lips pulled back into a sneer as he drew his gun. "You're gonna be easier to kill than your idiot father, kid."

Ruby yelped as a warning from the east of the clearing. Her father let out a painful howl, which was returned by another howl from the west.

"Ruby! Are you here?" Dylan cried out as he moved to the east of the clearing.

"Ruby," whispered Kent cautiously.

"I think all of the Hoods have joined our meeting. I wonder who invited them," Ken said, glaring at his son before peering into the Wood.

The bushes rustled and a large, grey wolf leaped into the clearing. Suddenly, shots rang out as Ruby howled. She didn't know who was shooting and at whom.

"RUN, RUBY! RUUUNNNN..." a barrage of voices screamed at her before another round of gunshots rang through the Wood.

Ruby crouched low among the woodland growth, unsure of what to do. Suddenly, she heard her Grams voice in her head. "Go dear, go now. Run! Don't look back! Be safe, my child." A moment later, Grams voice faded. Ruby threw back her head and howled before she tore off though the Wood.

She got to the top of the hill on the outskirts of Woodsville before she stopped to catch her breath, with the red cloak gripped firmly in her teeth. She dropped the cloak to the ground and howled.

"RUBY! COME BACK!" Dylan's voice pleaded, bellowing through the night sky.

"Go, Ruby," Kent's voice urged in a whisper, tickling her ear.

Her howl was returned. She had her answer. Quickly, she shifted back into a girl. Brushing the tears out of her eyes, she threw the cloak around her naked body, hopped in her car, turned the ignition and set her GPS for Kingman, Arizona. As she barreled down the road, she screamed hysterically trying to silence all the voices shouting at her in her head.

***

"Ruby, wake up, honey."

"WHAT?! Where am I? Ruby asked, scrambled to try and get her bearings.

~ *67* ~

"Shhh, honey. It's okay, you're fine. You were having a nightmare," Grams said soothingly, sitting on the queen sized bed next to Ruby.

Ruby shook her head, taking in the familiar surroundings of her room. Everything appeared to be in place. Her posters lined the walls, and her clothes were still strewn over the chair or bedpost just like she'd left them. She sighed dramatically and rubbed her eyes once she concluded she was safe. "Holy crap, Grams! That dream seemed so real."

"Do you want to talk about it, dear?" Grams asked, drawing her close.

"Nah, I gotta get up anyway." Reaching for her robe, Ruby pulled away slightly, but she didn't get out of bed. After she wrapped the robe tightly around her, she turned around to face her grandmother. "It was so silly, Grams. So many people I knew were in it, but they were different … and Dad," her voice trailed off. "Dad was still here." Ruby smiled wistfully, but quickly furrowed her brow. "Mom was gone, though." Ruby took a moment to swallow the lump in her throat, trying desperately to grasp the bits and pieces of the dream before they flitted out of her head. "Oh, yeah," she added, "I was a big bad wolf and there were people called Guardians and Huntsmen … like some fairy tale." Grinning, Ruby shook her head and laughed. "But I had a smoking hot boyfriend," Ruby said with a grin. She leaned across the bed and kissed her Grams on the cheek before hopping out of bed. "I gotta run, Grams. I tutor Kent this morning, then I have to meet Lilly to work on our 'Great Gatspy' project."

Ruby headed into the bathroom to start the shower. Then, she padded back to her closet to choose her wardrobe for the day. She grabbed her favorite skinny jeans, black tee and Dr. Marteen's. As an afterthought, she dropped the black tee and grabbed a tight red tee in honor of Valentine's Day. Just because she didn't really have a smoking hot boyfriend didn't mean she couldn't be festive.

Grams yelled up to Ruby over the music. "Breakfast?"

"Yes, please! Something to go with a large coffee? Thanks Grams!" Ruby shouted from the closet.

Grams mumbled softly to herself on her way out. "At least you don't have to worry about wolves, Huntsman and Guardians yet, my sweet girl. That day will come soon enough." Grams closed the door and headed to the kitchen.

***

On the walk to school, Ruby tried to think about her odd dream, but only bits and pieces briefly played through her mind. So much of the dream felt familiar, but the details were scattered and hard to discern. Smiling, she thought about Kent and Lilly's reaction to her dream. She was sure they would get a kick out of it. She climbed the last few steps into the library and rounded the corner.

"Good morning, Ruby. Happy Valentine's Day to my favorite tutor," Kent said, turning in his chair to face her, smiling. His steel blue eyes twinkled and he held a single perfect pick rose in his hand.

Ruby's lopsided grin spread across her face; he always had that effect on her. "Morning, Kent. Thanks," Ruby said, blushing. "Ready?" She asked sitting down next to him, her dream completely forgotten.

~The End~

My Forever Love

By: Theresa Oliver

Characters in this story are based on the book

Star, Starland Vamp Series, Book 1

by Theresa Oliver

Star

Rick and I had just left Washington D. C. in his black Mercedes GL450 SUV headed toward Cooperstown, New York, our home, after having just met with Sam Abbott, Zac's father and my boss. You see, Rick and I are members of a covert Special Forces CIA team ... and we're also vampires. In fact, according to the CIA, we don't exist. They only call us in times of dire emergency when there would be too much risk to human operatives. Abbott wanted to see us in regard to a new assignment, but none of the six members of our team are eager to get back to work. After our last assignment, all of us were nearly killed and now we're enjoying a bit of downtime. Personally, I was actually enjoying going to high school. I know, go figure.

Anyway, Abbott wanted to see both Rick and I. Although my best friend, Annie, loved going into the city, she couldn't come along because she was preparing something special for Rick for Valentine's Day. Zac—the love of my life—wanted to go, too, but Verus was helping him and John with their training. They couldn't afford to lose any time before they're forced to go on our next assignment, but who knew when that might be?

Rick and I have been friends since the Stone Age, or so it seemed. Actually, he knew my father during the Revolutionary War. That's how we met. He was known as Fredrick Lee, then. Although he shortened Fredrick to Rick, his last name has stayed the same over all these years. Since my father's death, Rick has been my father figure and mentor. He also saved my life, turning me into a vampire after I was shot in the back three times by Captain Clark on the first day of the Revolutionary War, but that's another story. My name was Abigail Starland, then, but now most people call me Star, although my alias is Lisa Miller at Cooperstown Central High School.

"Rick, do you mind if I ask you a question?" I asked, eyeing his expression.

Rick laughed, raising an eyebrow. "Since when do you have to ask?" Then, he took his eyes off the road to look into my eyes. "What's up?"

I laughed … Rick knew me so well. "Well …"

Now it was Rick's turn to laugh. "Since when are you ever at a loss for words, Abigail? Just spit it out."

"Okay, you asked for it."

Rick rolled his eyes, turning his attention back to the road. As we turned onto I-81 N., he gave me a look and raised one eyebrow. "Spill."

I laughed again. We had a bit of a drive ahead of us yet, so why not? "Rick, you never told me about your wife, Lucia."

Rick's grip tightened on the steering wheel and I immediately hated myself for bringing it up. "After all these years, why are you asking me this now, Star?" Obviously, it was a subject best closed and something he didn't want to talk about.

"I don't know. I guess since it's Valentine's Day, I was just curious," I replied, turning my attention to the passing trees outside the passenger side window. "You never told me about her. I know everything about you, but you never told me about her."

Rick sighed, eyeing the road, obviously debating on how much to tell me.

"Look, Rick, forget I said anything. If you don't want to talk about it …"

"Just give me a minute," Rick interrupted me. "It's been a long time." But vampires had perfect recall. I'm sure he remembered every detail, more so than a human.

"No problem, Rick. I know you can't get Alzheimer's," I said with a smirk. "If you don't want to talk about it, no problem."

Rick took his eyes off the road to look at me. "I was going to say that it's been a long time, but I still remember every curve of her face, her exact eye color and her scent, but, most importantly, her personality and … her love for me." He took a deep breath and turned his attention back to the road. "She was one of the kindest, most loving people I knew. She had one of the purest souls I've ever known."

I waited for a minute, debating whether to press him or not, but curiosity won out. "Tell me, Rick," I coaxed in a soothing voice.

A moment later his eyes glazed over a bit, remembering old times, long ago, times long gone, but not forgotten. Soon, his tale began.

Rick

When Abigail first asked me about Lucia, it really took me by surprise. Over all the years I've known Star, she never once brought the subject up. I had told her and Annie that I had just lost my wife not long before I met them in the Year of Our Lord, 1773. Star was only 16 years old then and

Acantha—as Annie was known then—was her best friend. However, I had lost my wife nearly a hundred years before I ever met them. For a moment, I decided if it was something that I really wanted to talk about. After all these years, Abigail earned the right to know.

I first noticed Lucia in the Year of Our Lord 1619. I said noticed, because, actually, we grew up together in a peaceful little village of present day Salisbury in the United Kingdom. I was twenty and had not yet chosen a bride, and she was sixteen, the same age Abigail was when I first met her. Although I was only four years older than her, she was still young, too young for courtship. But I pass by her house on my way into the village to trade furs that I trapped or wild game that I caught. With each passing day, she became more beautiful.

Her father owned a local apothecary in the edge of the village, which today would be considered more of a natural holistic healing shop rather than a drug store. I had to pass by it to get to the town square to do my trading. Each day I passed, Lucia was sitting out front on a rustic, wooden bench made of tree branches, working on her embroidery sampler or sewing. At first, I didn't notice her, but I politely returned her greetings of hello or smiles when I passed. The months passed and soon the cold came to claim the land and I thought nothing of not seeing Lucia sitting in the front of her father's shop. But when spring came the following year, one day I passed and she was sitting out front again, and my breath caught. She was no longer the lanky, blonde lass that I had known. She had grown into a beautiful woman. Her blonde streaked hair cascaded passed her shoulders, reaching to her waist and curled into lose waves at the ends. Her body had developed into curves in all the right places and her eyes were a mesmerizing blue, pools of calm ocean blue on a summer day. I stopped in my tracks, eying her beauty.

She tried to conceal a smile, but her eyes danced in obvious approval that I had finally noticed her. "Good day, Mr. Lee. How are ye today?"

"I be fine, Lucia, but I'm wondering something," I replied as one corner of my lips raised into a smile.

"And what might that be, Mr. Lee?" Lucia asked, clearly enjoying the exchange.

"I'm wondering where the lanky lass that used to sit before her father's apothecary shop disappeared to. Instead, a beautiful young lady now sits in her place," I said, adjusting the pelts on my shoulder.

She laughed aloud. "I think that lass is long gone, sorry to say."

"I'm not sorry at all," I replied, then knew the hour was getting on and that the daily trade would soon come to an end. "Will ye be here tomorrow?"

Lucia's smile broadened, reaching her crystal blue eyes. "Will ye be passing by, Mr. Lee?"

"I will."

"Then I shall be here," she replied, returning her attention back to her sampler, intriguing me all the more.

"Tomorrow, then?" I asked, hoping to regain her attention.

"Tomorrow," Lucia returned, rewarding me with a lovely smile that melted my heart.

"Pray, ye answer me one question before I go?" I asked, ready to sprint away.

"And what question might that be, Mr. Lee?" Lucia said, setting her sampler down onto her lap to look at me.

"How old might ye be now?" I asked with a smile.

"I'm seventeen years now, I will be eighteen in a few months," Lucia replied, then she thought of something as one corner of her lips raised into a curious smile. "And why might ye be asking?"

"Call it curiosity," I called back to her over my shoulder as I hurried toward the town square, unwilling to admit more.

"As ye wish, Mr. Lee," Lucia replied, returning her attention to her work.

Then, I stopped in my tracks as I took in her beauty. "And one more thing," I said.

"And what might that be?" she asked, as her eyes sparked.

"Please, call me Fredrick," I replied, pleased when a smile lit up her face. "And what might I call ye … Miss Collins or Lucia?"

"Ye may call me Miss Collins," she replied with a devilish grin.

I laughed out loud, intrigued. "As ye wish," I replied with a slight bow and ran off toward the center of town to do my trading, smiling like a lunatic when I reached the center of town.

"And here comes Mr. Lee!" Mr. Douglas replied, holding up a hand to motion me toward the group of men he was with. "What have ye brought for us today?"

"Some pelts," I said, still thinking of Lucia. "Ermine, mink and fox."

"Might ye have a squirrel or rabbit with ye?" Mr. Douglas asked, already going through the pelts.

"No, not today, but I'll be sure to bring the meat tomorrow," I said, watching the men carefully. Although I trusted them, you can never be too careful.

"Be sure that ye do! I have a hankering for some good rabbit stew, or maybe some venison?" Mr. Douglas asked, hoping.

I laughed at his enthusiasm. He was a plump old man who could no longer hunt for himself, and from the looks of his round belly, he didn't need to, either. "I'll see what I can do, Mr. Douglas."

"Pray ye see that ye do," Mr. Douglas said. Within minutes, my pelts were gone and my pockets were filled, but as I was about to bid farewell along with the other men, Mr. Douglas asked, "What made ye late today, Lee?"

I smiled to myself, remembering the exchange with the lovely young woman, wondering how much I should tell these men. "I was speaking with Miss Lucia Collins on the edge of town," I replied with nonchalance.

"The daughter of Mr. Collins? The owner of the apothecary?" Mr. Douglas asked, as his voice raised a few octaves.

Surprised by his reaction, I replied, "The one and the same. Why?"

"Oh, stay away from that one, lad," he said, shaking his head back and forth, then added, "for your own good."

"And why do ye say that, Douglas?" I asked, as my eyebrows pulled together in concern.

He looked back and forth to ensure that no curious ears were listening, then whispered in a low voice, "Because she's a witch, lad."

I laughed so hard that tears sprang to my eyes. "And what makes ye say that, Mr. Douglas?" I asked, dabbing at a corner of my eye.

"Because of the apothecary, dear boy! Everyone in town knows that they practice witchcraft in their shop."

"And why do ye say that? It's an apothecary! They sell herbs that heal!"

"Exactly!" Mr. Douglas replied, then added, "And they do incantations to heal, too. They are Druids! Witches, the whole lot of them!"

"Ah, go on with ye now!" I replied. "Just because they heal people doesn't mean that they be witches. They help people! They heal."

"Just mark my words there, Mr. Lee," he warned. "Remember what I said and stay away from that witch."

"I would kindly ask you never to speak of her or her family that way again," I asked him, as anger welled up within me.

"Have it thy way, but heed my warning," Mr. Douglas replied.

"I will not speak more of it and I warn ye not to speak of it again, either," I replied, then walked away, leaving him to his thoughts.

Witch! How could he be so naïve as to believe idle gossip? I wondered to myself as I stormed away. As I walked away, I decided not to think of it again. When I passed the apothecary, Ms. Collins was not waiting outside. I shook my head to clear away the thoughts, but they kept creeping back.

The next day, I rose early from my bed, took my homemade bow and arrows and headed toward the woods, remembering Mr. Douglas, the disagreement gone, but not forgotten. I walked through the woods on my route to check my traps, but I carried my bow, ready to hunt. I could use the money, after all.

I was looking along the forest floor through trees of oak, maple and various evergreens, when I heard a rustle in the leaves ahead. I darted behind a tree, ready, when from behind an oak stepped the most beautiful deer I'd ever seen. It was a stag, a four pointer, and had obviously been eating well. I brought him down with one shot to the head. I picked him up from the ground, swaying a bit under the weight, as I was still human. I arranged him so that his body was wrapped around my neck, holding onto its hooves, then headed toward town.

When I neared the apothecary, I vowed to take Mr. Douglas' advice and leave her be … until I saw her sitting on the rustic wooden bench in front of her family's store. Her beauty captivated me, but what held my attention the most was her smile. "Good day, Fredrick," she said as I drew near.

"And to thee, Miss Collins," I replied, unable to stop the smile from spreading across my face. As I saw her, I knew that I secretly had been looking forward to seeing her again.

Eying the prize around my shoulders, she placed her sampler down on the bench and asked, "What have ye there, Mr. Lee?"

"I caught this stag a bit ago," I replied, wondering if she

had cast a spell on me, but then I realized how silly that sounded and quickly brushed it aside. "I'm on my way to the town square."

"To sell it?" she asked as her eyebrows pulled together.

"Aye," I said with a nod. "In fact, I must be going while the meat is still fresh."

"Wait here a minute, pray ye Mr. Lee?" she asked, rising from the bench.

"Aye," I replied, and at that moment, I knew I would wait for her forever, if I had to.

She hurried inside the apothecary, and a moment later, her father came out the front door with her trailing right behind. "What do ye have there, Lee?" Mr. Collins asked, hurrying off the porch toward me. He looked over the stag still around my shoulders, picking up its antlers, and poking the meat.

"A stag I shot a bit ago," I said.

"Do ye aim to sell him?"

"Aye, I do," I said, then asked, "Are ye interested in buying it?"

"Aye," Mr. Collins replied, then asked, "How much do ye want for it?"

For the next few minutes, we haggled over the price of the stag, but soon came to an agreement. Secretly, I was glad not to have to face Mr. Douglas again so soon after our disagreement, fearing I might say more than I should if he said anything about the lovely Lucia.

"Sir, pray ye bring the stag in for me?" Mr. Collins asked. Off to the side, Lucia looked hopeful.

I glanced in her direction and then back to her father, which didn't go unnoticed. "Aye, I'd be glad to."

Mr. Collins looked over to his daughter, trying to hide her obvious approval. Then, he turned back to me. "Mr. Lee, might ye consider staying for dinner to enjoy stew made from this fine animal?"

I couldn't help but smile. "I'd love to, Mr. Collins. Thank ye for thy kind offer. I've been hunting all morning and haven't had time to eat."

"Well, then it's settled! Come in! I'll have the Misses set ye a plate," Mr. Collins said with a smile, then yelled into the house as I followed, "Esther! We have company! Set an extra plate!"

"Why, good afternoon to ye, Mr. Lee. What a handsome buck!" Mrs. Collins said, both happy and surprised to see me as she picked up the antlers of the deer I was still carrying across my shoulders. Then, she turned her attention back to me. "Might ye be staying for dinner?"

"Aye, he is, woman," Mr. Collins interrupted. "I already told ye so."

"Oh, quiet, ye! I'm talking to Mr. Lee here," she replied, then turned to Lucia, standing in the doorway. "Well … don't just stand there, girl! Fetch another plate!"

"Here, bring the deer into the back," Mr. Collins replied, leading the way. "I'll take care of it."

"I'll help," I said, following Mr. Collins.

"Nonsense!" Mrs. Collins interjected. "Pray ye come talk to us. We have very little company of late." She looked at her daughter as she came into the dining room with anther plate, nodding her obvious approval. "Come, child, keep Mr. Lee company while I prepare the meal."

I couldn't help but grin. "I'll be right back," I said to Lucia as she blushed. Then, I followed Mr. Collins to the back. The apothecary was in the front room, and their living quarters was in the back. We walked through the dining room into the kitchen and in the very back of the house was a place to skin and prepare game. I walked over to the wooden table and deposited the carcass on it, relieved to be out from under the weight of the heavy animal. "Here, I can help ye …"

"Nonsense! Ye heard the Misses. She would have my hide if I kept you all to myself!" he replied, obviously happy with the visit.

"Well, if ye insist ..."

"I do. Now, git!" Mr. Collins said, then added in a low voice with a wink, "Lucia's waiting for ye."

I didn't quite know how to take his comment, but smiled at his approval as I walked to the front room, leaving him to the animal.

"There ye be, Mr. Lee!" Mrs. Collins called out, hurrying across the room toward me as I entered the room. "Now, sit ye right here with Lucia while I prepare the meal," she added, slipping her arm into mine, then guided me across the room.

"But, Mother, I can help ye ..."

"Nonsense! Sit ye right here and keep Mr. Lee company," Mrs. Collins replied, then said to Lucia in a low voice as I suppressed a grin, "Do as I tell ye, girl!" And a moment later, Mrs. Collins disappeared into the back of the house, leaving Lucia and I alone in the sitting room.

"Pray, sit ye down, Mr. Lee?" Lucia asked, patting the seat beside her. "Or we can go outside and enjoy the afternoon breeze, if ye like."

"Aye, that would be nice," I replied, stretching out my arm to take her hand, and as soon as my fingers closed around hers, I knew I was home. In that instance, she won my heart. I tucked her arm into mine and escorted her outside. "The air is a bit cool. Shall I fetch thy shawl?"

"That won't be necessary," she said, sitting on the bench. "Come. Sit by me."

My heart fluttered as I did as she asked. I looked out over the forest stretched out before us on the other side of the road filled with oak and cherry trees as the breeze blew gently through the leaves.

"It's a lovely evening," Lucia said, for lack of anything better to say.

But I looked at her and replied, "Aye, lovely."

A slight blush colored her cheeks as she turned away. We carried on with small talk and I didn't even dare venture to touch her hand. She was strong, but gentle and loving. The sun began to set behind the trees when her mother finally came out the door. "Dinner time!" Mrs. Collins shouted, bursting onto the scene, breaking the spell of the moment. Inside, Mrs. Collins was careful to set my plate next to Lucia's. It amazed me that they so obviously approved of me. After all, I'd never had direct dealings with them, but they obviously knew me from my trading with the men in town. Mrs. Collins set a huge pot of venison stew on the center of the table. "So, do ye do well with thy trading business?" Mrs. Collins asked, reaching for the bowl setting on the wooden table before me.

"Now, be not rude, Esther!" Mr. Collins interrupted.

"Oh, calm ye self!" she replied to her husband as she ladled a large helping of stew into the bowl. "I didn't ask him how much money he earns!"

"I do pretty well," I replied as I glanced over at Lucia. She returned the smile, lowering her eyes, as her mother beamed, grinning from ear to ear.

We ate and talked animatedly about the weather, events in town, trade, foods … just about everything. I truly enjoyed visiting with the Collins family. Lucia's parents were loud and opinionated—completely the opposite of Lucia—but it was family … something I hadn't had in a long while. My parents died of the fever a few years before. I had tried to save them, but soon they succumbed.

As the sun began to set, I finally said, "Thank ye, Mrs. Collins, the stew was delicious."

"Ye aren't leaving already, are ye?" Mrs. Collins asked with a sincere look in her eyes.

"I'm afraid I must," I replied, then turned to Mr. Collins. "Thank ye for inviting me in, sir."

"Thank ye, sir, for the stag!" Mr. Collins countered. "Actually, it was quite delicious."

"Tomorrow, then?" I asked Lucia, hopeful.

"Tomorrow," she replied as a soft shade of pink colored her cheeks once again.

As I walked home that night, I found myself walking light on my feet in the moonlight thinking of Lucia, knowing that one day be my wife. It was just a matter of time.

The next day, I checked my traps and even shot a rabbit, then headed into town. On the way, I found myself rushing to get there, knowing I would see Lucia. As I neared the apothecary, my heart skipped a beat when I saw her sitting with her embroidery sampler on the rustic bench. She smiled as I drew near. "Good afternoon, Mr. Lee," she replied.

"Fredrick, please," I gently corrected.

The same delicate blush colored her cheeks as she replied, "Fredrick."

"I have something to ask ye, Miss Collins," I nervously stated, adjusting the pelts on my shoulder.

"And what might that be?" Lucia asked, as her ocean blue eyes danced.

"Will ye meet me to take a stroll in the moonlight tonight?" I asked, hopeful.

"Unchaperoned?" she asked, thinking.

"Aye ... I'm sorry ... but, aye..." I stammered, then thought I would just jump in with both feet. "Ye can meet me at the edge of the forest. I'll come by and get ye just after sunset."

"Well, I'm not sure ..."

Then, I knelt down on the ground in front of her and took her hands into my own. "Please, say aye. I promise you'll be safe. I respect thee ..."

"Shush ..." she said, placing a gentle finger over my lips. "Aye, I'd be glad to. I'll meet ye at the forest's edge ... just after sunset ... and don't ye be late!"

A broad smile spread across my face. "Ye don't know how happy ye just made me," I said, kissing her hand. "I'll be here. I promise."

"Ye better be," Lucia said with a teasing smile.

I hurried down the road toward town before her parents could see. In the center of town, Mr. Douglas motioned toward me. "There ye are, my boy! What have ye brought us today?"

"More pelts," I replied, hiding the rabbit behind my back.

"What? No meat?" Mr. Douglas asked, then a thought occurred to him. "And where were ye yesterday?"

"I was distracted. I had nothing to sell, anyway," I replied, determined not to tell him about the deer. I didn't want to open that can of worms again. "But, I brought ye this today," I said, holding up the rabbit by the hind legs.

"My dear Mr. Lee! Ye did not disappoint me, after all!" he said.

The day's trading commenced and I was glad that Mr. Douglas said nothing more about Lucia or her family. Once my pelts were gone and my pockets were full once again, I turned to go home.

"Mr. Lee, pray ye join me at the tavern … as a gesture of friendship … man to man," Mr. Douglas said, obviously feeling a bit uncomfortable with the words that were exchanged regarding Lucia. "Sorry about …"

"Think nothing of it," I cut him off. After all, apologies were not necessary. I thought about his offer for a moment, as I was not one to frequent the pub, then replied, "Aye, I'd be glad to join ye."

"And your money is no good, Mr. Lee."

"I hope that it's good!" I replied, "After all, ye were the one who just gave it to me!"

He laughed and slapped me hard on the shoulder as he walked with me in the direction of the tavern.

"I tell ye she *healed* him," a woman said to another woman as they passed by.

"Maybe she just helped the healing process and it happened naturally," the other woman replied. I couldn't help but wonder who they were talking about, but I had an idea.

"Nay! I tell ye she rubbed some herbs on his leg, chanted some words and the next day, he was completely healed!" the woman said.

"One would think a body would be happy that her husband was healed," I said loudly as I passed, knowing the women would hear. Some people just can't leave well enough alone.

"Humph!" one of the women snorted, sticking her nose up into the air, then said to the other woman, "Come, Gretta. Let us go to the Luvitt's store."

I grinned, shaking my head as the women passed. Idle gossips.

When we walked into the tavern, we sat at the bar. "An ale for my good friend Mr. Lee here," Mr. Douglas said, slapping me on the back, saying nothing of the women and what had transpired.

"I tell ye they're witches, they are," the bartender said to Mr. Fletcher sitting at the end of the bar, obviously in the middle of a conversation.

"Nay, they couldn't be! Mrs. Collins helped my Misses when she gave birth to our Jack," the man at the end of the bar replied. "Jack was being stubborn during his birth, but Mrs. Collins mixed a tea and soon he popped right on out, kickin' and screamin'. And to tell ye the truth, things haven't changed." Everyone in the bar laughed.

"I tell ye it's true! They're all witches!" Ralph Baker, the bartender, persisted.

"Why do ye speak of things of which ye knowest not?" I couldn't help but ask, slamming my ale down hard onto the counter. Suddenly, the whole bar went silent. Then, I turned to Mr. Douglas and said, "Sorry, Douglas, but I have somewhere to go."

"Now, don't ye be listening to the likes of them. They know not of what they speak," he said, patting me on the shoulder.

"Thank ye, nay," I said, rising to my feet. "I'll see thee in the square tomorrow."

Mr. Douglas frowned, closing his eyes and nodded. A moment later, I walked out of the bar, steaming mad, thinking of Lucia. She couldn't really be a witch, could she? But I knew that it really didn't matter; I loved her. Of that, I was sure. I hurried home and dressed into a clean shirt and trousers, waiting for the sun to set. When it was near dusk, I headed toward the edge of the forest where I promised Lucia I would meet her.

As I neared the forest's edge, there was my Lucia, waiting for me. A smile spread across her face and her eyes shone a brilliant blue as the moon began to rise. I hurried toward her and reached out to her. She skipped toward me and took my hand. "Let's go," I whispered, looking around to make sure that her parents weren't watching. We ran together into the forest for a while when we suddenly came to a clearing where several huge stones stood as a testament against time. I came to know it later as Stonehenge.

"Where are we?" I asked, stepping into the clearing. The moonlight lit up the stones.

"It's a sacred place," she said, "the sacred place of my people."

"Of thy people?" I asked, stopping as she walked on.

She turned to face me when she realized I was no longer by her side. "Aye, my people. Druids. I'm from long descendants of Druids."

"Witches?" I asked.

Lucia laughed. "In the literal sense, aye, but the magic we practice is natural magic that comes from Mother Earth."

Then, I realized that it did matter. "Let me take ye back …"

"Fredrick, I'm not evil. I call on the earth for the power of healing. It's not a bad thing," she said, trying to convince me.

"Why are ye telling me this?" I asked, taking a step toward her, truly curious.

"Because before we go any further in our courtship, I want ye to know everything about me," Lucia said, then continued, "but ye can tell no one of this. People do not understand and will burn us both at the stake if they find out."

The thought of my sweet Lucia burning at the stake sent a shiver down my spine. "Show me," I said, still unable to believe.

She closed her eyes and held out her hands to one of the huge, ancient stones standing before her. At first, a faint glow radiated from the stone, but then she began chanting in an ancient tongue and it glowed brighter until the whole stone light up the circle. Then, the next stone lit, and the next and the next until every stone in the circle glowed brightly, turning the night momentarily into day. Then, when she opened her eyes and stopped chanting, the light went out just as suddenly as it had appeared.

I watched her, wide eyed, unable to speak at first as she slowly walked toward me. "How did ye do that?" I asked, mesmerized.

"I told ye. This is a special place, the holy place of my father's, and there is great energy here," she replied.

"What is this place?" I asked, looking around at the stones spaced symmetrically within the circle.

"Years ago, it was a place of burial. Years ago when witches were ready to die, their families brought them here. At the moment of his or her death, their power was released here in this place and their spirit went on to join our ancestors. Then, the body was burned here in a sacred ceremony," Lucia explained, matter of fact, as she walked around the circle of stones, letting her hand trail over them as she passed.

"Used to?" I asked, beginning to regain my tongue. "Is that ceremony no longer performed here?"

"No, not any longer," Lucia replied, turning to face me. "Today, we realize that our power is released any place that we are and our spirit goes on to be with our ancestors, regardless of where our body is."

I nodded, trying desperately to understand. "Ye said that ye only perform good magic? Is there dark magic, too?"

She nodded her head, then said, "Aye, there is dark magic, but my family and I do not practice it. We practice only good magic. We want only to heal, to help people."

Then, I understood, and when she crossed the great circle of ancient stones walking toward me, I met her halfway in the middle. I reached up a hand to touch the side of her face, pushing back her long sun-streaked hair that glowed silver in the moonlight as she leaned into my hand. "Thou art so beautiful, Lucia. I'm sure you already know that I'm in love with thee." I pulled her into my arms close to my chest. "I love thee, Lucia, and I always will."

"It matters not that I am a witch?" she asked, as her blue eyes shone a pale gray in the moonlight.

"It matters not," I replied, wrapping my arms around her. "I love thee." And then I softly touched my lips to hers and she responded, returning my kiss. My heart raced as our lips moved together as passion enveloped us in the moonlight, here in this sacred place. And in this place, I knew she would be mine ... forever ... my forever love.

"I love thee, too, Fredrick," she returned, reaching up to press her lips to mine, and I had never felt such love and warmth before in my life. "Fredrick, there is the Summer Solstice ball coming up. The town will celebrate it with dancing and song, but it is very special to my people. It's lots of fun. Will ye come?"

I nodded with a grin, and my lips crushed down onto hers again. Passion enveloped us both as our lips moved in familiar ways, as if we had always been together, as if we were meant to be together. "Aye, I will go, but for now, I must bring ye home. Your family will miss thee."

She nodded sadly and replied, "Aye, you're right ... and my father is a light sleeper."

I laughed, then said, "Well, I guess we had better go, then. I want to keep my head this night."

We laughed and she laid her head onto my shoulder as we slowly started making our way back to her house. On the edge of the forest, I pulled her into my arms once more, pressed my lips to hers and they moved together, as one, until she pulled away. "I had better go," she whispered, her breath a soft caress on my skin.

"Until tomorrow?" I asked, hating to let her go.

"Until then," she whispered, then added, "I love thee, Fredrick."

"And I love thee," I returned, then watched as she skipped across the road and slipped quietly into the front door of her home.

The weeks went by and I saw Lucia every day, but never again in the moonlight until it was time for the Summer Solstice ball. That day on my way into town to do my trading, Lucia was waiting on the rustic bench as was usual. "Good day, Miss Collins," I said as I approached.

"Lucia, please," she said with a smile. "Will I see ye tonight?"

"For what?" I teased, but the confused look on her face was too much, so I burst into laughter. "Aye, dear Lucia. I understand the ball will be in the town hall?"

"Aye, it is," she replied, then added, "Mother and Father are going, as well."

"I'm looking forward to it," I said, taking her hand, "but please wait for me. I want to be the one to escort ye tonight."

"Are ye sure? I could go with Mother and Father and meet you there."

"Nay, I want everyone to see the most beautiful girl in town on my arm," I teased, as she laughed.

"In that case, I will be waiting," she said, smiling.

I walked into town to conduct my business and everyone was talking of the Summer Solstice ball. Nothing much ever happened in our little village, so this ball gave much needed excitement to the town.

"Will ye be going to the dance tonight, Mr. Lee?" Mr. Franklin asked, making small talk as he paid me for a pelt.

Next to him, Mr. Douglas caught my eye and shook his head, warning me not to say it. "As a matter of fact, I am," I replied, as Mr. Douglas rolled his eyes.

Mr. Franklin laughed as the eyes of every man present were on me. "Pray, do not keep us in suspense! The rest of us are married men, so who will ye be taking?" The rest of the men agreed as they laughed, obviously living vicariously through me.

"I shall be taking the lovely Miss Lucia Collins," I replied, as everyone grew silent and their faces fell. Some were looking at the ground, not wanting to meet my gaze.

"That witch woman?" Mr. Franklin asked, as his face contorted into a snarl.

"Mind thy tongue, Franklin," I corrected as the other men said nothing. "She is a lady and I want no one to say anything ill of or her family again. Is that clear?"

"Now, don't ye be ordering me around, Lee," Mr. Franklin replied. "That woman and her family are witches!"

"I'm warning ye to be on thy best behavior tonight …"

"Thou? Warning me?" Mr. Franklin sneered. "Worry not, for if she is going, then I will not."

"It's thy decision," I said, feigning nonchalance.

Mr. Franklin's face screwed up into a snarl as he stormed off, followed by a few of the men.

"Ye really shouldn't taunt the men like that, ye know," Mr. Douglas warned.

"But it's fun," I said, not heeding his warning.

He rolled his eyes. "I shall see ye tonight."

"You're getting the Misses to go?" I asked, clearly shocked.

"Actually, the Misses would go without me, whether I go or not!" Mr. Douglas said, laughing.

"Tonight," I replied, as I headed back out of town toward my home.

On the way home, I found myself looking forward to the evening, but a little worried about Lucia. I could handle the rumors, but I wondered if she even knew what the town folk were saying. Lucia and her family were very inconspicuous about their ways, but people still talk. At home, I dressed in my finery, which consisted of a nice black suit, white shirt and boots, and waited for the sun to go down.

At dusk, I headed toward Lucia's house, unable to wait any longer. The sun had set when I arrived, and she was sitting on the rustic bench in front of her parent's apothecary. She stood when she saw me, smiling, and I had never seen a sight more beautiful. Her blonde-streaked hair was pulled up on the sides as the back cascaded down to her waist. She wore a light blue dress that matched the exact color of her eyes in the moonlight. "Ye look lovely," I said, catching my breath.

"Thank ye, Fredrick," she said, blushing a faint pink in the moonlight. "Ye look very handsome; quite the gentleman."

"Thank ye," I said as concern colored my voice. "Lucia, there's something I need to tell ye …"

"What is it? What's wrong?" Lucia asked, suddenly concerned as she stepped off the porch and walked toward me, but how was I to tell her? As the silence wore on, she finally said, "Just spit it out, Fredrick. What's wrong?"

"Lucia, they are saying things about ye and thy family in town ..."

"Shush ..."

"Lucia, they're saying that ye be a witch! They know!" I said placing a gentle hand on each of her shoulders. "They don't understand."

"What's there to understand?" she asked. "I am a witch."

"But not a bad one," I said, taking a deep breath. "They don't understand."

She reached up and placed a hand lightly on my cheek. "Ye understand and that's all that matters."

"Are thy parents ready?" I asked, looking toward the front door.

"They already left," she said, then added, "Are ye going to offer me thine arm?"

I released a breath I hadn't realized I was holding, and offered her my arm with a smile. "Shall we?"

She nodded with a smile and, together, we walked toward town, but as we neared the square, shouts coming from the town reached our ears.

"They be witches, I tell ye, and they have the gall to come here tonight?" Mr. Franklin was shouting to the crowd, trying to incite a riot. "I say we string 'em up!"

"Look, sir, we came here tonight to enjoy the Summer Solstice and to dance, that is all," Mr. Collins replied to the crowd.

"I say they came to do a spell on us all, since it is the Summer Solstice!"Mr. Franklin replied. "Mark my words. When ye wake in the morning to boils all over thy bodies, you'll remember these words! Let's string 'em up before they have the chance!'

"Now listen hear, ye, Mr. Franklin," Mrs. Collins said, pointing a finger at him as she crossed the square. "I treated your wife when she had the fever just last month and now she be fine! And the lot of ye," Mrs. Collins said, pointing to the crowd as they stepped back. "I did nothing but help ye loved ones. Will ye turn thy backs on us now? And thee!" she said, pointing again to Mr. Franklin, now holding a rope. "No one believes thy words. After all, ye be just a sack full of hot air!"

"Those are my parents!" Lucia screamed, but I placed a hand firmly over her mouth and pulled her into the shadows before anyone saw her.

"Shush … stay ye here," I ordered, pointing to the shadows, "no matter what happens." I wouldn't let her go until she nodded. "If anything happens to me, meet me at the stones." She nodded once again.

"Franklin!" I shouted across the square toward where he stood with Lucia's parents. "Do ye not have anything else better to do than to harass innocent people?"

"Mr. Lee! I see ye came after all!" Mr. Franklin yelled across the square. "And did ye bring the lovely Lucia with ye?"

"Leave my daughter out of this!" Mr. Collins shouted as two men grabbed each of his arms.

"Leave my husband alone!" Mrs. Collins shouted, then advanced upon Mr. Franklin and slapped him hard across the face, leaving a red mark.

"String them up!" Mr. Franklin yelled to the crowd.

A few people in the crowd shouted "Yeah, string them up!" "They be witches!" "Do it now!"

"Now, let's just calm down a bit, shall we?" I asked, then turned toward the crowd. "They have done nothing but help thee! They have done everything from helping people with births to those very sick from the fever! They are innocent and have done nothing wrong! Let them go!"

"I say, let's not give them a chance! String 'em up!" Someone shouted from the crowd and then more shouted, until everyone wanted their blood.

"Go! I'll distract them and then ye run!" I said to Mr. And Mrs. Collins.

"I'm not leaving my home!" Mrs. Collins shouted at me, then yelled to the crowd. "I've helped ye! Will ye not stand with me now?"

But Mr. Franklin incited the crowd, preying on the naivety of the people until they were an angry mob. It was clear the crowd didn't understand the Collins family, and people—even good people—will kill what they don't understand. Suddenly, someone grabbed Mr. Collins and Mrs. Collins knocked the man to the ground. Within a second, they had a rope around her neck and around Mr. Collin's neck, as well. I tried to stop them, but before I could do anything, they were hanging from the end of a rope.

Lucia! I thought to myself, rushing toward the woods as someone tried to grab me, too, but I was too quick for them. I ran to the hiding spot where I left her and she wasn't there. Then, I remembered what I told her … that if anything happened, I would meet her at the stones.

I ran as quickly as I could into the woods, headed toward the ancient stones in the clearing. When I arrived, she was sitting on her knees, crying into her hands. "Lucia?" I softly asked, but she jumped a mile.

"They be dead, are they not?" she asked, looking up at me with tear-stained eyes.

"Aye, I'm very sorry," I said taking a step toward her.

"Touch me not!" Lucia shouted, hysterical.

"Lucia, all is well. I will care for thee," I said, then remembered something. "Lucia, we have to run … tonight. There is a ship leaving tomorrow … the *Mayflower* … and it's headed for the new country … America," I said, trying to talk some sense into her. I grabbed her shoulders, and continued, "But we have to leave … now!"

"But we're not married," Lucia said.

"No one knows that," I said, a bit surprised that she would think of such a thing with our lives on the line.

"I will know," she said, then looked into my eyes with the most pitiful look I'd ever seen.

"Tell you what …" I began, "Let's grab what we can from our homes and I know a preacher man who will marry us tonight."

"Can we get married here?" she asked, her eyes pleading, and I knew at that moment, I could deny her nothing.

"If we can. Let me talk to Paul first," I said, then added, "but no matter what happens tonight, we are leaving, married or not." Lucia nodded, drying her tears. "But we have to go … now." She nodded again and we were off. We ran through the woods as quickly as we could until we reached her house, but the apothecary was already ablaze. They wanted to make sure that they killed her, too, or that she didn't return. "Come on, let's go," I said, pulling her away as a new wave of fresh tears rolled down her face. She nodded and let me pull her away, in the direction of my home. In the surrounding woods of my home, I looked around and everything looked to be in place. "Ye stay here and wait for me," I instructed Lucia, kissing her hard on her soft lips. "I'll be right back, but if I don't come out, then go to Blackwall by tomorrow. I don't care how ye have to get there, but be on that ship when it sails. Maybe things might be different in the New World."

"Wait, let me do a protection spell over thee," she said, regaining her senses. Then she began chanting in a language I had never heard before. A moment later, she replied, "It is finished."

I nodded and headed toward the house, when suddenly a musket blast came from inside my own home. But suddenly, the bullet slowed in mid air until it fell onto the ground at my feet. I looked around and Lucia had her hand up, having stopped the bullet in mid air.

"See? What did I tell ye? She's a witch!" Mr. Franklin yelled from inside my house, then came onto the porch with four other men.

"Run!" I yelled to Lucia, but she held up her hands, as her blue eyes turned to fire. She held up both of her arms with her fingers spread and shoved. Suddenly, the four men heading toward us fell backward. "Nay, Lucia! Don't let them do this to thee!" I yelled, fearing that using this kind of magic would kill, not her body, but her soul. Then, with her hands still up, she slowly tightened her fingers into fists as the men on the ground started to choke. "Nay, Lucia!" I yelled, but she was way beyond hearing me. Suddenly, she began to chant in the foreign tongue and all four men stopped twitching, as they lay dead upon the ground.

The glazed over look in her eyes was gone and then she looked around, as if trying to understand where she was. "What happened, Fredrick?" she asked, then looked at the four men laying motionless on the ground as blood now seeped from their mouths, eyes and ears. "Good Lord! Did I do that?"

"Wait here," I said sternly, not answering her questions. "I'll be right back." She nodded and as quickly as I could, I ran into the house, grabbed all my money and a few clothes, then went out the back door toward a small barn where my horse, Blaze, waited. I led him out of his stable as he whinnied loudly. "Whoa, boy! Ye must be quiet tonight. We don't want to be heard," I gently cooed. As I patted the side of his neck, he quickly quieted down. Without bothering with a saddle, I slipped a bridle over his head, the bit into his mouth, and a riding blanket over his back and jumped onto his back.

When I walked Blaze around to the front of the house, Lucia was standing there, still looking at the four dead men laying haphazardly upon the ground and porch, with tears streaming down her cheeks. I quickly slid off the horse, wrapped my arms around her, and pulled her to my chest. "Lucia, we must go," I cooed gently into her ear.

"I didn't mean to do this! I didn't want to …" she bellowed as tears streamed down her cheeks. "It's dark magic … if I kill, I'll lose my soul!"

"Lucia, ye had no choice," I said, gently stroking her hair. "If ye hadn't, we'd both be dead now."

She nodded, coming to her senses as she dried her tears.

"We must leave ... now," I whispered urgently. It really was a miracle that anyone else hadn't come looking for us yet. She nodded again as I quickly climbed onto the horse then offered her my hand, and pulled her onto the horse behind me. Within minutes, we were racing to the next village. Through my trading business, I knew a lot of people ... and one was a minister.

"Where are we going?" Lucia asked, holding tightly around my waist as I pushed the horse as hard as he would go.

"Did ye not say ye wanted to be wed tonight?" I asked, listening, holding my breath for the answer.

"Aye, I did."

"Have ye changed thy mind?" I asked, again, holding my breath.

She paused for a moment, then answered, "Nay, of course not. I love thee, Fredrick. I always have and I always will."

"And I love thee," I replied as we raced onward against time, praying it would stand still just one night ... for us.

Within a short time, we rode up to a quaint little house, the home of Paul Davey. He was a protestant village preacher for the local church, who was married with eight children. How they all fit into his small house, I didn't know, but they all seemed very happy. The house was dark and I almost hated to wake him ... almost.

"Wait here," I said, but noticed the tears in her eyes as she nodded. I ran my fingers along her cheek, catching a tear. "Lucia, it really will be alright." She nodded again and I slid off the horse, hopped up onto the wooden porch and quickly beat on the door.

"What in blazes if going on?" a strong male voice bellowed from the other side of the door. "Hold ye shirt on!

I'm coming!" His eyes flew open wide when he saw me standing on his porch. "Fredrick? What in the blazes are ye doin' here? And at this time of night?"

"I have a favor to ask," I said, looking back over my shoulder at Lucia.

"Well, out with it then!" John ordered, then eyed Lucia on the horse, obviously upset and suddenly wide awake. "Fredrick, what has happened?" he asked, truly concerned.

"Who is it, dear?" a female voice asked from behind the door.

"Fear not, Susan," he answered, never taking his eyes off the two of us, concerned. "It's just Fredrick Lee."

"Well, ye should have said so!" Susan called out, as I heard footsteps getting louder until the door was pulled open wide. Mrs. Davey stood with the door open, holding a candle. Then, upon seeing me and the state Lucia was in, quickly asked, "Why, Mr. Lee? What has happened?"

"I hate to intrude, but might I have a word with thy husband … in private?"

"Oh! Of course," Mrs. Davey replied, then retreated back into the house. Mr. Davey waited, his eyebrows knit together, concerned.

"John, I have a favor to ask of thee," I began in a low voice. "Can ye marry us tonight?" I asked, nodding toward Lucia.

"What the blazes is this? Couldn't it wait until tomorrow? Thou art drunk, Lee. Go home and sleep if off. If ye still want to marry her in the morning, then I'll gladly make the arrangements," Paul said, pushing the door, but I put my foot in the door before it closed.

"Paul, I wouldn't be disturbin' ye if it wasn't important," I said, practically begging. "Please, the townspeople just hung her parents for witchcraft tonight …"

"Oh, dear God!" Paul said, quickly making the sign of the cross.

"Aye," I continued in a low voice. "I'm taking her away … tonight … but we must be married first."

John thought for a moment, concerned, then he looked directly at Lucia. "Do ye love him?" he asked and she nodded. "And ye wish to be married tonight?" Again she nodded. "Well, come in, then and I'll marry ye …"

"Would you mind marrying us in a sacred place?" Lucia asked, and I knew the exact place of which she was speaking.

"Well, here is a good place …"

"It would mean a lot to her … to us," I intervened, hopeful.

Paul took a deep breath. "And what place is that?"

"The meadow of the ancient stones," Lucia replied, raising her eyebrows.

Paul nodded. "Aye, that is a sacred place," he answered, then paused for a minute and, after a bit, nodded. "Aye, yes I'll do it. Just give me us a minute."

"Would you like me to ready the horses for ye?" I asked, knowing his wife would be coming with us, and that we had to go through the forest to get there. We needed a witness to make it legal.

"Aye, please ," he replied. "I'll only be a moment." From the tone of his voice, he knew the urgency of our request. I quickly prepared the horses and within a few minutes, Paul and Susan walked out of their house.

Susan walked over to me without hesitation and pulled me into a quick hug. "I'm so sorry to hear this, Mr. Lee," she said, patting the side of my cheek in a motherly way. Then, she crossed the short distance to Lucia, still waiting atop Blaze, took her hand and patted it. "My child, I'm so sorry for thy loss. Everything will work out."

"Susan, where are the children?" Mr. Davey asked, concerned as he helped his wife onto one of the horses.

"Annabel will watch them," she replied as she took the reins. Annabel was their eldest daughter.

Mr. Davey nodded and soon, we were off, pushing the horses as hard as they would go, and Lucia once again wrapped her arms around my waist, headed toward Stonehenge. Once we arrived, Blaze was a bit winded, but the Davey's horses were fine. I pulled Blaze to a stop and quickly helped Lucia down, as Paul did the same for his wife, Susan. Then, Paul and I quickly tied the horses to a tree, as Susan took Lucia off to the side.

"I hope ye don't mind or think me too presumptuous," Susan said to Lucia, "but I brought this along, thinking ye might like to wear it?" From under her cape, Susan pulled a lace veil, as tears sprang to Lucia's eyes. "I've had it for a while, but ye can have it, if ye like."

"It's lovely," Lucia replied, running a hand carefully over the lace shawl, then she turned to me, "I'll be right back."

I nodded, as tears sprang to my own eyes, as well. "Thank ye," I said to Mrs. Davey as she led my Lucia behind a tree.

"Well, my boy," Paul said, slapping me on the back. "Let's prepare."

I nodded, suddenly feeling a bit nervous. Paul and I picked a spot before one of the huge, ancient stones, facing the moonlight. It truly was a beautiful night. Moonlight illuminated everything, as if the earth was giving us its blessing. Then, Paul cleared his throat and I turned to face my bride. She looked lovely in the moonlight. Her long sun-streaked hair shone silver, and the lace veil was in perfect contrast to her pale, blue dress. She took off her sandals and walked barefoot along the soft green grass toward me, as a sheepish smile illuminated her face. Off to the side, Susan dabbed at her eyes. As soon as she drew near, I took her hand into my own, knowing we were one … forever.

"We are gathered here today …" Paul began, saying the traditional vows of our forefathers. It was a beautiful ceremony and even if we had planned it, it could not have been better. Soon, the ceremony came to an end with Paul's final words, "I now pronounce thee man and wife." Then he said to me, "Well? What are ye waiting for? Ye may kiss the bride." And I knew the moment my lips touched hers, I was finally home. A moment later, John cleared his throat and Susan giggled slightly, dabbing at her eyes.

"I love thee," I whispered, pulling my new bride into my arms.

"I love thee, too," Lucia returned, turning her chin up to me. My lips descended upon hers, a gentle caress, as I placed my hands gently on the sides of her face. When I pulled back, I knew I'd never forget the love radiating within her eyes as she looked into mine.

"I thank thee, Paul," I said, turning to face him and his wife.

"It be my pleasure," John returned, wrapping an arm around his wife. "This be the best wedding I've performed all year!"

"Well, let us be gone and leave these two lovebirds to themselves," Susan said, pulling her husband away.

"Go ye ahead, Susan, I'll be along in a moment," Paul replied, then turned to face me, and said in a low voice, "Do not be long. Ye do not want them to find thee. It's best if ye go."

I nodded, wrapping my arm around Lucia, pulling her into my side. "I understand. I don't know how to Thank thee …"

"Just take care of thyself … and this pretty little wife of thine," he added, as Lucia blushed.

"We'd better go," Susan said in a stage whisper, already atop one the mares.

"I'd better go before the Misses has my hide," Paul said with a smile, then patted my arm as he walked off. That was the last time I ever saw him, but I knew that I would be forever grateful to him.

When we were alone, I looked into Lucia's eyes and placed a gentle hand on her cheek as she closed her eyes and leaned into it. "We'd better go," I said, taking her hand, but she stopped me.

"Nay, Fredrick," she cooed in a husky voice, "Let's stay here tonight."

"But they might find us ..."

"Please ... I want to stay here ... with thee ... tonight," she said, with a lovely pale blush on her cheeks, as she looked down to the ground, embarrassed.

I place a gentle finger under her chin and slowly lifted it chin until our eyes met. "We can stay here," I agreed, knowing this might be our last night together if they caught us, but at least we would die in each other's arms ... as husband and wife. "I love thee, Lucia, my forever love."

"I love thee, too ... and I always will," Lucia said, then added, "Thou shalt always be in my heart."

Slowly, my lips descended upon hers as she closed her eyes. Our lips moved in familiar ways, gently, at first then passion enveloped us both as my lips moved with hers, as one. After a moment, I pulled back to allow her to catch her breath and slipped the lace veil from her sun-streaked hair, letting it fall to the ground. Slowly, I slipped her sleeve from her shoulder and let her beautiful blue dress fall to the ground beside the shawl, as both of our breaths quickened. She reached up and slowly unbuttoned my white shirt, exposing my muscular tanned chest, then she pushed my light brown wavy hair away from face and looked deeply into my eyes.

"I'll never forget this moment," she whispered, "It's what I've wished for all my life." Then carefully, I spread her lace shawl upon the ground, scooped my bride into my arms, and lay her gently down onto the ground. Then, I lay down beside her on the soft ground and in this holy place our bodies became one ... as husband and wife ... forever.

The next morning, I woke as sunlight danced across our bodies, caressing our cheeks, bidding us to wake. The birds were singing in the trees and then the reality of the night's events came rushing into my mind. I hated to have to do it, but I knew I had to wake my lovely bride. "Lucia, love, we must go," I said as I gently kissed her shoulder, brushing her long hair away from her face. "Lucia, love, wake up."

"If ye continue that," Lucia said, beginning to wake, "then we shant be going anywhere."

I laughed, continuing to kiss across her shoulders. "As tempting as that sounds, we really must go," I said, hating myself for suggesting it. Then, I suddenly remembered something. "The *Mayflower*! We must go. We must be on that ship." I quickly sat up, pulling on my pants and slipping into my shirt.

"Ye said the ship was to sail today," Lucia said, sitting up, reaching for her dress.

"Aye, but we might get lucky," I said, giving her shoulder one last kiss. "But we need to try."

Lucia nodded, slipping into her dress. "Aye, we should."

"Not so fast, Lee," a voice called from behind me, and my heart sank. In front of me, Lucia quickly finished buttoning up her dress. "Ahhh ... so, it's ye and the witch woman!"

"Watch how ye talk about my wife," I ordered, then turned around slowly to find Mr. Baker, the bartender, pointing a musket at my chest. He was alone. It would be a fair fight, one on one, but I didn't want my Lucia to get hurt.

"Wife! That's a laugh ..."

"We were married last night," I replied through gritted teeth. "Baker, ye don't want to do this. Put the musket down and go back to ye tavern," I said, edging toward him.

"I think not," he said with a sneer. "Everyone's seeking her! I'll be a hero ... when they string her up."

I inched closer to him with my arms up, then remembered the knife in my boot. "Baker, put the musket down …"

"Not on thy life!" he said, then pointed the musket at Lucia, watching wide eyed, frozen where she stood. "Hey, everyone! The witch is here!" he yelled loudly over his shoulder.

"Run, Lucia!" I yelled, then rushed at Mr. Baker, knocking him to the ground as I reached for the knife in my boot. He rolled over onto me, pinning me to the ground and I quickly flipped him off and bent down and hastily threw the knife with all my might, hitting him in the throat as the musket went off, shooting me square in the chest. I looked around as I fell to the ground and no one was coming … or, at least, I got him before anyone heard him.

"Fredrick!" Lucia shouted, rushing to kneel by my side as tears streamed down her face. "Oh, no, no, no!"

"Lucia … I don't have much time," I said, feeling my soul beginning to lift from my body, as my eyes began to close. "Lucia, listen to me … get to the *Mayflower* any way ye can. Go to Blackwall … it's leaving from there."

"I'm not leaving thee," she said, crying uncontrollably now, then she stopped short. "Wait. I can heal thee."

"Heal me?" I asked, smiling, knowing that my injuries were too great, even for magic to heal. "Lucia, no …"

"Hush … I can't lose thee, too … not now," she said, thinking quickly. Then, she ran off into the forest. I was relieved. I didn't want her to see me die. But a moment later, she came back with the branch from an oak tree and some leaves, I assumed were healing herbs.

Using a rock, she crushed the herbs, along with the oak leaves. Then, she stood and outstretched her hand over the field in the center of the ancient stones and chanted, *"Aquitus asparitus et parcium e tu. Aquitus asparitus et parcium e tu …"* over and again, until a small pool of water bubbled up from inside the ground in the center of the stones. Finding nothing to hold water with, she tore a length of fabric from the hem of her dress, ran to the stream and drenched the fabric. She hurried back and dribbled the water over the herb and oak leaf mixture, saying,

"Water of life, bring life to my love,
Oak or my fathers, heal from above.
Healing herbs, keep death away,
And forever, let my love with me stay."

It was the most beautiful prayer I'd ever heard, but I was losing blood and I could feel my life slipping away. "Lucia, I love thee …"

"Say not thy goodbyes to me, Fredrick Lee! Ye will not die," Lucia said as tears streamed down her cheeks. "The spirits are punishing me for taking the lives of those men …"

"Lucia, the spirits are not punishing thee," I said, reaching out to place a hand lightly on her cheek. "If I die today, then I die a happy man. Thou hast made me very happy. I will always love thee … my forever love." When I pulled my hand back, streaks of blood from my hand marred her beautiful face.

"Bring him back to me! Let him stay with me!" Lucia shouted to the heavens, as my eyes began to close. "No, NO!" she yelled, stroking my hair, then added, "I know what I must do …"

"No, Lucia. Don't use dark magic, love …"

"Hush! I'll do what I have to do … no matter who I have to bargain with."

"No! I won't allow thee to risk thy soul for me! Let me go, love," I begged, cringing from the pain, weak from the loss of blood. Then, I was beyond pain, beyond feeling. "Let me go."

"Nay, Fredrick," she said, then bent down to softly kiss my lips. "I waited for thee for so long … I'm not letting ye go." Then, my soul started to lift from my body when I heard her say, "I know what I must do." She began chanting and suddenly a snake crawled out from the forest's edge, coming toward us … a King Cobra … one of the most dangerous, venomous snakes in the world, but what was it doing here? They weren't indigenous to England. She chanted as she pulled my knife from Baker's head and slit her wrist with it, and held it to my lips. "Ye need blood … drink."

"What in the …"

"I said drink! There is no time to waste!" Lucia ordered as her blue eyes flared a brilliant green, and the snake inched forward, twisting and turning until it stopped before Lucia and me. I was starting to lose consciousness, but I drank the blood she offered. She began chanting in her ancient tongue, locking eyes with the snake. The King Cobra raised up half its body length, flared its neck and followed Lucia's movements, swaying from side to side, never taking her eyes from the snake. She opened her mouth wide into a snarl and bit down into the air, then the snake bit her arm. Then, the snake bent down and struck me, biting first my leg and then my arms, with Lucia guiding it. Searing pain flooded my body, setting it on fire as the venom spread through my body.

"Please kill me, Lucia! I'm burning alive!" I shouted into her face, as her eyes flared green. Then, she held her wrist that the cobra bit to my lips, forcing the blood into my system, as the ancient stones glowed brightly within the clearing. After biting me countess times, the snake slithered away, but disappeared before it reached the forest's edge. I sucked the blood and venom from her wrist, understanding that the great snake and I shared Lucia's blood. I drank until I was sure there was no venom tainting her blood, then pulled away, screaming and writhing in pain, burning alive from the inside out as she continued to chant in her ancient tongue.

"Now, ye are becoming a different creature," Lucia said, between chants. "Thou art no longer human, and human diseases will not harm you. Ye shall have the strength of a hundred men, but you will crave blood … above all else. Ye must needs learn to control it, but I will help thee." It was then that I knew she had bartered my soul … with her own.

"Lucia, what have ye done? Kill me!" I screamed as I writhed in pain for two days.

"No, ye shall be fine soon," she cooed, never leaving my side.

"Why did ye do this to me?" I screamed, "Let me go!"

"Sorry, but I just couldn't."

Then, just as abruptly as it began, the pain began to subside ... first from my fingertips ... then from my legs ... until I began to regain normal feeling again, and through it all, Lucia never left my side. As I started to regain control of my senses, I felt stronger than ever before ... invincible. It was an incredible feeling, but a thirst like I've never felt before overwhelmed me. "Lucia, what have I become?"

Lucia thought for a moment, then replied. "I'm not quite sure, but ye will no longer be human."

I nodded, letting the information sink in. If I wasn't human, then what was I?

"I'm sorry, Fredrick, but I just couldn't let ye go," she said looking into my eyes.

"We'll figure it out together," I said, then pulled her into my arms, but I could smell her blood ... pulsing in her veins ... beckoning to me to feed ... to bite ... Suddenly, I pushed her away.

"Fredrick?" she asked, bewildered.

"Lucia ..." I said as my breath quickened. "This is going to sound strange, but I ..."

"What, Fredrick?" she asked, taking a step closer, but I immediately stepped back. "Whatever it is, just say it."

"Lucia ... I don't know any other way to say it ... but I want thy blood ... to drink it ... I hear it pulsing in thy veins ... calling to me ..." I quickly turned away, ashamed for even saying such a ludicrous thing, for even thinking it.

"What have I done?" Lucia asked, taking a step back.

"Lucia?"

"Fredrick, there are stories of blood drinkers … monsters," Lucia said, not sure what to say or do. "They are killers …"

"But I don't want to kill! I don't want to be a monster!"

"Then, don't be," she said, taking a step closer to me. Then, she picked up my knife and punctured her wrist in the same place that she did before. Immediately, blood dripped down her wrist …

"No, Lucia! What are ye doing?" I asked, taking a step back, horrified. "I don't want to kill thee …"

"Then don't," she said, offering me her freshly punctured wrist. Blood was flowing from her wound on her wrist, falling toward the ground … but I caught it before it was lost. I lifted it to my lips and the overwhelming sensation of blood … the coppery, salty-sweet taste … the life-giving force of blood … My breath quickened as I tried to fight the desire to taste … to feed. Unable to take it anymore, I took her wrist into my hand and looked into her eyes as her luscious blood dripped onto my hand. She nodded, and I held her wrist to my mouth and drank of her goodness … her life-giving force … her blood. I noticed she started to sway on her feet, so I immediately stopped before I drained her completely. The sensation was euphoric … better than anything I had ever experienced before … almost better than sex, but not quite.

"Oh, my Lucia," I cooed into her ear, pulling her to my chest as I wrapped my arms around her. "Lucia, I'm so sorry."

"Nay, don't be," she replied in a weak voice. "Don't be."

"We have to get thee something to eat," I said, picking up my white shirt from our wedding night. When Fletcher shot me, I had just enough time to slip into my pants and my chest was bare. I looked down at my chest, wiped away the blood and it was completely healed. "Thank ye," I said to my Lucia as I slipped into my white shirt, hoping the blood stains on my chest wouldn't bleed through before I could bathe.

"Do not thank me," Lucia said as tears streamed down her face. "Look what I've done to thee."

"Lucia ..." I gently cooed, pulling her into my arms. "Ye saved my life."

"But ..."

"But nothing," I cut her off. "The rest we will work out ... together." She nodded and I helped her onto the back of my horse, knowing I had to get her some food ... soon. "Lucia, when is the last time ye ate anything?"

"Before the dance," she replied.

"That was two days ago, at least," I said as I folded Lucia's lace veil and slid it into my leather pouch along with my clothes. Then, I slid into the saddle in front of her and she quickly slid her arms around my waist. "We have to head toward the *Mayflower,* but we shall get ye something to eat on the way."

"Do ye not think that it already sailed?" Lucia asked, resting her head on my back as I ran Blaze through the woods, staying hidden. "I know of a tavern in the next town ..."

"Nay, we need to get as far away as possible," Lucia interrupted sleepily. "I can wait." But deep down inside, I wondered if she really could. Then, I had an idea. "Lucia? Can ye wait until we get a few towns away?" She nodded into my shoulder, but said nothing. I ran Blaze all day into the night until the sun had gone down completely. Even though it was dark out, I could see with complete clarity. I knew that Blaze needed to eat, too, but grass would have to do for now.

I pulled Blaze abruptly to a stop and Lucia nodded awake. Relieved, I slid off the horse and helped her down. She was weak and needed food ... now. I took the heavy blanket from Blazes' back, doubled it up and laid it on the ground. "Lay down for a bit. Ye need to rest. I'll be back straight away." She nodded, too tired to resist, and let me place the blanket under her head for a makeshift pillow as she lay under an old oak tree. I knew that to Druids, oak trees had healing powers. I didn't know if it would work, but I snipped a fresh green oak leaf from the tree and held it to her lips. "Here, suck on this for a bit," I said and she complied. I wasn't sure if it would work, but it was worth a try.

I quickly built her a fire and left to hunt ... for her. I was amazed at the speed at which I could run, but there was too much at stake. Suddenly, I smelled some white-tailed deer to the right in a clearing. As I drew near, they were drinking from a crystal clear lake. I slid behind a tree, staying downwind from them, so they couldn't catch my scent. Then, a doe lifted her head and sprinted toward the woods while the others followed. As quick as a flash, I darted after them and caught the doe, bringing her down with ease, careful of her sharp hooves. I heard her heart pushing her luscious blood through her body. It didn't smell as good as human blood, but good enough. Quickly, I sank my teeth through the folds of muscle and sinew of her neck, finding the main artery, then let her heart do the rest as I drank my fill. She struggled futilely, then one of her hooves caught me on the forearm before I was finished. Suddenly, she grew weak as her heart inadvertently failed.

Then, I knew. I could survive on animal blood. It didn't taste as good as human blood, but it would do and I wouldn't have to kill humans. I didn't want to kill ... to be a monster. I picked up the doe like it was a feather and slung her over my shoulders, around my neck. Then, I ran swiftly back to Lucia. As I neared the place where I left her, I knew the fire would keep the wild animals away from her, but she needed sustenance ... now. Within a few minutes, I was back at the fire where I left Lucia. "Hello, love," I gently cooed into her ear.

"Thou art here," she whispered, looking weak and very pale.

"Aye, love. I'm here. I will never leave thee," I said, giving her a kiss on her forehead. She gave me a weak smile and closed her eyes. I left her to rest and used my knife to cut up the deer. I whittled green sticks, ran them through the meat and held them over the fire. I quickly discovered that fire wasn't my friend and was careful not to get too close to it.

I also knew that Lucia needed water. She needed fluids. While the meat was cooking, I thought of running back to the lake where the deer were drinking, but I had nothing to carry the water in. Then, I had a thought. Would my blood help her the way it helped me? It was crazy, but without giving it a second thought, I slit my wrist and held it to her lips. She struggled a bit, but was too weak to resist, as I let my blood drain into her mouth and down her throat. Already, I could hear her pulse growing stronger. It was then that I learned that my blood had healing powers for humans. Soon, the meat was cooked and I cut it up into tiny pieces and placed it into her mouth, feeding her. Before the front hind quarter was gone, she sat up, took the meat into her own hands, and hungrily fed herself, digging in, biting off huge chunks of meat. "Well, I'm so glad ye are feeling better," I said, clearly enjoying watching her eat, knowing she would be fine.

"Sorry," she sheepishly replied, holding a hand to her lips, and the blush on her cheeks was an exquisite shade of pink.

"Nay, don't be! It's grand to see that ye feeling better!" I said, laughing.

"I have a question," Lucia asked. "Did ye feed me thy blood?"

"Aye, I did," I replied, then added. "I think it healed thee."

She nodded. "That makes sense."

"How is that?" I asked, intrigued.

"Well, I healed thee, so now thy blood can heal me … humans. It makes sense," she said, taking another bite of the venison as I laughed. She ate for a good while, then finally slowed down. "That was delicious. Thank ye."

"Thank ye, my love," I said, then wrapped my arms around her shoulder, leaning her back beside the fire, as she curled into the crook of my arm. Get some rest, love. I'll stand guard. Ye shall be safe."

"Are ye not tired? Do ye not need to rest?" Lucia asked, lifting her head to look into my eyes.

"No, not at all," I replied, and she nodded. Soon, she drifted off to sleep.

The next morning, the fire died out and I scattered the ashes. "Lucia, love," I whispered into her neck, smelling her sweet scent. "Time to wake."

"I'm hungry," she said, sitting up.

Luckily, there was plenty of cooked venison left from the night before, so I cut off some of the meat, handed it to her and she eagerly accepted. She sank her teeth into the venison and ate her fill, as I prepared Blaze for the journey, knowing I would have to find some grain soon. He couldn't survive on grass alone for a long period of time. "Ready, love?" I asked when she stood, holding Blaze steady. She nodded and I slid into the saddle and helped her up behind me. We rode silently for a while, but sometimes we laughed or talked about our hopes for the future. Then, a thought occurred to me. "Lucia, why are ye such a powerful ... witch?" The word seemed awkward on my lips when referring to my beloved Lucia.

She grew silent, and I immediately regretted the question. "When a witch dies, their energy goes to the next of kin. Since both my mother and my father died and they were both witches," she paused for a moment, remembering, "their power was released into me, along with all of my ancestors that were witches." She was silent for a bit, then said, "I come from a long line of witches."

"So, ye inherited the power of all the witches within thy lineage?" I asked, truly amazed.

"Aye," Lucia said, then her voice broke on the last part, "That is why I couldn't save my parents. I didn't have enough power ... until they died."

I sat for a moment, taking it all in. "I'm so sorry for ye, Lucia." And deep down, I wish there was something I could do to make it up to her.

We rode for days, traveling within the shadows of the forest by day and resting by night. Once, we came to a barn and I was able to get some grain for Blaze. I hated to take the grain, but Blaze was growing thin and we needed him to remain strong. Also, he had been my horse since he was a colt and I loved him. He was a great horse. At another house, there were clothes drying on a clothesline, so I was able to get a clean dress for Lucia and a clean shirt for myself. We needed to save what money I had from trading for our journey that lay ahead.

It took us five days to get to Blackwall. I just hoped that the *Mayflower* was still there. It promised freedom in the New World—freedom from oppression, freedom to worship, freedom to live ... freedom. Maybe there, my Lucia will be safe. When we arrived, to my amazement, the ship was still there. So, Lucia changed into her new dress as I slipped into my new shirt and we approached the ship. We both felt exposed and vulnerable in the open, having traveled in seclusion for so long.

We both looked around as we rode up toward the ship setting in the harbor, looking for anyone from our village that may be looking for us. Even though it was doubtful that anyone followed us out this far, we kept a watchful eye nevertheless. "Try to act natural," I said to Lucia, riding behind me on Blaze. I could feel her nod her ascent.

"Might I help ye, sir?" a gentleman with short, blonde hair asked, carrying a musket, standing guard.

"Aye, may I speak to the captain?" I asked as Lucia waited.

"Aye, what about?"

"Passage … to America," I said, awaiting his response.

The gentleman nodded and lowered his weapon. "Ye be in luck! Our passage has been delayed. We've been waiting here in port for a week now, but we should be shoving off soon."

"What are ye waiting for?" I asked, making small talk.

"Ah, some pilgrims … church people."

I nodded, feigning concern. "Who may I ask is the captain?"

"Aye, Captain Christopher Jones," he replied with obvious pride. "I'll go fetch him."

I nodded my ascent.

"Do you think we'll gain passage?" Lucia asked, worried.

"We shall see, but let's just wait a bit," I said, trying to sound comforting.

A few moments later, a middle aged, tall gentleman with dark, wavy hair brushing his shoulders approached with the blonde man. "This be the gentleman I told ye about, Captain Jones."

Captain Jones looked up at me sitting atop Blaze and said, "Well, are ye coming down from there, or shall I look up at ye all day?"

I smiled, already liking his spunk, and slid down off the horse, then helped Lucia down, too. "My wife and I have journeyed long to seek passage," I said. "Might ye have room aboard your (thy) ship?"

Jones sighed, then looked at the blonde gent. "Well, we are waiting for some church people, and we can use the money … can ye pay for thy passage? For ye and the Misses?"

"Aye," I said, hoping he wouldn't ask an astronomical amount, but we couldn't wait. It was just a matter of time before the town folk of our village caught up with us.

Jones scratched the short stubble of his brown whiskers on his chin and said, "Well, if ye be going, what do ye plan to do with thy horse?"

"Sell him, I guess," I said, then added, "unless ye have room?"

Jones laughed, enjoying the joke. "No, but we have room for the likes of the two of thee; however, ye need to pay now."

"Aye. Thank ye, sir," I said, reaching into my pocket for the money.

Once I counted it out, Jones said, "Well, right this way, Mr. ... Mr. ..."

"Lee," I supplied, taking Lucia's hand. "Fredrick Lee, and this lass is my lovely wife, Lucia."

"Lucy, It's a pleasure to meet ye," Jones said, taking her hand into his, then raised it to his lips to kiss it chivalrously.

"Lucia, please," she corrected, smiling sweetly.

"So be it ... Lucia," Jones said in acknowledgement. "We are awaiting supplies, along with the passengers, then we shall set sail."

"If ye have a bow and arrows, I can hunt for ye," I offered, knowing we could cure the meat before we sailed.

"That's a fine offer," Jones said, slapping me on the back with a smile, then looked at Blaze. "Ye horse is a bit starved, but I can fatten him up before we go, then ye should fetch a fine price for him. It'll help ye on the trip."

"I'd be much obliged," I replied, moved by his offer of kindness.

"We have a stable here for our horses. You may keep him there, if ye like."

"Aye , Thank ye."

"Come ... I'll show you where it is," Jones said, then said to Lucia. "My Misses can show ye to your quarters."

"Thank ye," Lucia said with a smile.

"Ye should wait 'til ye see it before ye be thanking me," Jones said, laughing. "Ye might change thy mind."

"Nay, never," Lucia said, clearly amused. "We're just looking forward to a safe passage to America."

"The name's Brandon ... Peter Brandon," the blonde gentleman said, offering his hand. I shook it, but then his eyebrows pulled together, concerned. "Ye hand ... it's so cold."

"Well, it be cold out here and we've been traveling in the open for a bit," I replied, trying to cover, making a mental note not to shake hands with people unless it was necessary or unless I wore gloves. I knew that would be the first thing I bought, when I could. Then, I turned my attention back to Jones. "Where be the stables, again?"

"Right this way," Jones said, slapping me on the back. "Worry not about thy wife. My Misses will show her to your quarters and then ye can join her."

"Thank ye," I said. As I followed Mr. Jones to the stables, I gave Lucia a worried look over my shoulder. She gave me an encouraging glance back, telling me not to worry, but after what happened in our village, I didn't want to leave her alone for long ... no matter how much power she possessed.

Not long after, I joined Lucia in our quarters. The room was small, but private, knowing that being a vampire on a long voyage would be taxing to my control. And on a ship— no matter how big or small—word would spread quickly.

"How are ye, love?" she asked, running a finger along the dark circles under my eyes. To a human, it probably looked like I was just tired, but in reality, I needed to feed.

"I be fine," I said, pulling her into my arms. "How are ye?"

"Fine," she said, but I could tell she was tired.

I nodded. "Why don't ye stay here and rest while I borrow Brandon's bow to hunt."

Lucia laughed. "Dearest, ye needn't a bow."

"Aye, but they don't know that," I replied, enjoying hearing her laugh again. "Rest and I shalt return soon."

She nodded and I helped her settle into the small bed meant for the two of us. Of course, I didn't need as much sleep as humans. We can go for extended periods of time before we need sleep, but then we go into a coma, of sorts, appearing to be dead.

Brandon obliged, loaning me his bow and arrows and I came back shortly with a stag. It was enough for everyone on the ship, but for only one meal. I made a deal with Jones, telling him that I would hunt every day to save our supplies until we set sail. Meanwhile, I loaded up on blood to the point of gluttony in preparation for the long voyage ahead. It worked out well, but Brandon soon became suspicious.

Within a few more days, we set sail. On the *Mayflower,* there were many shops where a person could buy supplies for use in New World, so Lucia and I enjoyed walking the deck in the evening before the ships closed, collecting supplies that we would need. The ship made its way down the Thames into the English Channel and on to Southampton Water, where we waited.

"Why have we stopped, Mr. Jones?" I asked him one day on the deck while taking a leisurely stroll.

"We be awaiting the arrival of another ship, the *Speedwell,*" he replied. "They will sail with us to America."

I nodded. Although I was concerned, I concealed it well. I knew that the longer it took for us to reach America, the harder it would be for me to find blood and to conceal my vampirism, as it later came to be known. "How long will we be waiting?" I asked.

He shrugged. "They're on their way, so it shant be long," Jones replied, then one corner of his mouth curled into a half smile. "Why? Are ye in a hurry to get to America?"

I laughed, then said, "Aye, a bit, I guess." If the circumstances were different, I knew that Captain Jones and I could have become great friends, but after what happened to Lucia's parents, I trusted no one with my secret.

We waited another week until the *Speedwell* finally joined us. We started for the New World but the *Speedwell* sprang a leak. We had to go back and repair it quickly, but when we started out again, it sprang another leak. Jones suspected foul play, as the captain of the *Speedwell* always appeared nervous when America was mentioned, but this time, the *Speedwell* went back and we finally embarked on our journey.

Lucia and I stayed in our cabin as much as possible, but the effects of having no blood was wearing on me. At night, I crept down to the hull of the *Mayflower* and fed on the blood of rats that lived there. The blood was rancid, but it sustained me temporarily. Then, one night Lucia surprised me. "Feed from me," she said as she once again touched the slight purple patches beneath my eyes.

"Lucia, I cannot take advantage of ye …"

"Take advantage?" she said with a laugh. "I was the one that made ye into what ye are." She took a step toward me, but picked up a knife that lie on the small dresser and slit a wide cut on her hand. Then, she held it out to me, as her blood pooled into her cupped hand. "Feed from me," she repeated, and this time, I couldn't resist. In an instant, I was at her side, holding her cupped hand within my own. I looked pleadingly into her eyes, warring with my love for her and my insatiable need for blood. She nodded with a smile and I raised her cupped hand to my lips and drank, careful to stop before I took too much. Soon, I pulled back, cut my own hand, and fed it to her. A moment later, her hand was completely healed, and she didn't feel the effects of the blood loss as much, either.

Afterward, I held her within my arms, then my lips descended upon hers hungrily, craving another need almost as strong as my need for her blood. Our lips moved in familiar ways as passion enveloped us both within the privacy of our cabin.

The journey was arduous and Lucia and I continued in this way, but I tried to wait to feed from her for as long as I possibly could. I didn't want to kill her accidentally by taking too much blood too soon. So, I kept up my trips to the ship's hull and the rats, as well. One night after one of my trips from the ship's hull, Mr. Brandon was waiting for me. "Out for an evening stroll?" he asked.

"Aye indeed," I replied, straightening my shirt. "Lovely night."

I tried to pass by, but his words stopped me. "In the ship's hull?" he asked suspiciously, as I stared at him, waiting. "What do ye do down there?"

"Just checking out the cargo …"

He suddenly grabbed my arm, and I turned around and looked into his eyes, as mine flared. "Ye saw nothing. I've been asleep in my cabin with my wife all night," I said.

His eyes went blank, then he repeated, "I saw nothing." Then, he walked on his way. It was the first time I knew that vampires had powers to control the mind. I also started hearing the thought of others within my own mind, as well, at first, afraid I was going crazy. I had to learn to control listening to people's thoughts, learning how to block them out until I wanted to listen in. After that night, I started listening to Brandon's thoughts often, and he remained suspicious.

As our journey droned on, the days grew colder. One good thing was that the sun wasn't so bright. It actually does nothing to me, but my skin glows as if slathered in baby oil in the direct sunlight. Today, it doesn't present a problem, but in those days, it could. Most people looked pale, some sick and frail. If I walked around looking like a model who had been lying out in the sun, people would notice.

After the night that Mr. Brandon spotted me coming up from the hull of the ship, I tried to wait longer periods of time between feeding, so as not to attract attention, but waiting too long created a risk of exposure. We were halfway through our voyage and I had waited too long between feeding, when Brandon spotted me on the deck again one night. "Out for another midnight stroll, Lee?" he asked sarcastically.

"Aye, and thee?" I asked, hearing his strong heart pump luscious, life-giving blood through his veins …

"Aye, and what brings ye out on such a night?" he asked, looking around at the gale that surrounded us. The storm was beating the ship, spraying water onto both Mr. Brandon and myself.

"Nice night," I said sarcastically. "And thee? What brings ye out on such a treacherous night?"

"Just out for a stroll," he replied, as he added within his mind, *and watching out for ye. I know ye are a monster, no matter what anyone else thinks.*

"So, is that what ye think?" I asked, unable to resist responding to his thoughts. "That I'm a monster?"

Shock, then anger flitted quickly across his face. Then, he quickly composed himself and said, "So, I was right."

"Aye, ye are," I replied, then grabbed him, pulled him into the ship's hull, and sank my teeth into his neck. Despite his sour disposition, his blood was sweet and delicious, and slid down my throat, filling the far reaches of my capillaries. I drank my fill, but stopped before I drained him dry. To my horror, he was screaming that he was burning from the inside out. That was when I realized that I was venomous. If I bit my victims, then I had drain them dry, or they would turn into vampires, too. He begged me to kill him over and again. His shouting was so loud that if I didn't do something quickly, he would expose Lucia and me. So, thinking of Lucia, I broke off a wooden stake from a nearby crate. "I am so sorry that this happened to ye," I said, then drove the stake through his heart as his eyes opened wide in horror. Blood pooled from the wound and I took his arm and bit into it, draining him dry. After his death, I carried his limp body up the stairs of the hull. Before walking onto the deck, I looked around to ensure no one was watching, and threw his body overboard, knowing the sharks that followed our ship for scraps would take care of his body. I told no one about that night—not even Lucia—but when Brandon was discovered missing, I'm sure she knew.

After Brandon's disappearance, everyone was a bit more careful about walking the decks at night, creating less watching eyes for me. After that night, I could go down to the hull to feed on the rats as often as I needed, then I carried their bodies up to the deck and threw them overboard so no one became suspicious. The blood was hideous, but served its purpose.

We finally reached America, landing at Plymouth in November, the Year of Our Lord 1620. Our landing was none too soon, as I wasn't the only one that was starving. Many of the passengers onboard were starving, as well. It was already cold in the New World, and looked to be uninhabited. I tried to hunt game for everyone, but there was little to be had, but one day I was lucky enough to catch a bear before it hibernated. I drained it dry and I shot it with an arrow in the neck to make it look good. Then, I went back to the village to get some men to help carry the carcass back. Of course, I could easily have carried it back to the village, but they would suspect even more than they already did.

Before long, the humans started dying off. We tried to build shelter in time, but the cold was brutal. At night when everyone slept, I worked on it at super speed without anyone knowing, but it still wasn't enough. Also, the food supply was dwindling and children were dying of the fever, as well. It was a brutal time. And it was very hard to stand by helplessly and watch as so many humans died, many of which had become my friends. But soon, we finished the shelter and I hunted rabbits or bears sleeping in their dens. Of course, I told the others that the animals had ventured out of their dens, but most of the humans were so hungry that they didn't care. Food was food, after all, no matter the source. But I worried the most about Lucia. She was growing weaker by the day, even though she did a protective spell over herself. She was so weak that I didn't dare feed from her, so often times, I went longer than I should have between feedings, which wasn't good.

By Spring, the worst was over. The American Indians had made themselves known by then and were helping our small village as much as they could by bringing us grain and food. They even taught us how to plant and grow food.

But by then, many had begun to suspect that something was different about me … and Lucia. So, we decided to go off on our own. Deep in the woods, I built us a cabin and it was some of the happiest days of our lives. Over time, we realized that I wasn't aging, so Lucia performed a spell to keep herself from aging, as well. We lived happily deep in the woods for the next seventy years with neither of us aging.

Of course, many of the passengers of the *Mayflower* had died off, but rumors still circulated about blood drinkers, which became worse, having been added upon by the villagers due to ignorance and fear. Many of the rumors included that vampires burst into flames in the sun, was warded off by garlic, and was afraid of crosses and holy relics—all of which are untrue. In fact, I have many holy relics that I still cherish today.

Over time, Lucia grew hungry for the company of others, so we journeyed to another local settlement that sprang up as the population grew. We didn't want to go back to Plymouth for fear that the rumors of blood drinkers were still running rampant. And after what happened to Lucia's parents, we understood that people killed what they didn't understand.

I built us a small cabin on the outskirts of town, much like the apothecary that belonged to Lucia's parents. Over time, Lucia began collecting herbs and planting flowers in the style of the old days.

"What are ye doing?" a small voice asked Lucia one day.

"Planting flowers," Lucia replied, jabbing her finger down into the soil to plant another seed. When she turned around, a young brunette girl was there, wearing a calf-length dress and a bonnet. Her hair was in two braids and she couldn't have been over twelve years old. "Would ye like to help?" She nodded, and soon Lucia showed the young girl how to plant. "What's thy name?"

"Elizabeth Hubbard," the young girl replied, clearly enjoying working alongside my Lucia.

I walked out the door, smiling. "Well, it looks like thou hast made a friend," I said to my lovely wife. Both Lucia and Elizabeth looked up and smiled, then continued their work, laughing as they planted. "I'm going hunting and will be back later," I said with a bow and a sheath of arrows slung over my shoulder to make it look good.

"Bring us back some venison," Lucia said over her shoulder.

"That's the intent," I replied, returning the smile. In the safety of the woods, I ran as quickly as I could, enjoying the Spring day of 1692. The wind blew through my hair as I ran almost to Canada, enjoying the feel of letting my muscles stretch. Then, I caught a familiar scent and slowed as the scent of white-tail deer came rushing to my nostrils. I came to a stop and hid behind a tree. Two doe and a stag were drinking water at a small natural watering hole, taking turns keeping watch. Headed for the stag, I took off in a flash as the three deer sprinted away. I caught the five-point steer by the antlers as the two does ran off. It was between us men now.

The deer pawed frantically with its razor sharp hooves and one caught my arm, tearing the sleeve and leaving a gash deep into the skin, but before it healed, I bared my teeth and bit into the thick skin, fur and muscle of the steer's neck. Immediately, blood rushed into my mouth and down my throat, filling every capillary of my body. You see, vampires metabolize blood for food. It carries oxygen to every part of our bodies, just like a human's body, but a vampire's body uses the blood for food. If a vampire goes for too long without eating, his or her body would cease to function and would become a living corpse—unable to die, unable to move, unable to live.

After I drank my fill, I slung the steer over my shoulders around my neck with ease, then I ran it back to my Lucia. When I arrived back to our cottage, Lucia and Elizabeth were just finishing planting flowers. "There's my man," Lucia said, eyeing me over her shoulder.

"And I brought ye back some venison, just as ye asked," I replied, giving her a quick peck on the cheek as Elizabeth watched.

"What happened to thine arm?" Elizabeth asked, concerned, noticing the scratches on my arm and torn sleeve.

"I be fine," I reassured her. "Just a little scratch."

Lucia quickly turned her shoulders around until she was pointed toward the road. "I think it's time for ye to go home now. Thy mother might be worried." Then, she added. "It was nice to meet you."

"Nice to meet ye, too," Elizabeth said, worried, but did as she was told and hurried down the road.

But I had a sinking feeling as I watched her go. "Lucia, I think it's time for us to move on," I said, still holding the steer around my shoulders.

"Nonsense," Lucia said, smiling. "I feel like we're finally fitting in here."

I took a deep breath, then let it out slowly. "Just be careful," I said.

"Well, let's go in and enjoy this venison, shall we?" Lucia said, smiling as she took my arm and I led her into the cabin.

Over the next few months, Elizabeth visited Lucia every day, and Lucia loved working in the garden beside her. On her visits, they talked of many things, but I had cautioned her never to tell her of the magical arts. After what I had seen in the past, I knew that mass hysteria could happen in one night, as it did with Lucia's parents.

One Summer day, Elizabeth brought a friend with her to visit Lucia, who was working in the garden, planting medicinal herbs. Her backed was turned and she didn't hear the girls walk up. Steadily, she held out her hands over the seeds, closed her eyes, and sprouts began to spring up into tiny plants, then blossomed. The girls hung back, whispering, darting behind a bush. "Did ye see that?" the other girl whispered to Elizabeth. "She be a witch!"

"Now, Abigail, don't ye be starting that again," Elizabeth said, then walked out from behind the bush, as the other girl followed. "She's a nice lady."

"So were the other ladies. We shall see," Abigail replied, then walked up to Lucia.

"Hello, Miss," Elizabeth said, touching Lucia on the shoulder.

"Well, hello, Elizabeth!" Lucia said, returning her warm smile. "I'm pleased that ye came back for another visit."

"Yes … hello, Mrs. Lee," Elizabeth said timidly.

"Please, call me Lucia," she said, then turned to her friend. "And who do we have here?"

"This is my friend, Abigail Williams," Elizabeth said, frowning.

"What seems to be ailing ye today? Ye don't seem to be quite yourself," Lucia asked, placing a gentle hand on her shoulder.

"Her stomach seems to be ailing her today," Abigail replied, looking at Elizabeth sympathetically. "Might ye have something that will help her?"

Lucia looked at the girl suspiciously, then replied, "I think ye should go home and ask thy mother."

"But it's a bit of a walk," Abigail said, as Elizabeth held her stomach, not knowing what to do. "Please, can ye help her?"

Lucia reached for an herb out of the garden, when I stepped out onto the porch. "Lucia, I don't think we should be entertaining guests today," I said, concerned. "I need thy help inside."

"I'll only be a minute ..." Lucia said, picking the herb, as Abigail sneered. Elizabeth's eyes darted back and forth between us, obviously afraid to stand up to her friend.

"No, my love," I interrupted, then stepped closer to Elizabeth. "I'm sorry, but I need for thee to go home now and forget what ye saw."

"Forget what I saw ..." Elizabeth repeated as her eyes glazed over.

"What form of sorcery is this?" Abigail asked, her eyes open wide as she took a step back. "Witches! Ye both be witches!" she said, then ran down the road toward town.

Quickly, I looked into Elizabeth's eyes and said, "It's time for thee to go home." Then, she obeyed, turning around to walk back down the road.

Once the girls were gone, Lucia turned to me and said, "What have ye done? She was my friend!"

"Lucia, she is not thy friend," I said, taking her shoulders to look into her eyes. "I have to go after Abigail. I shall be right back."

"Fredrick, she's only a child ..."

"Lucia, she saw thee in the garden ... with the herbs. She knows ye are a witch," I said, looking into her eyes. "I have to catch her before she reaches town."

I darted after her, leaving my stunned wife at the house, knowing the implications of my words. If the girl reached town before I caught her, the whole town would think she was a witch. The wind brushed by me as I darted down the woods toward the girl, but I was too late. Abigail was already standing in the town square, shouting at the top of her lungs to anyone who would hear, "Mrs. Lee ... down the road ... and her husband ... are witches!" she screamed, doubled over, trying to catch her breath. Then, Elizabeth reached the town square, walking slowly, with a dazed look in her eyes. Hysterical, Abigail grabbed her by the shoulders and turned her around to face the growing crowd. "See? Look in her eyes! She's been bewitched! Mr. Lee spoke to her, telling her to forget and … and … look at her!" The crowd gasped as a gentleman with a top hat stepped forward to Elizabeth, "Is this true, Elizabeth?"

"Is what true?" Elizabeth asked, as I breathed a sigh of relief. For a moment, I thought maybe I'd pushed her mind too hard in my haste. Care must be taken when using mind control. If I pushed her mind too hard, she may have spent the rest of her days without any memories at all.

"Are Mr. and Mrs. Lee witches?" the man asked, as his eyebrows pulled together in concern.

Elizabeth looked over at Abigail with fear in her eyes. Abigail nodded to her and she closed her eyes, warring with herself, trying to decide what to do. "Aye, she be a witch," she finally said, as Abigail smiled and the crowd gasped.

I cringed, remembering the night Lucia's parents were killed, knowing it would be just a matter of time before they came after us. I was so angry that I would have slaughtered the whole town, but I thought first of Lucia. "She was thy friend, Elizabeth!" I yelled, walking purposefully toward the girls, as Elizabeth began to cower behind Abigail. "And ye betrayed her! How could ye?"

Suddenly, the girls started screaming and rolling around on the dirt pulling at their hair, and the crowd started shrieking "Look! He's bewitched them!" "He must be a witch, too!" "Let's get him!" I snarled and ran straight toward the girls, when a wooden arrow shot me in the back. I kept running, when another, then another shot me, then I fell helplessly to the ground when one shot me between the eyes. They left me for dead when my eyes slowly began to close, and my last thought was of my Lucia … my forever love.

Stunned, I listened to Rick's tale of his love, Lucia, as we neared the city limits of Cooperstown, and I couldn't help thinking of my forever love, Zac. What would I do if the same thing happened to him? Now, I knew why the vampire community kept their existence secret from humans. Although we didn't live in the Stone Age any more, mass hysteria could happen at any time, as it did in WWII with Hitler, and with Lucia and The Salem Witch Trials. I knew I should let the tale stop there, but I had to know. "What happened to her, Rick?" I asked, my voice barely a whisper.

"When I woke up, I was still laying in the street. I pulled the arrow from my head and as many from my body as I could, but no one noticed. Everyone's eyes were on a figure in the center of town," Rick said. Tears started falling from my own eyes, for I knew what he was going to say. "And when I looked to the center of town, my Lucia was hanging from a rope, like a common criminal. I caught her eyes just before they closed, silently telling her that I loved her, willing her to do a spell so she could live, but she shook her head no. Then, I knew that she had been waiting for me. She did a spell that would keep her alive long enough to tell me goodbye. I have no idea for how long she hung there … alive … before I woke." Rick took a deep breath and wiped away tears from his own eyes.

"Did you try to save her?" I asked.

"Yes, I did," Rick replied, "but it was too late."

"Why didn't you turn her into a vampire?" I asked, truly curious, needing to know the whole story now.

Rick took another deep breath and I knew that, even after all these years, it was still difficult for him to talk about. "Lucia and I had talked about it in the past, but Lucia didn't want to become a vampire. She always felt bad about what had happened to me. She never felt bad about saving my life, but had always regretted turning me into a blood drinker. She never wanted it for me. At the time she turned me, she knew there would be consequences, but she never knew to what extent."

"But you're a good vampire …"

"Yes, I am, but there are many others who are not," Rick replied.

"Why didn't she try to save herself?" I asked, watching his face. "After all, she was a powerful witch."

"She didn't want to lose her soul," he said, shaking his head. "For each time she killed, she felt the darkness enter her heart. She knew that if a witch continued to kill, then she would become evil, something she never wanted to become. Throughout her whole life, she only wanted to save people … to heal. She never wanted to take life … from anyone … even stupid little girls accusing others of witchcraft. That's where the true danger lies. People begin to believe lies when they have no explanation for something they don't understand."

I nodded, understanding. Lucia was a great lady … perhaps a martyr, representing victims throughout the centuries who suffered and lost their lives at the hands of ignorance. "I'm sorry, Rick. I had no idea that Lucia died in the Salem Witch Trials."

"Actually, she never even got a trial. They lynched her right in the street, just on the word of two little girls," Rick said with a faraway look in his eyes.

Deep down, I was glad that Rick told me the story of his Lucia … of his forever love. Now, as we pulled up into the driveway of our two story stone cottage in Cooperstown, New York, I was glad that after all these years, he had finally found Annie.

"Love you, Rick," I said, much to his surprise. On this Valentine's Day, I was reminded that there are many kinds of love out there … romantic love, the love of parents for their child and a child for her parents, and the love of friendship.

"Love you, too … daughter," he replied, teasing me, breaking the spell of the moment. To Cooperstown Central High School, Rick was my father, and in many ways, he really was.

Suddenly, Annie ran from the house and Rick stepped out of his Mercedes GL450 SUV. When he saw her, his eyes lit up, then he looked over at me. "Go," I said, and he smiled and gently squeezed my hand. Then, he quickly jumped from the car and scooped Annie into his arms, spun her around and crushed his lips onto hers. I watched them as I got out of the car, hoping that he and Annie had many more years together … even more than he had with Lucia. After Lucia's death, he waited a long time before he and Annie finally found each other. They both deserved every happiness in the world.

Then, I looked onto the porch, and out stepped Zac. A strand of his sun-streaked hair fell lazily over one eye, but he quickly flipped it back, revealing his beautiful green eyes. He smiled watching me, and I ran quickly across the lawn and into his arms, much quicker than human speed. "What's the hurry?" he asked.

"No hurry," I replied, looking into his eyes. "I just missed you."

He brushed away a strand of my long brown wavy hair from my eyes and asked, "Are you okay, love?"

Then tears sprang to my eyes as I thought of the story … and of everything we'd been through so far in our short lives together. Then, as his full lips descended upon mine, I knew I was home … safe in the arms of … my forever love.

Be Mine

By: Jennifer Paquette

The characters in this story are based on the book

The Awakening of Agnostos

By: Jennifer Paquette

The man looked like a Greek god.

No, she thought. She knew what a Greek god looked like, and this man was even more perfect. His eyes had the sweetness of a cherub, yet his cheekbones looked like they were chiseled from the finest Italian marble. His hair was spun gold and she knew if she closed her eyes the softness would be like a warm wind through her fingertips. He sat serenely on the balcony of a modest whitewashed stone house, staring into the shimmering blue Aegean as if he were waiting for her. Her lips ached to touch his.

Aphrodite leaned farther out of the window of her glorious temple on Mt. Olympus to gaze at the perfect mortal man. Apollo had nothing on this guy. She sighed deeply as she thought of her fellow Olympians. Zeus was off somewhere with Hecate, Goddess of Magic, thinking they were fooling everyone. Aphrodite didn't know why they thought their affair was a secret, since it was obvious everyone knew. Everyone but Hera, that is. Zeus' wife and queen was too busy pampering her silly, precious peacocks and bossing around cloud nymphs to even notice what her slick husband was up to.

Aphrodite dismissed her thoughts and focused on something she could control. This man was hers for the taking, but at the same time, she sensed something special about him. He exuded a certain sensitivity and radiance that she had not seen before in a mortal. She sensed that he had much love to give, but no one to share it with. Aphrodite turned to gaze at her image in the mirror. *Instead of sending him a woman to love and cherish,* she mused, *perhaps I will send him me, Aphrodite, Goddess of Love and Beauty.*

She studied her delicate features again in the mirror, thinking of what look would please the perfect mortal man most. Her buttery curls framed her heart-shaped face and cascaded over her shoulders. She piled her hair high on her head and posed a bit. Too sophisticated. She transformed her hair into a shimmering chestnut brown color and fluttered her eyelashes playfully. Her eyes then changed from a deep violet to a piercing sea green. She played the ingénue and changed her eyes again to a sparkling baby blue and gave a sultry wink in the mirror. Which one would he prefer? She pouted her lips, changing the color into a coral pink, then ruby red. She stamped her sandaled foot and flung the folds of her dress aside as she marched across the stone floor in frustration.

Her husband, Hephaestus, would think she was totally nuts. Hephaestus, dark and moody with his misshapen figure and large hands, was actually the kindest of the gods. She had been flirting forever with Ares, when Hephaestus walked up to them and bellowed, "Make love, not war!" Ares was furious. As the God of War, it was obvious Hephaestus was mocking him, but Aphrodite was delighted. She had "make love, not war" engraved on the back of her chariot right after she married Hephaestus.

But Aphrodite had tired quickly of the unsightly Hephaestus, who spent his days forging metal and iron among the hottest flames of Olympus. She tried to visit him once to get involved in his work, but her hair was singed and she was immediately covered in soot, so she never went back. Now, they kept separate temples and only saw each other at Council meetings. Aphrodite was aching for a new man.

Back to the task at hand, she pondered how to woo the magnificent mortal. She did not want to appear directly in her godly form, as it was usually too overwhelming for mortals to bear. She walked to the far side of her temple and gazed out the east window, which showcased a craggy decline down the mountain where Aphrodite had planted her famous rose garden. The air exploded with the heady scent of thousands of roses, creating a rainbow of colors from creamy white to soft peach to brilliant red. A gust of wind blew across the garden and several supple petals were plucked from their blossoms and danced in the air before floating downward. She had an idea.

Aphrodite carefully stepped through her rose garden, skirting around the thorny branches that reached out to her. She peered deeply into each rose bush, analyzing the color and texture of the flower. *The rose she chose, must be perfect,* she thought as she continued down the mountain. She then came upon a small bush, the newest of them all, as it only had a handful of blooms. The sunlight warmed the petals of the rose and brought out their brilliance in a manner that made Aphrodite stop in wonder. The color was magnificent. The rose was a deep crimson at the base and a warmer hue near the top, the color of a sunset. She very gently caressed the petals and found them to be so soft she was afraid they would shred beneath her touch. She bent to smell them and was rewarded with the sweetest of scents, light and perfumed. *I will send him a gift of rose petals from the Garden of Aphrodite.*

She knelt beside the bush and spoke softly. "Forgive me, my lovelies. I promise you will grow back more brilliant than before, but for now, I need your help." Then, she gently blew into the rose bush, multiplying the petals and sending hundreds of them soaring into the sky. She watched as they formed a loose whirlpool shape, then cascaded down Mt. Olympus, as if riding a mighty wave.

Moments later the sunset colored rose petals wafted around the mortal on the balcony. He slowly looked up in amazement, as if the petals from the sky were falling stars. He gently picked a petal off his sleeve, studied it, then placed it on the ledge of the balcony and walked inside the house.

Aphrodite stared at the empty balcony littered with the petals from her precious rose bush. *How dare he?* Her eyes turned a stormy blue as she tried to keep her temper in check, staring at the sad little bush, now just a jumble of branches and tiny thorns. She was just about to march back to her temple to mix a sleeping potion for her most unfavorite mortal, when he came back out onto the balcony, but she gasped when she saw what he was holding: an elegant, sleek vase, made of heavy crystal. He carefully picked up the petals and placed them into the vase. As the vase was filled with the petals, he smiled. After every single petal was in the vase, he held it up to the sun to catch the light. Caressing the vase against his chest, he walked inside.

Aphrodite clapped her hands in delight and ran back up the hill.

***

The next morning was February 1. Usually, Aphrodite didn't pay much attention to the calendar—she would just look at the moon or the tides every now and then—but it was her wedding anniversary and she wanted to do something special for Heph. She put on her darkest dress so dirt wouldn't show as much and changed her hair color to a warm cinnamon. Then, she accented her look with amber eyes and her favorite apricot tinted lip gloss. She even sprinkled glitter across her face and neck. She went back to the rose garden and gathered an armful of roses tinted in bright yellow, deep orange and fire-red. Thinking her husband would appreciate her attempt to honor his name with the colors of fire and warmth, she headed down to his workshop, but immediately upon her arrival she knew something was wrong. It was freezing and no light glowed from the fires.

"Heph?" she called out in her sweetest voice. She waited for a minute. Receiving no reply, she threw the flowers onto the floor. "I spend half of my morning fixing myself up for this man and today is the day he decides to take off?" She turned on her heel and marched back toward the sunlight.

***

Aphrodite knew she should have tried to find her husband, but she really didn't have the patience. Plus, she wanted to see what the perfect mortal man was up to. So, she hurried to the window and was not disappointed. He was standing on the balcony, staring out at the sea again, with the vase of petals setting next to him on a small decorative table. She decided to send him another gift, but what would be worthy of him? What could possibly be better than a vase of a hundred rose petals the color of a sunset? Suddenly, it hit her. She turned and ran down the circular steps in the middle of her temple, almost tripping over her dress. She hadn't been down here in months, because the temptation was so great. Just the smell was enough to make her crazy. The last time she was here she stayed a week and gained eight pounds.

Luckily, she remembered the combination of the vault. As the door creaked open she almost passed out as the scent of luscious chocolates wafted to her nostrils. She steadied herself against the door, willing the craving away. This is for the perfect mortal man, she reminded herself, not for me. She gazed upon the rows and rows of high shelves with their tiny symmetrical cubbyholes. Each row was carefully labeled in beautiful, curlicue handwriting. Aphrodite started on the left, at the very first row. She would take samples from each section, taking the best of the best. With a flick of her wrist she produced a beautiful, ornate box with a cover inlaid with sapphire chips to place them in. She approached the next row of cubbyholes labeled "Creams" and gazed lovingly at the contents. Each tiny cubbyhole held a morsel of the finest, richest chocolate, with creamy centers of strawberry, vanilla, citrus and mint. She delicately plucked the choicest squares and gently placed them into the box, fighting the urge to grab a handful and stuff them into her mouth. Then, she moved to the next row labeled "Caramels". Here were the chocolates with the gooiest, sweetest and stickiest of centers, luscious caramels, nestled into each square of heavenly chocolate. Her mouth watered as she continued choosing the finest pieces for her perfect mortal. She continued down the main aisle to "Nuts," then "Fruit," (her least favorite) "Truffles," "Cherry Cordials," "Peanut Butter," "Marshmallow," and finally "Coconut." Each row also had a section of dark, white, and milk chocolate. Zeus also wanted her to add a sugar free section, but she refused. She smiled at the memory as she lazily made her way down each row, looking carefully through the wide variety. Finally, the box was so heavy she could barely carry it. If this didn't get his attention, nothing would. Aphrodite stumbled out of the vault, drunk from the smell of chocolate, but proud of her willpower, as she hadn't snatched a single morsel.

She made her way back up the spiral staircase, holding onto the railing with one hand and the precious box of delicacies in the other. She was sweating by the time she reached the top and her bouncy curls were now plastered to her forehead. She was surprised to see her temple bathed in moonlight and the stars twinkled rapidly, as if trying to tell her something. She couldn't believe it was nighttime already. She put the box down and went over to her washbasin to freshen up. As the flowing waters cooled her tired hands, she gazed up to check the calendar. Could it really be February 13?

Aphrodite groaned as she realized she had been down in the chocolate vault for almost two weeks. This was the longest time she had ever spent there, and she didn't eat anything! Then she gasped. Two weeks? The perfect mortal man must have surely forgotten about her by now. She silently cursed her weakness for chocolate and vowed to sell her entire collection to Artemis in the morning. Artemis was always hunting and could certainly use the energy and caffeine fix. She could also feed her silly deer the chocolate if she wanted. Aphrodite really didn't care.

Although it was clearly the middle of the night, she leaned over the windowsill, hoping to catch a glimpse of her precious mortal, but she couldn't see a thing. Aphrodite fought one last urge to eat the entire box of chocolates, then remembered the awful sugar crash from the last time and decided against it. She would deliver the chocolates personally in the morning after a good night's sleep. She was so tired she didn't even bother with her beauty creams, and she was asleep before her head even hit the pillow.

*** *

The next morning was filled with abundant sunshine and fresh breezes. Aphrodite hummed a tune as she dressed. She highlighted her hair in soft shades of gold and butter cream, and let it flow loosely down her back. Her eyes shone as blue as the sky, and her lips were frosted in pink and silver. She chose her favorite dress—a pastel pink confection that hugged her curves in all the right places. Then, she decorated her arms with silver bangles and bands, and shimmering pink teardrop earrings dangled from her ears. She smiled at herself in the mirror. She was gorgeous.

She picked up the box of chocolates and glanced at the calendar. February 14th. Then she hurried out of her temple and down the mountain, grabbing a single red rose from her garden as an afterthought.

Aphrodite reached the house and suddenly was very nervous. What if he didn't like chocolate? What if he didn't like her dress? What if he found someone else in the two weeks she was stuck in the chocolate vault? She chided herself for being so silly. After all, she was Aphrodite, the Goddess of Love and Beauty. There should be no question that any man, immortal or mortal, should not immediately fall in love with her! Still, she had never felt like this before about anyone; not even that pumped up Ares. Then, she peered around the corner and saw him. Her breath caught in her throat and a thin sheen of sweat formed on her brow. He truly was perfect.

She gingerly stepped onto the balcony and waited for him to notice her. She saw that the vase of petals was still on the table and she breathed a sigh of relief. He was standing against the balcony wall, leisurely studying the foamy waves of the sea stretched out before him. The blue-green water churned and rolled, creating a mesmerizing show. Aphrodite silently cursed Poseidon for sidetracking her perfect mortal man today. She wasn't in the mood for the sea god's tricks. Her feet hurt and the box of chocolates was getting heavy.

"A-hem," she said, clearing her throat.

The perfect mortal man turned around at the sound of her voice and stared at her, squinting in the bright sun. For a split second, Aphrodite thought she totally blew it and wanted to just sink into the stone wall behind her. He looked at the vase of petals, then back at Aphrodite, and his smile grew warm and inviting as he opened his arms wide.

"I've been waiting for you," he murmured.

Aphrodite slowly walked across the balcony, as her mind raced, trying to think of the perfect thing to say in return. All of a sudden a thought came to her that she didn't quite understand, but she knew it was right. It was also important, and would immortalize her and her actions for thousands of years to come.

"Happy Valentine's Day," she purred, as she fell into his arms, still holding the box of chocolates and a single red rose.

Fin

Hungry
By: Amber White

The characters in this story are based on the book

Tonight the World Dies

By: Amber White

The gun felt heavy in her palm. She was terrified.

Why is this happening? she thought. *Why now? Why us? And where is he? Is he safe? Oh, God why?* It became a chant, barely escaping her lips. "Why? Why? Why?"

Gravel shifted to her right, making her jump. People were walking closer. They were careful, not like the shuffling steps of *them*.

"We've got a survivor!" someone said. It was a male voice. He sounded urgent.

She cowered lower into the wreckage of the car.

"Ma'am?" The person knelt down a few feet away.

She gripped the pistol tightly in both hands, aiming wildly at the figure.

A rustling noise resounded around her, the sound of several guns being cocked and leveled at her hiding place.

"Don't come any closer. I'll shoot!" she cried.

The figure swatted it away easily. "Don't worry, we're here to help," he said.

"Help?"

"Yes, but you need to put your weapon down."

Suddenly, a flashlight beam illuminated the figure from behind. She gasped at the sudden brightness, shielding her eyes as she peeked out at him. He was in his mid-thirties, wearing camouflage pants and a matching long sleeved shirt under a heavy looking vest, pant legs tucked into light brown boots and his hair was hidden beneath a helmet. He was laden with guns and canisters.

She threw her pistol down, letting him slide it away from her. Then, he checked it before handing it to someone behind him.

"Who are you?" she asked.

"Special Forces, Ma'am," he said.

"Like the military?"

He nodded. "You want to climb out of there?"

She slid out from under the twisted metal, looking around nervously. There seemed to be a whole team of them, but no sign of *him*.

"Do you need medical attention?" the man asked, helping her to her feet.

She shook her head, still searching. "Did you find anyone else?"

The men looked behind them at a body strewn across the pavement.

"Link!" She wailed, running to him.

She elbowed her way past the soldiers trying to stop her. Falling to her knees, she clung to the unmoving body of her boyfriend. She sobbed, holding tightly to him, praying he was all right.

"He's gone," One of the men growled, trying to pull her away, but she held on, unwilling to accept what she knew was true. It was too late. Lincoln had died saving her. She kissed his lips softly. They were cold. It took three soldiers to pry her from him.

"Was there anyone else here with you?" the first soldier asked.

"It was just us. Then those ... people came. He tried to fight them off while I hid."

"Did they look sick?" The soldier who first tried to pull her away from Link asked, intense, with his eyes narrowed.

She nodded meekly.

"Were you bitten or scratched? Did you come in contact with their blood?" His fist tightened around the grip of his assault rifle.

"No," she squeaked.

"Sir, we need to keep moving. There's a safe location up ahead," another soldier said.

The first one seemed to be in charge, because when he motioned once with one hand, the others fell into formation.

"Stick close to me," he said, catching her gaze.

They moved with starling precision, rapidly covering the distance between where they found her and the cement building half a mile away, checking every corner and every car along the way.

People were already inside the building, which turned out to be an old gas station. The military guard entered through the rear, which was locked and sealed behind them. The soldiers spoke briefly with a few people in a circle, then left through the front door, ordering her to stay behind.

They kept her gun; not that she wanted it. Link had pulled it from one of their attackers and forced her to take it. She hid with it while he used another gun to fight them off.

Rural America, where everyone has a gun, she mused. *At least it's not like the city, where it's mostly gangsters and criminals.*

"Are you okay?" someone asked.

She jumped with a start, looking around to see who had spoken to her. It was a woman, slightly older than she.

"I'm ... fine," she said.

"I'm Jean," the woman said.

"I'm Steph," she said, smiling slightly.

Jean returned the smile. "Come sit with me. Here. Take some potato chips. We can talk," she said, offering her a bag of chips.

Steph followed her to the side of the room, where they sat in small fold out lawn chairs in front of the freezer.

"I'm staying away from the beer," Jean said. "It's safer."

"I don't know. People can get pretty rabid about their ice cream," Steph replied, pointing her thumb at the shelves of ice cream behind them.

"That's exactly why I picked out this spot," Jean said, smiled brightly. "So why don't you tell me what happened to you out there? You look like hell, and I know I'd want to talk about it if it were me. Help to make sense of it all."

Steph looked down at her hands. They were scratched and bloody, resting on top of her bleeding legs. Tears welled up in her eyes.

"I was with my boyfriend. Link was taking me to this little romantic place by the lake. He's good to me like that. Or, he was." She paused and Jean patted her arm. "We hadn't been listening to the radio until we saw all the traffic. It was too late to turn back, but he saw a side road and we went for it. He really wanted us to have that vacation. Anyway, another car came out of nowhere and hit us. We flipped over. I was so scarred. We both got out and went to check on the other car and then they attacked us," she explained, trembling.

"But you made it out okay," Jean said.

"Link fought off the guy that was grabbing him. He saw a gun and shot him in the leg, but the guy didn't stop. He sounded like a hungry animal. Link shot the arm off the man grabbing me and he let go and I ran around the car to get behind Link. Oh God, they chased us! He shot them so many times, but they kept attacking until he hit them in the head. He pulled another gun away from the dead passenger and shoved it into my hands. When other people started coming toward us, we knew they were going to kill us. He ordered me to hide in our car and I did. That was the last time I saw him alive," Steph said, as tears rolled down her cheeks.

Jean pulled her into a hug. "You're not alone," she whispered. "Most of us have lost someone to this already."

"But what is it? Why did they attack us like that? Why didn't shooting them stop them?" Sheph asked, sniffing back tears.

"I don't know. I don't think anyone really knows."

"Is this why the military is here?"

"Yes. They were sent here to protect us," Jean answered, trying to sound comforting.

"Then they must have some idea what this is," Steph reasoned.

"If they do, they aren't telling. It wouldn't help knowing now, though."

"You're right."

Jean hugged her again. "But everyone in that whole Special Forces team was cute, weren't they?" she asked with a wink.

Steph couldn't help herself. She laughed, but the reality of just losing the love of her life was too much, stifling the humor.

And all this time, with the soldiers, with Jean holding her hand, no one noticed the blood on her lips, or her increasingly bad cough.

***

It had been hours since she said good-bye to him, but she could still taste him on her lips. Not even her violent scrubbing in the bathroom could remove his blood, or the blood on her wounds—blood that wasn't altogether hers. It was already in her, already flowing through her veins and mouth, spreading.

The pain wasn't bad at first; she hardly noticed it, but soon it was worse than anything she could have imagined. She writhed, screaming, on the floor, as the people around her edged back in fear, contemplating running.

"What's wrong with her?" someone asked.

"Oh God, she's sick!" someone else shrieked.

Those two small words started a stampede. People bolted for the door. An employee locked himself in the break room behind the counter.

Steph stopped moving and fell silent as her vision went black.

Everything was different. The first thing she noticed was that she wasn't in pain anymore. She couldn't feel anything at all, not even the broken bottle she accidently cut her hand open on when she got up. The shards dug deeply into her palm and fingers, but she didn't feel it. She didn't feel her fingers grasp the pieces as she pulled them out.

"Hello?" she tried to call out, but it came out a short moan. *Where is everyone?* Steph wondered.

She shuffled to the door, unsure of her feet which were completely numb. She stumbled a few times, catching herself on the shelves, scattering food everywhere.

When was the last time I ate? she asked herself.

She was hungry, but the food around her looked and smelled disgusting. She wanted something else. She wanted meat … raw meat.

Steph made her way out the front door, as her instincts told her to head right, away from her overturned car. There were more cars facing her to the right … and all were full of meat, but they weren't. They were mostly empty. She had walked for a long time and she was starving. She had almost given up hope when she saw someone quivering in the back seat of a car.

Yes. Meat, she thought.

Without thinking, she fumbled with the handle. The door was locked.

Meat.

She slammed her fist through the window as the person inside shrieked as she grabbed her with both hands, dragging them out and onto the pavement. They caught briefly on the window frame, but Steph quickly pulled them free. She didn't care if it was a man, woman, or child. She just wanted to eat.

When they had stopped kicking and screaming and when she had had her fill, she staggered to her feet and walked on. She didn't know what she was looking for; she just knew she had to keep moving. *It* was out there.

Soon she was hungry again, so she searched more cars. The people she found inside were already dead. They wouldn't taste right.

So hungry, she thought as she shuffled down the street. Then, she tripped, landing face first on the asphalt, but when she looked back to see what she had tripped over, she did a double take.

"Link?" She said, sounding more like a word than anything she'd tried to say since she woke.

"Steph?" he asked. It sounded more like a groan, but was clear enough to understand.

It was him. It was really him.

"I thought you were dead," she said, touching his face.

"I thought you were, too. I woke up and I couldn't find you." He pulled her into a hug over the half eaten body lying in front of him. "Eat," he said when he caught her staring down at the body in front of them.

So, so hungry, she thought. A part of her wondered why she was eating human flesh, but she was too hungry to care. Lincoln was alive, and they were back together. That's what really mattered.

As they devoured what was left of the body in front of them, Steph couldn't help sneaking glances at Link. He was really there. He was alive!

"We should walk up there," he said, pointing up a small side road when they finished.

"Why?" she asked.

"It's right," he said.

Steph shrugged and followed. His logic was as good as hers.

"You and me, Steph. Just you and me," he said, throwing an arm around her.

"You're so romantic. Candlelight, a bear skin rug, 'Oh darling, could you pass the legs?'" she laughed.

He kissed her. It was the first time they had kissed and not felt something, anything. There was no heat, no passion, no little sparks. They just felt … cold.

***

It was morning when they reached a cabin. Steph hung back, chasing after a squirrel while Link ate his squirrel in full view of the windows. There might be meat in that cabin, but they couldn't wait that long. They were hungry. Once Link finished his food, he walked up to a back window.

"Is anyone in there?" he asked in his groaning voice, tapping on the glass.

"Maybe they can't understand you," Steph said quietly.

He acknowledged her comment, and moved on to another side of the cabin, his hand trailing along the wood.

"Hello?" he called.

Steph followed him from the trees. If the people inside were other zombies, she didn't want to get close.

When he got to the front, someone started shouting. Then she heard a blast as Link was propelled backward. He landed hard on the sidewalk. Steph screamed and tried to run to him, but her feet wouldn't move fast enough. Her legs were tangled in bushes, trapping her out of sight.

She watched in horror as he rolled over, and a teenage girl stood over him in the now open doorway. He asked her to put it down, to stop, but she yelled over him. He grabbed her leg and pulled, wanting to take the gun away, but the girl kicked him in the face. Steph's stomach rolled.

The girl latched onto the gun she had dropped, and shot Link in the face, and he didn't move again.

Steph worked as hard as she could to free herself from the plant, kicking and pulling. It wasn't until the girl had left with her friends that she had stumbled out from the trees, running to Link's side, but he was gone.

Steph roared a string of swears, as her body shook with dry sobs. She couldn't look at his face. There was nothing there to look at. She had lost the love of her life for a second time in twenty-four hours. That girl was going to pay. Steph would rip her apart and eat every last bit of her if it was the last thing she did. She had heard them call her Jo, which was a strange name for a girl, but it didn't matter. She was going to destroy her. She just had to follow them. They would have to stop eventually.

Steph stumbled after them back to the main road. They were driving slowly, making their way through the cars. She couldn't move fast enough and their truck was vanishing down the road. She had to keep following. She was so hungry. She couldn't let that girl get away with killing Link. Then, a loud bang echoed within her ears and she fell forward, hitting the ground. Looking behind her, she saw a shaking woman holding a gun in a trembling hand.

Maybe if she had a bite, she'd be able to move faster.

The woman crept closer, her whole body shaking like a leaf. Steph tried to sit up and the woman aimed the gun at her head. Then, everything went black.

Some part of her knew she was finally, completely, dead. She couldn't see and she couldn't hear, but she could feel Link next to her, as his hand was in hers. She squeezed him tightly and he pulled her into his embrace, as his scent filled her nostrils ... and she was home. Dead or alive, she was home.

A Heart That Cannot Beat
By: Elaine White

A collection of short stories about
the Charcot clan members

The characters in this story are based on the book

Runaway Girl
The Secrets of Avelina Chronicles

By: Elaine White

Valentine's Day 1503

Damian sat on the windowsill, staring at nothing in
particular. One foot was pressed against the frame, while the
other dangled freely in the air. He was one story off the
ground, sitting on the windowsill of the bedroom that he had
once shared with Angela … so many years ago. There was
nothing to see in the room, but his brain pulled many
memories to the forefront of his mind. One was entering the
house as husband and wife, with Angela holding onto his
arm. Another, the night his father died in the downstairs
bedroom while he watched helplessly from the window as an
outsider. Long years of being Angela's Peter Pan before that

boy had ever existed, flitting in and out of her window, and her life. Watching the woman he loved grow old and live a life without him by night and babysitting her killer by day. It was impossible for him to see Amelia as anything else in those early days; the days before he loved her.

Little did he know that he had been followed by Trey, his brother-in-law, best friend and Angela's closest living relative. He hated watching Damian torture himself over and again. "Damian, leave this place to your memories. Come away with me. Torment yourself no longer," he begged, but it was no use. Damian sat forlorn, watching the memories play out within his mind's eye.

Trey was forced into action. He raced up the staircase and straight into the bedroom that had once been his sister's straight at Damian, pushing him out of the window. Both men fell out of the house, plummeting to the ground. When they landed, unharmed, Trey pinned Damian to the earth. "This is folly! Angela never would have wanted this," he argued, trying to talk some sense into him, but it was useless. The pain was too raw, too soon. Damian pushed Trey away with little effort and rose to his feet. He stalked into the forest without a word or a care, thinking only of his Angela and the life that had been ripped from him. It wasn't fair, and it wasn't right. He could still remember that fateful night, so crystal clear in his mind.

They were about to turn in for the night, sitting by the fire in their bedroom, when a scream roused him from his thoughts and drew him to the doorway of the house. They had no neighbors on the outskirts of the forest, so without seeing anything outside his door, Damian ventured out to walk the perimeter of the house. It was unsettling times; witches were being burned and tortured. The council often snuck into people's homes at night, hoping to see some sign of witchcraft within. On this particular night at the back of the house, he had found a man nosing around.

"Amelia! Do not go far," the man called out, concerned.

Damian approached cautiously. "What seems to be the problem, sir?"

"My daughter ran off. It is late … she may get into danger," the man confessed, panicked.

Damian did the only thing he could and offered to help search for her. As he walked, he caught sight of a little girl running through the trees, faster that he would have imagined could be possible. Damian heard a sound behind him and turned, but nothing was there. Damian stopped walking as he reached the thick of the forest, sure that Trey wouldn't follow him in there.

He laughed remembering how naïve he had been. In those days, he never knew vampires existed, nor did he really believe in witches, but he knew hysteria when he saw it. It was the entire reason he had built a house on the outskirts of the forest; it was away from so called civilization and large enough to house his family and Angela's comfortably. He had never supposed that it might be the one thing that had put him into danger.

Amelia—as he later knew the little girl to be—had played with him for only a short time, teasing and tormenting him with sightings, crying and long chases. When he finally caught up with her, she was huddled on the ground, crying. Angela had always wanted a child, but their marriage was still new and they were unsure of when they might be able to afford a family on his pitiful wages. He had approached Amelia in hope of giving his wife a few hours of joy spent with a child, warming her and her father beside a fire before they had to leave. But it had all went terribly wrong.

The moment Damian was within her reach, the sweet little girl turned into a monster. With a snarling face, fangs and blood red eyes, she lunged at him and secured her mouth to his throat before he even had enough time to scream. It was the most terrifying moment of his life. Only two thoughts had occupied his mind at the time; surviving to see Angela again, and the sound of his own heart beat fading away. Amelia had fed from him for what felt like hours, but that he knew couldn't have been very long, as Angela never came looking for him. He lay in the dirt with Amelia hunched over his limp body, listening to the sound of his own failing breath in his ears and the sound of someone sucking the blood from his body. Damian sank to the ground within the forest, hugging his knees, believing that he would die … until that last moment.

When Amelia finished feeding from him, she had abandoned his body on the ground and skipped off into the trees. That was the last thing Damian saw—Amelia skipping away happily after killing him. It was an odd memory, not quite complete with his fading life, but the last real emotion he ever felt. He didn't remember seeing Lucius again when he discovered his dying body and the great tearing wound in his throat, but he recalled the sensation of being saved. He remembered the way his body lifted off the ground almost magically, even though he now knew that it had been Lucius' strong arms lifting him. In his near-death state, the blood that had poured into his mouth was like the cleanest water given to a parched man as he drank thirstily. It wasn't until years later that he realized death was not necessary. The process of turning required only two blood donors, one vampire, one human; one gave and the other received.

Damian wished that he had been sensible enough to refuse, but he hadn't understood at the time. He believed that some kind person had found him and attempted to heal him with healing waters, or at least offer him one last taste of pure affection before he died. Now he knew better; he would have refused, but he didn't have the choice anymore.

Later he was told that two hours had passed before he was fit to stand again. He had been weak, uncertain and confused; not a good recipe for someone who now had strengths and abilities beyond his understanding. Later, Lucius explained everything in the forest, as his little daughter stood by innocently, smiling at him. He had explained that they were vampires and that his daughter was dangerous, unruly and would be condemned as a witch if anyone knew. She was the child of two pure blood elders and, therefore, a vampire from birth. If captured, she would die. He had begged for his secrecy and Damian, with his soft heart, had agreed … on the condition that he make Angela a vampire and take her with him into his new life. Lucius understood his heart then.

Damian had climbed the side of the house and crept inside through the open window, while Angela slept by the fire. Damian would never have done anything against her wishes, so he woke her and explained about the little girl and her father. Then he told her what had been done to him, to save his life. To his relief, Angela had wanted nothing more than to share her life with him. So he laid her upon the bed, where she would be comfortable, then he lay down beside her. With a gentle kiss and a profession of his undying love, he had done as Lucius had instructed him and bit her neck and drank until he felt the flutter of her heart. Tears were in his eyes when he pulled away, but Angela just smiled a dreamy, sleepy smile and touched his face tenderly. Damian kissed her lips, about to open up a wound on his wrist and offer it to her, but before he could do so, Amelia's scream pierced the air.

Damian was forced to leave his wife, lying peacefully on her bed, as blood stained her throat. He could hear the movement downstairs and didn't doubt that his father was rushing to check on Angela, but he couldn't risk being caught. Lucius had warned him of that. If he changed out of anger or surprise, his own family would surely turn him over to the Witches Council to keep Angela and themselves safe from him. With one last promise to return for her, Damian rushed to the window and jumped to the ground.

Damian had returned to Angela nightly after turning her, only to find that no matter how many times he fed her, her system would not accept it. Finally, Lucius and Angela convinced him to stop. He still felt the pain in her voice when she told him she would always love him and that if they couldn't spend their life together, she still wished to see him from time to time. It broke his heart. After that, he spent every moment with her that he could spare without putting himself at risk of getting caught. When he wasn't with her, he was at the vampire clan house on the other side of the forest where Lucius lived. Over time, he became like a son to the man who had saved his life. Trey often wondered about his sister's happiness at a time when her husband was believed dead.

Trey had never stopped looking for Damian, after that first night when he was discovered missing. It was believed that the screams in the forest were Damian's and that he had been killed, but Trey wouldn't accept that until he found his body. Night after night he ventured into the forest searching for a newly dug grave, or a body disguised by leaves, but he found nothing, and he could never understand Angela's insistent pleas for him to stop looking. Then, he knew. On his search one night, he noticed the window to Angela's bedroom was wide open, and a light was shining brightly within. He knew that Angela had suffered terribly from the cold since her affliction which had only lasted twelve days, to his relief. It was a chilly night, so he made his way back to the house to scold her for putting her health at risk. That was when he saw a dark shadow climbing the outside of the house and sneaking in through the window. A moment later, the shutters were closed.

Trey was curious, so he rushed to the house and hid behind a nearby tree to see if he could see who was climbing in through his sister's window. He recognized the dark outline even before he reached his hiding place. Without thinking, he jumped out and embraced the shadow in a heartfelt hug. "I cannot believe you are alive," he whispered, sure there was some reason for secrecy. When his cold hands gripped his arms and pushed him away, he knew. When Trey saw this face for himself, it was not the Damian he knew. He had a deep brow, eyes like the midnight sky, and snarling lips over white, elongated fangs, but it was Damian all the same. "I do not understand this ..." he said. Unmindful of the vice grip Damian had on his arm, he lifted his hand and touched the deepened brow of his best friend. "... but I want to know the truth. You cannot leave me behind, Damian. We are brothers ... friends ... family. If there is a reason Angela does not leave with you, tell me and I shall change her mind. We three shall go on adventures together, just as we always have," Trey asked excitedly. Then, Damian knew he was never going to be left in peace if he risked visiting Angela every hour he could spare.

Damian had taken Trey into the woods, to a hiding place, and explained everything. When he knew what happened to his sister, he feared the same might happened to him as well, but he asked Damian to try regardless. If Damian could live as a vampire, then so could he. And in the safety of the woods, they wouldn't be interrupted. It was his right, as his brother that they share the adventure. They had returned to the house together, and Damian had waited impatiently in his old bedroom, pacing the floor as Angela watched from her seat by the fire. He had talked to her about Trey's request, and Trey promised that he would visit her, too, hoping that his sister would give her permission for him to leave the family.

Damian had known the minute Trey walked into the room and Angela smiled sadly at him, that her mind was made up. A moment later, she told them both that she would rather they have each other than forever be separated, and if she couldn't enjoy the adventure with them, then they would just have to enjoy it even more for her, and occasionally return to tell her of them.

The next seventy years had been spent that way. While Damian became guardian over Amelia, he and Trey had limited their visits to Angela until they only saw her once a month, then once in six months, hoping that she could move on with her life, but Angela never re-married, she never considered herself a widow or heartbroken. And she died in her bed, eventually, with a smile on her face and memories of a life she had never been allowed to live. And Damian had fallen apart.

Deep in the forest beside the house that was no longer his home, Damian began to cry. Trey sighed and offered him what little comfort he could; a comforting hand on the shoulder of friendship. Damian buried his face in his knees and mourned the loss of his wife ... the woman he loved ... and the man he had once been. Along with Angela, everything within Damian died ... his hopes, his dreams, his emotions.

Now, just a month after Angela's death at the ripe old age of seventy, he truly wished that he had died that day, too. It would have been better for Angela to live a widow's life and have the chance at another happy marriage later than to leave her as the wife of a man she couldn't be with. Damian heard the rumors that had spread about him throughout the town: that he found another woman and ran off with her, that he had abandoned Angela, even that he had been murdered by a man who wished to have Angela to himself. Each rumor was more ridiculous than the other. No one knew that he had been killed by a spiteful little girl or that he had risen after death.

After seventy long years of watching his wife grow old and finally die, he wished that he had been thinking clearly enough to take Angela with him. Unfortunately for Damian, a vampire's first instinct is to protect itself and seek the quickest escape. Even now, his vampire brain told him that if he had attempted to take Angela with him, they both would have been caught and punished. Even now his instinct told him that it was better that Angela lived a human life away from the stain of vampirism, than to burn at the stake as a witch ... but his human heart disagreed. It ached to see her again, to kiss and hold her. His heart told him that life wasn't worth living without Angela.

"Brother, do not despair. I know it should be the three of us together, but it was not meant to be. I am only thankful that my transformation was completed so you won't be alone." Trey's voice caught Damian's attention. He raised his eyes from the ground knowing that much was true. If they had been interrupted again, preventing Trey's transition as it had Angela's, he truly would have been alone in the world. He indicated for Trey to sit with him and together they each silently remembered Angela, each silently mourning her.

From that day on, Trey watched Damian with regret and a silent prayer to his sister, whom he hoped was smiling down upon them. He wished that Damian would rediscover his humanity. He wished that she had died happy, and he hoped that one day, Damian would learn to live again.

Valentine's Day 1524

Samuel choked in his desperation. The blood simply wouldn't go down his throat fast enough, but it was delicious and addictive. It was the third time that night he had fed from the poor young woman in his clutches; the third and not likely the last. What a Valentine's Day gift it was!

When it had happened, he couldn't say, but somewhere between the arrival of the young teacher and that moment, as he felt her warm, coppery blood flowing down his throat at a rate not even close to fast enough, Samuel had become infatuated with her. Nisha had been paid to reside within the vampire clan house and teach the elders' children about the latest century. The elders could cover all of the previous centuries, but no one knew better about the present time than a human. So Nisha, down on her luck and without a penny to her name, accepted a teaching job at the clan house. She just hadn't known what she was getting into.

Nisha had been a cobbler's daughter. Her hair was closer to silver than gold, and she was nothing but skin and bone, but exceedingly smart. Being smart wasn't enough for a single, young woman in the early days, but it was enough of a hindrance to make her wish to travel the world and leave behind the family business. She had left home at fourteen, refusing to learn the family trade, and spent the next year with a travelling physician, learning all she could. By the age of twenty, she had returned home to show her father her progression in the world, only to discover that her father had died two years before, having drank himself to death, heartbroken at the loss of his only daughter.

Nisha was beside herself with grief, but then she was saved. A young man had ventured into the tavern and asked the barman if there was anyone he knew who could teach children. The barman told him of Nisha, one of the best teachers in the land. The next night, Nisha came to the tavern and presented herself. Almost immediately, Samuel found himself captivated by her wit and good looks. Nisha was such a beautiful young woman, talented and intellectual. They had spent the next four days discussing the extent of her knowledge in the tavern, meeting every evening for a meal and a discussion. Before the week was out, Samuel invited Nisha to live at the clan house. Samuel told her the truth of his people; they were vampires. Nisha hadn't believed it at first, but after she discovered the truth for herself, she had no other choice. So, she accepted the truth and decided to stay. That was when the trouble started.

That was why Samuel choked another three more times on Nisha's blood before reluctantly pulling away. He coughed violently for a few seconds as Nisha barely managed to stumble back into a waiting chair. The experience was heady for them both, but it was worse for Nisha. She couldn't continue feeding Samuel as he needed, but neither could quite force themselves into the next step.

She was yet only twenty-two years old. How could Samuel ask such a thing of her?

Nisha closed her eyes and leaned back against the headrest of the chair, dizzy and weak, but more so than usual. She could feel her heart beating. It no longer hammered against her chest as it used to, but instead, just flitted around and then stopped for long seconds before beginning its dance again. The more Samuel fed from her, the stranger and more distant it felt. She knew that it couldn't go on much longer. When she opened her eyes, Samuel was standing over her with a wet cloth in his hand. He placed it onto her brow and Nisha closed her eyes, feeling is cool relief, but she didn't want to see those eyes … not now. Not looking so hurt, so disappointed. Samuel knew that the charade would have to end soon.

There had been talk in both the clan house and the human village the moment Nisha began spending long hours with Samuel in the study, just days after she had moved into the house. The talk from town wasn't worth hearing—though Nisha knew what they were saying—but the talk from the clan members was more difficult to ignore. Samuel was an elder, the master of the clan. In that respect, he could do as he wished, but in another respect, he should never have left the safety of the clan, nor should he have opened his heart and mind to a human, but neither saw any harm in discussing literature and the world together. Samuel told her of vampires and their history, while she shared what she knew of humans. It had been a strange relationship, but the first real one Nisha had ever experienced. Two weeks after her arrival, things had become worse.

Now, Nisha opened her eyes and forced herself to look at Samuel, and she really couldn't imagine spending Valentine's Day with anyone else. The day had existed before, but it was only then, during the fifteenth century, that it became about love and romance. Who knew how many decades and centuries he had lived through, and yet she hadn't the courage to ask. Nor did Samuel look a day over twenty-three. He had the most shiny golden hair and green eyes she had ever seen, and his six feet held him a good foot taller than Nisha. His shoulders were broad and the scars on them proved he had seen a few battles in his time. Who would have thought? The warrior and the scholar. It almost pained her to see Samuel turning away from her with that look in his eyes. She held the cloth to her own head, closed her eyes and allowed Samuel his moment of torment.

Samuel could remember the very moment things had become intolerable. At the end of Nisha's second week in the house, the council had called a meeting to discuss and compare human and vampire medicines and he had not been included. Samuel had never told her what had transpired then, nor would he wish to hurt her delicate human emotions by admitting so now, but he knew that something had to be done. The council had accused him of losing his head and had called for his relinquishment of power, but he would never do so freely, and he told them so, yet that didn't stop them from wanting his resignation. He fought with them for three hours until they reached an agreement; if Nisha were to remain within the clan house and in Samuel's confidence, he either had to turn her or claim her. He had stormed out of his own council room and retreated to his chambers for no more than ten minutes before Nisha came to speak with him, concerned and worried.

Samuel did what was necessary; he claimed Nisha as his own with a kiss. That afternoon they became lovers and Nisha had offered her blood to Samuel for the first time, in a final expression of her love. That night, Samuel fed and nearly drained Nisha of every ounce of her blood.

Afterward, he refused to look at the young woman for two weeks out of shame. He would never have forgiven himself if he had killed her.

Then one day, Nisha broke the silence between them rather craftily. They had agreed that they needed to discuss the children's progress with their learning, so Samuel met her in the library and listened as Nisha talked of the children, and accepted an empty glass, then filled it from a pitcher on the table. The moment the blood hit his lips, he was consumed. He emptied the glass in one go, and then refilled it immediately from the pitcher. Nisha silently sat across from him, watching him drain three, four and then six full glasses of blood without so much as batting an eyelash. It was her blood, collected over long days. When the pitcher was empty, Samuel came back to his senses, staring across at his willing victim, confused.

"Now, you must accept that you can never again refuse me. From this moment forth, if you do not feed from me, I shall feed you against your will. Can we come to an agreement?" Nisha asked. Samuel walked out of the room, only to return after a long, thoughtful walk in the gardens … and agreed.

From that moment on, Samuel fed from Nisha almost daily. With each time, the need grew stronger. Each time, the hunger could not be satisfied; each time he came closer and closer to killing her. The more Nisha tolerated his vampire nature, the more Samuel loved her for it. They quickly fell in love, but they both knew that Nisha's life would be vastly shorter than any amount of time Samuel would live through. Samuel never suggested the alternative for fear that the idea would be rejected, and Nisha didn't suggest it because she knew Samuel would regret it the moment it was done.

Samuel turned back to Nisha, and saw that she still had her eyes closed. The cloth still lay on her forehead and he almost didn't wish to disturb her, but he knew he must. After being fed from, Nisha needed to sleep and eat … and not in a chair. Samuel approached his love and gently removed the cloth from her forehead. It was only then that he saw her lifeless arm hanging at the side of the chair. Samuel came to his senses and found that no heartbeat assailed his ears. He knew what must be done. He must make his choice now, whether he wished to or not. Should he allow Nisha to die a human, or should he make her a vampire? As they had never talked of it, he had no idea as to how Nisha would feel if she woke and found herself a vampire. Would she feel disgust, hatred or betrayal? Or would she rejoice and thank him? Samuel hadn't enough time to think it over logically. Emotion won out.

Biting into his own flesh, he let the blood flow from the wound and held it over Nisha's parched lips, hoping. Long moments passed as the blood tricked down her chin and onto her clothes, but Samuel didn't care. All he cared about was Nisha. His stupid thoughts had distracted him from the danger and he lost track of time as he allowed his blood to flow into Nisha, until the loss grew too much and loss of blood and heartache sent him to his knees. Samuel despaired as he sat by the rocking chair, his eyes closed in prayer, unmindful of the continual pour of blood from his self-inflicted wound.

It felt like hours, sitting and praying for time to reverse before a soft creak and the light touch on his arm awoke him from his thoughts. Samuel raised his head and believed himself suffering the hallucinations of starvation, as he gazed into Nisha's bright blue eyes. "You claimed me for your own one last time, Samuel. Now it is my turn," she said softly as light fingers traced the wounds on his bleeding wrist. Samuel looked down at the same spot where Nisha's eyes were focused and noticed that he had torn the flesh of his wrist badly in his attempt to feed his companion. Nisha frowned disapprovingly before she lifted Samuel's wrist to her lips, and kissed the wound gently. Within seconds, the shredded skin healed. "Feed from me, my love. Then you shall be well again, and we may live out our lives as we have done so far. We shall share our lives, our food and our hunger as we have always done," Nisha said with the lightest spark of emotion in her voice. Samuel was flooded with relief that not only was his Nisha saved, but he relished the opportunity of spending a lifetime with her, as well. It had been a whirlwind of a Valentine's Day, but it had all come together in the end. Samuel did as he was asked and fed from his love, safe in the knowledge that his life was now complete.

Valentine's Day 1630

After losing Angela, Valentine's Day had always been difficult for Damian. Amelia had been in confinement to her bedroom chambers for a full century already, and it wasn't a good phase in their relationship, especially since Damian was her guard and the one to keep her in confinement, no matter what she said or did.

"I cannot understand why my father will not allow me my freedom. I have been incarcerated long enough. Tell him that I will not suffer it any longer!" Amelia shouted at him ... again. She had always been difficult and aggressive, and even a century alone in her chambers, with only Damian as her guard to talk to and spend time with, hadn't improved her disposition.

"You know that you will not be free until you can show your father you are responsible enough not to run away. If you wish to have your freedom, you know what you must do," he reminded her again. She needed to apologize to both himself and her father. It was the only way she would be allowed out of her rooms again, but she didn't seem to understand that. She huffed and sniffed, pretending to cry, but nothing moved him from his post. He stood inside her bedroom door, watching over her to make sure she behaved.

Amelia had no idea that Damian loved her. He never had the strength to tell her, but he hoped to do so that day. It was Valentine's Day, and he didn't know a more appropriate day to say it, but not until she calmed down. Not while she screamed at him and ordered him around like a servant. He had loved her for so long, and it had been a long time since Angela's death. He had finally come to terms with the fact that he must move on with his life if he was ever to be happy again. His best friend, Trey, had finally managed to drill that into him. Now, he was determined to do as he was told and live his life.

"Please, Damian, I beg you. Speak to my father ... ask him to release me ... even if just for this one day. I need to see the sunshine and smell fresh air. I need to live. He cannot keep me prisoner forever," Amelia said, turning her big brown eyes upon him with that pouty, pleading smile of hers and Damian could feel himself melting. He hated himself for it. After all, he was a vampire ... a soldier. He shouldn't melt at anything, least of all an unruly girl fluttering her eyelashes at him, whilst trying to manipulate him. To show her that he was resisting her attempt to wrap him around her finger, he stayed silent, staring straight ahead. "Well, if you do not care about me or my feelings, then stay silent. Keep your distance. But if you must do so, do so on the other side of the door where I do not have to see your steel eyes and your harsh mouth. If you do not care then spare me the torment."

Damian was so surprised at the apparent anguish in her voice and the tears in her eyes that for a full moment he stared at her, confused. It almost sounded as if ... it couldn't be, could it? Did she have feelings for him? Or was this just another attempt to wrap him around her finger to do her bidding? The moment she began to cry, hiding her face in her hands and throwing herself down upon her bed, Damian let out a deep sigh of hope. He couldn't bear to see her so sad. As quietly as he could, he left the room and stood on the other side of her door as she had asked, contemplating what to do.

For a full two hours, he stood at the door, as a cloud of uncertainty ruled his mind, feeling as if his heart was about to burst. Could she love him? Was it really true? He knew that if he went to her father, Lucius, and told him that Amelia loved him, her incarceration would be over. They would be united as a pair before the sun came down. Married ... but did he want to get married again? It was such a big step, especially for a vampire. Only elders and masters were allowed to unite, under vampire law. It was a method of control that Damian didn't approve of, as only united couples could have children. Considering how few of their people were left in the world and that they were forced to turn humans in order to gain more vampires in times of war, it seemed a ludicrous law, but it was the law all the same. Damian shook his head. He hadn't even told Amelia that he loved her yet. It was not the time to be thinking of unions and children, but it was Valentine's Day and it always did some unpleasant, strange things to his brain. "It turns to mush, that is what it does," he scolded himself under his breath, as he made his way downstairs toward the council room where he hoped to find Lucius. He was in luck. The master sat reading a book at his desk. "Master, may I have a word?" Damian asked, silently walking into the room before capturing his sire's attention.

"Damian, come in. Have a seat," Lucius offered with a smile. He was battling his mind and heart, trying to decide if he was glad to see the young soldier, as Damian was like a son to him already, or if he dreaded speaking with him because it meant Amelia had done something terrible again. "What can I do for you, my boy?"

"I would like to ask if you would remove Amelia's sentence of confinement for one day ... today," he asked, wanting to get the words out before he changed his mind. Lucius raised an eyebrow, sitting silently, waiting for him to continue. "I have decided to tell her how I feel. With your permission, I will take Amelia out of the house for one day, tell her of my feelings and then return her to her period of confinement before midnight." Damian held his breath for a full two minutes as Lucius stared at him, contemplating whether or not he approved. Lucius had always known of Damian's feelings for his daughter. He already loved Damian like a son and had turned him into a vampire. He knew there was no other he would wish her to unite with, but it was complicated. He was her guard. She deserved, and needed, to be in confinement.

Allowing her one day of freedom seemed innocent enough, but once Damian told her of his feelings, she might return them. If her feelings were real, then it would warrant the end of her confinement. If not, she may claim they were in order to be set free. Could he trust her to be honest? Thinking it over, he knew he couldn't; she had done too much over the years for that to happen. She lied freely to anyone and everyone she could in order to get her own way or to keep herself out of trouble. And being her father seemed to make him a prime target for those lies. She didn't care who she hurt, or how much they loved her. It couldn't be allowed.

"I will grant you this one day, Damian; however, I must insist that Amelia not be set free of her confinement, even if she returns your affection. She cannot be trusted and I would like you to remember that. I do not want her to hurt you again." Lucius spoke solemnly, scared that his soldier would have his heart broken once again by the deceitful girl he loved. She had taken his human wife from him; she had ruined his life entirely, and whether or not he loved her, she was still dangerous and was never to be trusted until she could prove herself worthy.

"Thank you, sire. I understand. May I also ask that another be put on guard for the next hour? I have some arrangements to make." Damian asked one more favor of the man who had saved his life and it was granted. He was so happy and relieved, that he actually smiled for the first time in many, many years.

Lucius' heart turned over at the sight and sunk to the pits of his soul as the young soldier left the room to begin his preparations. As he watched him go, he had an awful feeling that things were not going to work out well. Would Damian forever be alone in the world?

Amelia was confused by the change of guards. When she had opened her door to plead with Damian one more time, she found Chandler in his place. Although she was confused, she was not ungrateful. The way Damian looked at her was bordering on scandalous, so she invited Chandler into her room—despite his protests—and sat him down in a chair. Then she began her pleas all over again. "I must escape this prison, Chandler. I truly must. I feel as if I cannot breathe here … and Damian … he looks at me so …" she prattled then, seeing the flash of jealousy in his eyes, making her smile. He really was very sweet. He had guarded her often when Damian's particular talents were needed elsewhere, but she had never really paid him much attention … until now.

Amelia was about to open her mouth and say more to encourage his jealousy when the door opened and Damian walked in. "Thank you, Chandler. You may return to your duties," Damian said calmly, as he always did after he had disappeared for God knows how long. Amelia didn't understand. Damian could be gone for minutes, hours, even days or weeks when Chandler took over his guard duties, but never once had he displayed any kind of emotion toward her. She never knew what he disappeared off to do, and no one was likely to tell her.

"Have you spoken with my father? Am I to be released?" she wondered, hopeful. Damian watched as Chandler left with a glare, wondering what had happened in his absence and why Amelia was suddenly clutching his arm, beaming up at him as if she was going to get what she wanted. He was a little confused by her changed attitude, but he kept things simple and admitted to the truth. "Yes, but just for today only. Gather your shawl and we shall go into the village," he instructed her gently, waiting as she rushed to gather up a warm covering. Then he held the door open for her and accompanied her downstairs.

Damian had planned a full, romantic day for them both. He took her to the beach, watching her adoringly as she built sandcastles and ran from sea creatures, giggling and laughing to herself. They walked through the meadow behind the mansion and then he returned to her room when the sun had set and the hour was late. Even then, when Amelia thought it was all over, sitting in her room, reminiscing about their day, Damian kept his secret. Out on her balcony—if she only looked—was a special display where he would profess his love for her. Two seats set at a table where they could watch the stars, with candle light, fresh flowers, a special jug of rich blood and a brand new dress that he had bought from her favorite seamstress that morning. It was all ready and prepared, hidden behind the long drapes that shut out the drafty windows.

"If you will excuse me for just a moment, Amelia, there is one more thing I must do … then I have a special gift for you," he explained with a slight smile. He wasn't surprised to see that Amelia looked excited and promised to wait patiently for his return. He left her alone for barely more than ten minutes, going back to his room to talk himself into a confession, wanting it to be just right. He didn't want to make the mistake of trying to tell her that he loved her and having the words come out confused or end up saying something completely different. He changed into a fresh suit, checked his hair and took a few deep breaths to calm himself before returning to Amelia's chambers … only to find her gone. He sighed in frustration; this was so typical. Of course it was only natural for her to ruin everything by running off. It was so typically Amelia.

After searching her best friend's room, the store room and kitchens, he made his way to the council room to see if she had gone to plead her case to her father, but at the bottom of the stairs, Damian froze in his tracks. Amelia was at the bottom of the stairs, talking to Chandler, but what made matters worse was she was flirting with him. "Damian won me a day of freedom. He says there is a surprise for me and I rather think it may be another day of freedom tomorrow. I would so love for you to share it with me. Perhaps, after my surprise, you may take me on a moonlit walk?" she asked, beaming up at the soldier ... just as she had always beamed at him. Chandler nodded his agreement and gently touched her hair in a show of affection that, rightly, shouldn't have been allowed between a soldier and a princess. Then, he gave her a single rose, and Amelia's face lit up with love. Damian was heartbroken.

"Amelia, it's time to return to your room. Chandler may join you for tonight only," he interrupted suddenly, unable to ignore her guilty smile, as if she knew what she was doing to his emotions, but Damian tried to ignore her as best he could. Chandler snapped back to attention outside the council room, fearful that he had been caught doing something he shouldn't have and that he would now be punished for it. "It's alright, soldier, I'll take over your duty. It's Valentine's Day and Miss Amelia has a rare opportunity to enjoy it, without confinement to her room. It is your one chance, if you wish to take the opportunity," he offered, trying desperately to ignore the lump in his throat and the way his stomach turned into knots.

Chandler looked at Amelia for a clue as to what he should do, but her hopeful smile said everything. She wanted him to go with her. "What of the master, sir?" Chandler wondered as he reluctantly handed his spear to Damian. It was his duty to stand guard outside the council room, after all.

"I will explain if the master wonders why you are not here. You may as well enjoy yourself, soldier ... for both of us." Damian said, faking a smile as best he could, watching as Amelia ripped out his heart and threw it away once more, as she took Chandler's hand and rushed him up to her chambers.

Damian was devastated, but he stood guard all the same, taking up Chandler's position outside the council room. He was only mildly surprised by the way Amelia rushed back down to him five minutes later to gush over the presents left for her. To his relief, she thought her father had sent them up and he wasn't going to correct her. It was only when Lucius appeared that he was caught unaware.

"Damian? I thought you were with Amelia?" he wondered, looking around curiously, looking for Amelia.

"We had our day together, sir. She wishes to spend her night with another," Damian confessed through gritted teeth. Somehow, he could never hide his true feelings from Lucius, no matter how hard he tried.

"The young soldier whose place you have taken? I was afraid of such a thing. I had noticed that he took a rather long time whenever he was sent to run errands for her. Now I know why," Lucius replied, contemplating whether or not to ban Chandler from ever seeing her again without making it seem like he was punishing the poor solider. "Why did you allow such a thing? You love her, do you not? Why allow her to spend Valentine's Day with another man?"

Lucius had no idea how his words stung him. Damian took a deep breath and admitted the truth, whether or not anyone understood. "It will make her happy and that is all I care about," he confessed, unashamed of his feelings or how easily Amelia twisted them. One day he would either move on and forget about her and find love elsewhere, remaining a solider his whole life, or else he would finally confess his feelings to her and find that she reciprocated them. Miracles could happen. It was Valentine's Day after all, and he had actually enjoyed himself.

"Even at the expense of your own happiness?" Lucius asked, placing a hand on Damian's shoulder, feeling the tension that ran through his whole body. No matter what he said, he could never convince him that he was alright knowing that Amelia was spending Valentine's night with another man.

"Yes. Amelia and I do not have the best relationship, but that is one thing that will never change. Now, matter how I feel about it or what sacrifices I have to make, her happiness will always come first," Damian replied, smiling to himself. It was true. No matter how many Valentine's days they shared throughout their lives, no matter how many other men she wished to spend those days with, he would always put her happiness first ... no matter what.

Valentine's Day 1675

Shiloh had never known anything like it. Her life had always been far too simple and innocent. Now, it was so far beyond complicated that she barely knew what to do. She had been a college graduate looking for a way to make some easy money; that was all, and quite innocent. Well, not anymore, but it had been at the time. Now she was so far out of control that she barely knew any other life. To make matters worse, it was Valentine's Day, and instead of being in love with some local village boy, she was alone ... so, so alone.

She had found a small ad in a local newspaper, looking for a nurse to care and feed a man of ninety. Since she had spent two years as a volunteer nurse, she went to the interview to see if she could be of any use. She wasn't sure how much medical knowledge they required, but she was willing to give it a shot. She hadn't expected to arrive at a mansion in a sleepy English town an hour's drive away from campus to find it buzzing with life. Once invited inside, she saw at least a dozen young women her own age, mulling around a table looking at magazines. Shiloh wondered at the necessity of the advert, but then she had managed to convince herself that maybe they didn't have any medical knowledge.

Upon her arrival, she was shown into a small study just off a large hallway. She was interviewed in a slightly strange manner. The questions were more personal than she was used to, but she thought it was probably because she was from out of town. Quaint little villages like this one always had strange people, but she accepted the job anyway. She was taken to a room upstairs and was told that she would be taken to greet her charge, Laurence, in a short while. Then, they left her to settle in.

Shiloh immediately began unpacking her things and getting acquainted with her room in the old mansion. She was, therefore, only mildly surprised when there was a knock on her door an hour later, followed by the entrance of a very handsome looking man, who she gauged to be around twenty-five. "Good evening, Shiloh. I am Laurence," he explained, extending his hand to her.

She had been so stunned that she held her hand out to shake his before his words really registered. She laughed, at first. "Laurence? Is that a family name?" She asked politely, as the young man gave her wrist an adoring stroke with his thumb.

"Not especially. My father had the same name many years ago, but he's no longer with us, you see," he mentioned with a smile, gently lifting her hand to his lips. Just when she thought he was going to be gentlemanly and kiss it, he didn't. He took the tip of her finger into his mouth as if to taste her skin, and then smiled at her as she attempted to remove her hand.

She hadn't been sure what was happening, but even back then she had an inclination that it wasn't good. As she sat in a rocking chair by a window reading her book, she knew that it was her only chance to get away. But that had been years ago—two years to be exact. So, when her bedroom door creaked open behind her, she didn't give it a second glance. Not even when Laurence sat himself at her feet and smiled at her for the hundredth millionth time. He ran a caressing hand over her ankle, up the calf of her leg and pushed up the skirt she wore. Shiloh became far too used to it, but she paid him no mind. Yet, the moment his sharp fangs pierced the skin on the inside of her thigh, her head lolled back against the seat and she closed her eyes. The feeling was still delectable … even now. Laurence was hungry and he had no patience. Instead of asking her to move onto the bed, or feeding from another wound, he gently lifted her leg from the floor and positioned himself between her knees. His back touched her left thigh only partially, while he gorged himself on the blood from her veins. Shiloh gasped as his fingers dug into her leg and he impatiently removed his fangs from the wounds he had made and pierced her skin two inches higher, where the blood was fresh.

Shiloh's mind went back to the first time Laurence had fed from her. Another Valentine's Day spent alone, but at least back then, she had had some hope. He had left their first meeting unsatisfied, telling her to rest and that they would discuss her duties the next day. She began to wonder if perhaps his father had died and he didn't want to break the news to her that, just moments after getting the job, she was without work. It struck her how silly the human mind was, making up excuses for something that should have been so obvious. So, she read and unpacked for the remainder of the day.

It was only that night, dreaming forbidden dreams of Laurence and the clear attraction he had already displayed toward her, that the dream was disturbed. She woke to pain, her eyes and mouth flashing open in a wordless scream as two strong fangs pierced her neck. A body lay across hers, warm and strong as she felt the life being sucked from her. The moment he knew she was awake, Laurence pulled back and smiled at her with a bloody grin. "You are mine now,

Shiloh. You may never leave this house until the day I die," he warned her, planting a tormenting kiss on her lips before resuming his feed. She had been so weak then, so unable to fight back from shock and surprise and loss of blood. All she could think about for a long moment was that he had kissed her, and placed the taste of her own blood on her lips. But she knew his words were true, and she knew what he was.

Laurence had visited her almost daily after that first feed. He would taunt her with small words of belonging and ownership, and always fed from her when she had no chance of refusing him. She only fought back once, a week into her stay at the mansion. Shiloh remembered it clearly, even as Laurence made a third wound in her thigh to feed from. She had discovered his secret, that he only bit her when she was least prepared, and she had rearranged the room to suit her needs. She made it impossible for him to creep up on her— from the door or window—and laid traps down at night, so that if he came in while she was sleeping, she would wake. She had been sitting by the window that day, facing the door, ready for him. When he walked in silently, she noted his immediate surprise.

Laurence had squared his shoulders and advanced toward her, then casually lifted her wrist to his mouth. When she retracted her touch, he glared at her in confusion and tried a second attempt. Again he failed and his anger didn't go unnoticed. He spun around and left the room. She didn't see him again for two weeks, in which time she was denied food or water and was left to starve in her room. Shiloh would gladly have allowed herself to die then, refusing him his blood supply except for two things. Her strong fighting sense had kicked in, telling her not to give him the satisfaction of killing her out of frustration because he couldn't have his way with her. The second was the knowledge that if she did die, he would only get another girl to take her place, and she couldn't allow that. Then, Shiloh did the one thing she hadn't yet had the strength to do. She had got dressed up into the nicest outfit she had, struggled to the door and threw it open. It had been difficult going down the stairs in the state she was in, but once there, she managed to compose herself and make her way toward Laurence's office.

He was surprised to see her. So were his ten companions, each one staring at her as if she were some disgusting creature they abhorred. "Laurence, I wish to speak with you … alone." She managed to make the words sound strong rather than weak, and the other men appreciated her a little more for it. They rose without a word and left the room, leaving her alone with her tormentor. She had been careful about it, walking across until she was right beside his seat, and allowed him to take her hand and kiss it. Then, as casually as she could, she had asked him if he was hungry. The glitter in his eyes when he finally looked up at her was triumphant, and he wasted no time in dragging her wrist to his mouth and feeding from her. But after only a few seconds he pulled away, obviously dissatisfied as he frown at her. To Shiloh's surprise, a hand had appeared on her forehead, she was ushered into a seat and Laurence had called a young woman into the room. "She is dying, sire. She must eat and rest for many days before she is herself again," the young woman explained with a small curtsey before leaving the room.

She had known he was angry, both with her and with himself, for allowing her to get into such a state. For a full week Laurence didn't visit to feed from her, but had her constantly watched by a young woman who cared for her. It seemed strange at the time, but she had recovered, and Laurence had resumed his feeding from her on a daily basis.

When he pulled back from the third wound and looked at her hungrily, Shiloh had no idea what he was thinking. He had never been so hungry for her blood before; he had never fed from her more than once a day. Something had happened and now he looked almost guilty with an unquenchable thirst in his eyes. She met his gaze out of curiosity, for the first time in a long time, and found that he looked away far too quickly. She thought for a moment that it was out of shame, but to her surprise, he rose. It was only when she heard the squeak of the door as he opened it that she ventured to speak. "What is wrong?" she wondered, unsure whether he would tell her. But the door didn't close. Shiloh fixed her clothing back into place and stood up, rather unsteady on her feet. When she found herself wavering as she stepped toward him, she almost let out a sigh of relief when his strong arms caught her.

Laurence lifted Shiloh into his arms and carried her across the room to the bed. They had shared the room for a year and six months, but they had never shared anything remotely intimate together, not conversation, not feelings and certainly nothing physical. Again, she asked him what was wrong, and this time, he chose to answer her. "You are sick," he replied and were not the words she was expecting. Shiloh frowned and shook her head, not understanding what he was talking about. But she didn't think she wanted to know, so she didn't ask. Instead she tried to tell herself that he was tricking her somehow, but his eyes were filled with fear. "It is sudden, yes? But not to me. I, who have tasted your blood, know the truth. There is a sickness in your blood … a doctor told me to continue feeding from you, that it would remove the sickness, but each time you recover from a feeding, so does the sickness in your blood. I could only hope that if I fed too much ... if I took more than was mine to take …" he began again, but Shiloh was shocked to see that emotion choked him. She was stunned to hear that he thought he had a rightful claim to a certain amount of her blood, but she had to push that aside for now. He looked away and cleared his throat. "You must go away. The doctor will care for you and you must never return." He spoke without looking at her and then rose from the bed and left the room, but she couldn't understand what was happening. What did he mean? Why was he sending her away? He once told her that she would never leave the house until he died.

Shiloh spent the rest of the day alone, contemplating Laurence's words. They just didn't make any sense. But, for some reason, when the doctor arrived and examined her, tsking to himself and telling her nothing, she refused to go. The porters came with the strong vampire guard she had seen downstairs upon many occasion, ready to carry her to the waiting ambulance, but she just found that she didn't want to go. She sent them off with the foulest language she had ever used, then barked orders at the vampire guard to bring her Laurence. She had never known herself to be in such a state before.

But Laurence wouldn't come. The guard gave his excuses verbatim, or so they said. "He says he does not need a goodbye from you, miss, as you were only a source of nourishment. You do not mean enough to him for goodbyes."

That made Shiloh's blood boil. "Go away and ... guard something," she snapped back, forcing herself out of bed and stalling in her room only long enough to lift the silk dressing gown from the back of a chair. She was really quite undressed for company, in her opinion. She wore only a silk negligee that a young nurse had changed her into, with her hair down, but it was enough for what she planned to do. Slipping on her dressing gown as she walked out of her room, Shiloh made her way unsteadily down the stairs and found Laurence standing in his office, talking to one of his friends. The moment he saw her, he tried to feign indifference and look away, but it was at that moment that she lost her footing on the bottom step. Before she hit the floor, Laurence raced across the room and caught her within his arms with a distinct look of panic on his face.

Shiloh leaned her head against his shoulder, exhausted from her efforts, watching everything pass by as Laurence carried her back up the stairs to her bed. She wanted to say something, but the moment he laid her down, he stopped her. "Why do you act so reckless? You sent the doctor away … without his healing, you will die," he protested, clearly worried about her. For some reason, she was delighted. During her time in the house with him, she had always considered herself a victim who couldn't leave. Somehow, when he had told her to leave and that she meant nothing, she realized that she wanted to stay for Laurence and not for any other reason.

"Why are you going to send me away?" she asked, her voice faint and gentle.

"I cannot keep you. You are sick and you need a doctor," he said with a sigh, then took her hand into his own. It was the most expressive and personal he had ever been.

"I won't be sick if I stay with you … if you make me one of you, but only if you want me …" Shiloh found it difficult to get her words out. "If you don't want me here when you can't feed from me …"

Laurence stopped her with a kiss. "I feared you did not wish to stay. I was afraid to ask in case you did not wish to," he confessed, giving her hand a squeeze. Shiloh smiled, but she felt so weak that she decided not to bother waiting any longer.

"Turn me, Laurence, and I will stay with you forever," she promised in a whisper. Her voice wasn't up to much more. "But you must choose … I do not feel well at all."

Laurence was worried about the confession and how quickly she was deteriorating. The doctor already warned him that she may have been ill for a long time, before he was able to taste it within her blood. Without him, she may never have known of her sickness until it was too late. Now that they had prior warning, he agreed that he had to make a choice. He tried to move from feeding from her to becoming more personal, but all attempts had been met with stony silence from Shiloh, and he understood that at the time. Without being able to make personal progress, it seemed wrong. He didn't want her to feel compelled to love him just because he fed from her. "If you love me, I will turn you," he promised finally, smiling hopefully. Shiloh appreciated the compromise and agreed, only just managing to lift herself to kiss him. It wasn't easy and she smiled as he took a gentle grip of her shoulders and eased her back onto the bed. "Do not move until you are well again. I will turn you, if that is what you want," he agreed, waiting for her nod of agreement before lowering himself to bite her neck.

Shiloh's blood was like a favorite childhood blanket, warm and comforting, always guaranteed to do what was needed. Laurence fed from her until he felt her heart falter. He hadn't done so before; he had never pushed his feed so far, for fear of hurting her, but now he knew it would save her life. Her heart attempted to keep beating, but found it difficult, and finally, when he felt the moment it stopped, he withdrew. Without wasting time, he pierced a wound in his own wrist and held it to her mouth. Turning her was his only option if he was going to save her life. When she pulled back, he knew that she had fed enough. He waited patiently, sitting on the side of the bed, as her eyes slowly closed and she allowed his blood to do its work. Over an hour passed and Laurence was beginning to worry that he had waited too long to act, but eventually, Shiloh opened her eyes. There was such a life in her as she moved toward him that he knew the transition was successful. He gave in to the passionate kiss she gave him, and relished the thought of spending eternity with her. And for the first time in her life, she had someone of her own … maybe there was something lucky about Valentine's Day after all.

September 1888

He couldn't believe his luck. Just when he thought it was safe to prowl the streets, Jack the Ripper had struck again.

~ *178* ~

Twice in one night. There was no way he was going to be able to feed now.

Wilhelm retreated from Whitechapel and returned to his carriage, directing it to take him home. He lived not far from that seedy place that Jack had made his haunting grounds, but by all rights, Wilhelm had the monopoly on its inhabitants. He had been hunting there for decades, long before Jack ever came to be. Now, he was being ousted by an equally bloodthirsty rookie. Maybe it was time to give in, time to hang up his coat one last time. Maybe he should go to his clan elder and ask to have it over with?

Actually, Wilhelm didn't mind. He liked the smell that Jack's handiwork gave the streets; a stench of blood and fear that he fed from almost as much as the blood itself. The moment he was safely inside his cab, he drew the curtains and took a brief peek outside every now and then. It was dangerous being a single man out on the streets at night nowadays. With Jack the Ripper remaining so mysterious a character, no one knew whether he was rich or poor, tall or short; any man seen walking alone after dark could be accosted by the police, especially if there was any sign of blood on him. Wilhelm had just escaped being interrogated that night.

She was young and unusually pretty for that area, especially for being out at that time of night. She didn't reek of alcohol like the others, but of the sweetest perfume. She had been on her way to work, a long walk in a dangerous place. Wilhelm smiled to himself as the carriage drew him home; her smell, her skin, her eyes. They were all so expressive of who she was … or had been.

He could remember the way the wind had caressed her scent through the air towards him. She hadn't been his original target; he had been looking for a more susceptible woman. He would probably have ended up with another prostitute, hanging around some corner or other, only too happy to go off into the shadows with a man, had she not come along. He didn't know her name, but then, he never knew any of their names. Not unless he chose to make them special. And this girl was indeed very special.

He had changed course the instant her smell had captured his senses. It wasn't difficult, as no-one ever noticed him lingering in the shadows. He had been silent as he walked up behind her, his eyes closing as his nose explored the smell of her dark hair. They were just inches apart. He closed the distance, whispering soft Latin words to her that held her spellbound to do as he pleased. With a smile, he stepped up beside her, extended his arm and reveled in the sensation that swept through him. She blushed and placed her arm through his. Wilhelm had never known a smile so captivating before.

Even as he sat in his carriage heading home, he couldn't stop thinking about her. Even as he peeked out at the street he passed, watching the groups of men going through each alleyway, trying to make it harder for Jack to prowl the streets, he thought of her; mysterious, and wonderful, nameless her. Even as he cursed the confounded Mr. Lusk for setting up such a neighborhood scheme, he thought only of her. He cared not that his hunting ground would be off limits until Jack was caught or disposed of. He cared not that he may have been seen with that wonderful woman and become a suspect for being a single man out alone with a woman so late at night. None of it mattered.

Wilhelm waited just a few moments, seeking the shelter of shadows, before brushing her dark hair back from her luscious neck and swooping in to claim his prize. He didn't have the patience to wait any longer. He could still feel the ache of his fangs in the carriage, aching for her, for her blood. He recalled the faint gasp of breath that left her lungs as his fangs pierced the delicate, beautiful flesh of her neck. The taste had been intoxicating. He knew then what he was going to do. He hadn't done it often; there had never been any reason to. He had never cared if his victims lived or died once he was through with them, but not with her. He couldn't allow *her* to die. The moment he felt that small flutter of her heart, ready to give way to his hunger, he had stopped and gazed down at her for a long moment. Then, doing something he had never planned to do that night, he bit into his own leathery flesh, creating two small puncture marks on his wrist and then held the bleeding wounds to her mouth with such force that she couldn't resist.

Wilhelm knew at the time that she never would resist him. His Latin spell had worked too well for her willpower to make a difference. She had gulped down his blood by natural instinct to stay alive, and yet, even as he felt the bumps of the cobbled road through the carriage, anger and frustration welled up within him, for she was lost.

Moments after he had withdrawn his own blood from her lips, he had been about to carry her to his carriage waiting just a few feet away, but those wretched men were there, still trying to scare off Jack the Ripper. They had been far too close to discovering him with a bleeding victim in his arms. He only had time enough time to cover her with his cloak in the darkest part of the alleyway before retreating to his carriage, knowing that he would return for her soon, before she starved to death. He only hoped she didn't die. If she did, they might have another Jack on their hands. He wouldn't rest until he found the person who kept him from his prize.

"Master," a voice drifted into Wilhelm's thoughts on the carriage ride home when it came to an abrupt stop. He looked up from the window toward the carriage door in front of his house. His footman was holding it open, waiting for him to exit. With a sigh, he stepped out and withdrew into his unassuming home. It wasn't in the least ostentatious, but it wasn't really home either. He had been in voluntary exile from his vampire community for far too long. If it hadn't been for the girl, he might have stayed away indefinitely, but now he thought that perhaps he might go back after all … if only to show off the beauty he had discovered when he reclaimed her.

Wilhelm was lost to his own thoughts as he entered the library and took a seat before the fire his housekeeper had prepared for his return. He always felt the cold lately—ever since he left his family and friends. He knew fine well that vampires weren't supposed to live alone. They became dangerous to others as well as to themselves, they stopped taking care of themselves and their feeding, they got caught and punished, or heaven forbid, sloppy. *He* would never be accused of such things. He hadn't forgotten the old ways.

He picked up a book, to take his attention away from his thoughts, when he was surprised by a faint, but somehow familiar smell. It tickled his nose and his senses alike, until he was forced to look up from the cover of the book he held, only to behold an even more enrapt beauty. "How is this possible?" He asked aloud, fearful that his senses had deserted him. Had he not fed enough? Was he drifting into that dangerous starvation that could kill him, or was he really hallucinating?

Wilhelm knew he wasn't imagining anything the moment the young woman stepped forward, placing her body before his. She was the most beautiful creature he had ever known. As he reached out his hand to caress her face, her features distorted to mirror his own hunger. Her blue eyes blazed almost transparent and her fangs descended. They faced each other, vampire to vampire, for barely three seconds before she threw herself at him and bit into his neck. Wilhelm held still. His beauty, his creation was still weak. He could hear her heartbeat fluttering, trying to decide whether to die or fight, but she had made her choice out of hunger. She came to him to feed from her sire, to grow strong, so Wilhelm helped her. He held one hand to her raven dark hair, leaned his head to the side and used a strong arm to hold her to him until she had fed adequately.

He was so enchanted by the flow of energy between them that he barely noticed time slipping by, until he found himself, once again, face to face with her beauty. "What is your name, child?" he asked as she wiped a spot of blood from the crease of her mouth.

"I am Victorie, sire," she replied as she curtsied, as was fitting to his high born status and her low birth.

"Yes you are … you are my Victorie … and mine you will stay." Wilhelm wasted no time in reveling in his victory. She—such a beautiful, wonderful she—was his, and her name epitomized everything he had suffered in his life. She was his final victory, and he celebrated it with a kiss. Now he had something … someone … to live for. Now, he had love and romance and hope in his life again, and he had the silly thought of doing something spectacular for her, for Valentine's Day.

Valentine's Day 1892

Damian could never understand why a simple name was so difficult to get right. He had adopted the surname Gray over the last ten years as a necessity to ensure that his real name did not continue creeping up on the census. But what was so difficult about Damian that he changed it to Dorian? That damned writer had really messed things up now.

Damian recently read the published version of his life story, Dorian Gray, and he was not pleased. Since when had he been anything of the sort? Of course, his best friend and brother-in-law Trey found it most amusing, but Damian did not. The only portrait picture hanging on his wall was without a photograph. It represented a life, a family and a wife he had long since lost. There were no photographs of Angela, so he kept the empty frame above his fireplace to remember her by … to remember their life. That small offering was even more important on her favorite holiday, Valentine's Day … the day he missed her the most.

"You must forget about this silly book and come hunting with me. I really am very hungry and you are the worst host for not offering me sustenance," Trey teased him, taking the hated book from his hand and throwing it into the fire, to signify his agreement to how little it represented the man before him. Damian was a vampire, that much was true, and he could live forever, his features never changing. That was also true. But he was in no way cursed never to look upon an image of himself for fear that all his years would return to him. Where the silly man had got that idea from, he didn't know, but Damian was brooding about it. He hoped for something true to life, something that explored his pain and anguish and the loss of his dear, deceased wife, Angela.

"I should have asked that Doyle chap to write my memoirs instead. He would have done it justice," Damian lamented with a sigh, before forcing himself out of his seat. "Very well. We shall hunt," he reluctantly agreed.

He had always hated feeding from humans. It might have been the only thing to sustain him for his unnaturally long life, but that didn't stop him from wishing it were another way. Prowling through the darkness, creeping up on victims, watching the light go out in their eyes if he fed too much were all the things other vampires loved, but Damian hated. However, it wasn't his choice; he had to live the life he was given. So he threw on a cloak and stalked to the door after Trey.

It was foggy outside the clan house, dark and depressing. Trey laughed and talked of how the hunt would be easy, but Damian wasn't so sure. Something felt wrong. It was nothing he could pinpoint exactly, just something not quite normal. They walked for ten minutes, chatting quietly about this and that, until they reached the outskirts of their town, Avelina. This was where vampire land ended and human territory began. They could smell the difference. The human land stank of beer, cheap perfumes, sewage and unwashed bodies. Damian wished he could just turn around and go home again, but as was Trey, he was starving. He needed blood, so he pointed silently at a small barn that led away from the center of the village, as Trey nodded in agreement.

Damian headed toward the barn and sank down in the hay, waiting patiently, while Trey walked into the human village and into the public house. He would bring back two warm bodies that he and Damian could feed from; he was better at retaining his human nature than his brother in law. "Who is up for a round of drinks … on me?" Trey asked, laughing as he approached the bar. A few eager eyes turned his way and he immediately spotted two women, probably from the brothel upstairs, eyeing him like a prize turkey. If he had money enough to buy lots of drink, they might try and get their share from him, as well. But Trey spotted an even more intriguing dinner in the corner of the room.

Two young girls sat in the corner, trying to avoid being seen. After a quiet chat with the barman, he discovered that their carriage had broken down on the road going through the village and they were forced to stop while the blacksmith worked on it. Trey tipped his hat to them then walked across the room to their table. "Good ladies ... if you do not mind my inquiring, what prevents your carriage from going further?" he asked politely, not presuming to sit down as the two young women glanced up to see a well dressed gentleman sitting beside them.

"Our carriage wheel has broken sir, and our horse is lame. Once the blacksmith has replaced a broken shoe and the broken wheel, we shall continue our journey, though it may take hours," one of the young women replied.

Trey nodded and smiled.

"If you do not mind my suggesting, there is a very elegant home just in the next village. Its inhabitants would very kindly offer you rooms for the night … away from this outrageous crowd," Trey suggested with a twinkle in his eyes. The young girls glanced at each other and then at the gentleman, considering the matter seriously. Then, eyeing their concern, added, "Of course, I will accompany you to ensure that you will not be harmed."

Trey knew he had won them over already, but for good measure, he assured the young women that there were many ladies already within the elegant house who would gladly care for them, and the matter was settled. He walked out of the public house with the two women, and led them toward the barn where Damian waited. He ventured in alone. "My brother, I have found some lovely young girls to join us, and they will be returning home with us. Can you fake an injury of some sort? Or shall I claim you shy?" Trey asked in amusement and laughed when Damian threw a fistful of hay at him. Shy, he decided. He exited the barn with Damian, and presented him to the young ladies, as his brother-in-law, widowed and painfully shy in company. They each looked upon him favorably, and gave their apologies for the loss of his wife, as they walked the short distance to Avelina.

Once within the safety of clan house, Trey offered to escort the girls to their rooms, as he offered them his arm. To Damian's surprise, one girl turned and blushed at Damian, requesting his arm. He gave it reluctantly and followed Trey up the staircase. Trey glanced back at Damian with a wink, and followed the young girl he had escorted, into her bedroom, where he intended to feed from her.

Damian saw the expectant look on the face of the girl who held his arm and fear thudded through his chest. He led her to an empty chamber, and held the door open as she walked inside. "How beautiful! What a lovely room," she said, as Damian quickly closed the door behind her. His breath caught as he leaned momentarily against the door … for she looked too much like Amelia as memories came flooding back. Brushing the memories aside, he walked back into the hallway toward his own room. There, he locked himself away for four days and four nights, until the young women had left the clan house. He couldn't feed from her— from any woman—not on Angela's day. When he reappeared, he was starving and emaciated but with Trey's care, he quickly recovered. Trey later reminded him of the danger he had put himself through ... and all because a young girl looked like Amelia.

Then Damian remembered that reckless girl who had stolen Angela from his life; that forbidden girl; that wild, uncontrollable girl that he couldn't hate, and didn't want to love. But he did love her, and he was going to have to face it.

Valentine's Day, present day

Damian paced the floor of his office. It was Valentine's Day ... again. He never understood how it came around so quickly each year. Normally, the years went by so fast he barely noticed, but somehow, when February came around, time stopped completely for three days. The day before Valentine's day, the actual day of love, and the day after, when he thanked his lucky stars that it was all over yet again for one more year, at least. It was the one day of the year that had haunted him like a ghost since he lost Angela, but this year, he decided it would be different.

When Angela was alive, and he was with her, he had at least enjoyed the day of love by sneaking into her house and spending the day with her, whenever he was able. It had been her favorite holiday. At least then he had been able to face the day without dreading it. After her death, it all changed. For centuries, he had hidden away and wallowed in self-pity on every fourteenth of February. Then the impossible happened. He decided to tell Amelia, his difficult and moody charge, that he loved her. He had never wanted to love her, but he hadn't been able to deny that it was true. It had been his first and last attempt to celebrate Valentine's Day … until now.

Damian returned to his desk and tried to calm his hectic thoughts. Valentine's Day wasn't the end of everything, not anymore. He just had to remember that and learn to appreciate that his life was different now. Now, he had Kaitlin and it was their first chance to celebrate Valentine's Day together. He couldn't help but laugh to himself. He had been weak and pathetic to believe the lies Lucius had put into his head … lies that told him that he loved and couldn't live without Amelia. He had always thought he was strong enough to resist any mental tampering, but Lucius had proven him wrong. He fell for the lies and believed that he loved Amelia for not just weeks or months or years, but for centuries. Now that the lies were gone, he felt light, free and happy … for the first time since losing Angela.

Valentine's Day would no longer cause his heart to race from fear and regret. It would no longer cause him to break out into a cold sweat and send him running for his chambers and locking the door. No, this year he was going to enjoy himself and treat Kaitlin to the wonders that, being a vampire on Valentine's Day, could bring to her life. Much to her surprise, he had tucked himself into his office for the first two hours of the evening, trying to gather his thoughts and calm himself down. Now, it was time for the surprise.

"Darling, may I steal you away?" Damian asked with a smile, the moment he found her sitting in the library, chatting with Emily, her new best friend. When she smiled at him, he felt the same strange, warm sensation running through his whole body. He had no idea what it was, but Kaitlin was the only one who could manage it.

"You know fine well you can have me whenever you want," Kaitlin teased him, reaching out and slipping her hand into his.

Damian left the library, leading Kaitlin through a door in the basement she had never seen before. Since he was now the Master of the three clans, he had already arranged to have Trey hold down the fort while he was gone, telling those needing to know that they would be gone all night, but it didn't stop him from being excited. He had been perfectly calm until he saw Kaitlin, who was now his wife. Now, he was eager to share everything with her.

"Slow down," she said, laughing to herself, struggling to keep up as he rushed along the secret underground tunnel. She had no idea where they were going, but she was excited about it.

When they finally emerged from the darkness, Damian simply stood to the side and let her take in the wonders before her. A glittering lake sat directly ahead surrounded by forest trees and, to top it all off, there was a picnic basket, blanket and candles decorating the ground right next to the lake. Soon, the sun would set, the stars would come out and it would be the most romantic night of her life. "This is beautiful," Kaitlin whispered, unaware she was holding her breath until she let it out. When she turned to look at her husband, he just smiled at her with such a light in his eyes that she almost wondered if it was a dream. She hadn't seen him so happy since their union. She thought that night, watching him being dubbed an elder, watching them become united in heart, soul and blood, and then watching him take his place as the rightful leader of the three united clans had been special. But this ... this was beyond all that. This was private and personal, and just for them.

Kaitlin let Damian lead her to the blanket. She made herself comfortable while he lifted a boulder with such ease that she almost gasped, until she saw that it was fake. Beneath it was a secret hole with two boxes inside. "This is a secret place. In times of war, when we have to run off or if the leader must escape, then supplies are left in this place so that the leader may survive until he can return home." Damian smiled as he explained, handing her the first box.

She was surprised to find that a very ancient looking telescope was inside, lying on a velvet cloth.

"I haven't actually celebrated Valentine's day before. There was no such thing back home and when I got here, I didn't have anyone to celebrate with. Are we going to do some star gazing with that old thing?" she asked softly, laughing as she inspected her first gift, wondering how old it was and if it would still work. It wasn't until after she spoke that she realized how insulting her words could have been to a gift that, obviously, Damian had kept safe for many years.

But Damian just smiled and laid out a veritable feast of delights that included human food that Kaitlin had once loved, and plenty of blood for them to enjoy together. "Yes we are. That *old thing* happens to be one of the first telescopes ever made. It's a refracting telescope that was used in the Netherlands in 1608, so be gentle," he teased her gently, well aware of how much she loved the history of his world. She never had enough time to look into all the things she wanted to know about. Her world—a magical Island—had never had the same progress or technology and he was her soul mate, her husband, he didn't want her to feel left out. If someone was going to teach her about the history of his world, he wanted to be the one to do it. "I love it," Kaitlin blushed.

On her request, he sat and told her about the telescope, its invention and how it worked, while they waited for the stars to come out. They talked about everything; his previous hatred of Valentine's Day and how she had never known it existed. Then, he presented her with the second gift, a set of books on magic that Kaitlin delved into right away. The books were old and well read, but very special. The elders told him of them recently, and as Kaitlin had her own magical gifts, he knew that reading of ancient magic that the vampire elders had discovered centuries ago would be something of a joy for his queen. Then, Kaitlin did something that surprised him.

"Well … I have a gift for you, too. Since this is my first Valentine's Day, I've been worrying over what to get you for a gift, but as it turns out, I waited so long that nature kind of took over," she explained with a nervous smile. She wasn't sure how to say it, so she went silent for a moment, thinking it over. She took so long, chewing her lip so nervously that Damian began to worry that something was wrong.

"Kaitlin … if there's something wrong … if something has happened, you must tell me," he begged, desperate to know what was going on. He took her hand into his and held it tenderly. He was so afraid that he had missed something, done something wrong or had neglected her and that she was upset with him.

"We're pregnant."

For a moment, Damian was speechless. He stared at her as if she was an alien he couldn't believe was real. And, truly, he wasn't sure he *could* believe it. Then it sank in and he was so pleased, so happy that he caught her up in his arms and kissed her passionately, before realizing what he was doing. "Okay, we have to be really careful. You have no idea how incredible this is! Elders … masters … they are the only people in our world who have ever been allowed to be united. That gift we were given … without that, we couldn't have children. Not in our world," he grinned, handling her very gently. He lifted a spare blanket he brought along and wrapped it around her shoulders, and then removed all the human food and put it back into the basket, insisting that it wasn't good for her or their baby. Kaitlin was so amused that she just laughed and held his hand tightly, until he was able to calm down.

"I'm not sure I understand. Please talk a little slower," she asked softly, intrigued to hear what he was saying.

"Our people need a blood bond and a sanctioned union before they can bear children. We were given that gift because we were chosen to rule, but others are not granted it. If Trey had not united with an elder's daughter, he would not have been allowed a union at all. They would be together, but would not have been given the blood bond and union. They would never have been able to have children. But because they … and we … were given that chance, we can. I can't believe we did this," he said excitedly, but for the sake of her understanding, he calmed down enough to explain the stupid rules of the clan. The elders had thought they were controlling the population and controlling who was worthy of children and who wasn't, but he could never agree with it.

"Then, as the new leaders, we can change that law, can't we? We can let anyone and everyone be united if they wish. Then they can have that blood bond and children if they wish to," Kaitlin said with a smile, adamant that while they were in charge, there would be no more barbaric, ridiculous rules or laws. And Damian agreed that it sounded perfect. After all, they ruled the united clans; therefore, they could decide what they wanted. And if it made Kaitlin happy, then he would do it.

"I love you … more than I could possibly say. And we are going to have a wonderful family," he promised gently, leaning in to kiss her in thanks for being so beautiful and smart. He had never known anyone like her. He needed to remember and thank Trey for his loyalty over the years, for without him, he would never have gotten over Amelia or Angela and then, he might not have had the sense and the room in his heart … to love Kaitlin.

Fat Chance My Love
By: J.S. Wilsoncroft

The characters in this story are based on the book

Fat Chances

By: J.S. Wilsoncroft

The smell of bacon made my mouth water as I quickly walked down the stairs, nearly tripping over my own two feet. I love our family Sunday breakfasts, especially now that Cory became a part of it. I still couldn't get past the idea that we have been dating for over a year now. Sometimes when I'm lying in bed with him, I would secretly pinch myself to make sure I wasn't dreaming. One time I think he caught me when I heard him chuckle to himself.

Just as I stepped on the bottom stair, the doorbell rang and my heart beat wildly against my chest. I quickly wiped the bacon induced drool from my lip with my sleeve, opened the door and sighed heavily. Just seeing his gorgeous face and perfect body took my breath away.

"Good morning, sweetness. How's my favorite girl doing today?" Cory smiled wide, stepping over the threshold. Following closely beside him was "our" little cocker spaniel, Annie.

"Good morning to my favorite guy and … girl," I said cheerfully. I leaned down to pick up Annie and held her tight against my chest, as her little, black stub wagged vigorously. Annie was our 'baby' and between Cory and I and her 'grandparents', she was the most spoiled dog in town. I think she knew it, too.

"Annie's been pacing the living room since seven o'clock this morning. I think she knows it's Sunday." Cory laughed as he took off his leather jacket and hung it on the coat rack.

"Of course she knows its Sunday. It's when she gets to eat her Pappy's pancakes," I laughed along with him.

"Where's my grand doggy?" my mom asked as she walked into the hallway. I could feel Annie's stub thumping against my armpit as Mom walked over and petted her.

"Good morning, Kathy," Cory smiled. Mom looked up and winked at him.

"So glad you could join us today," I sighed happily. Everyone that I loved deeply was now under one roof; life is grand.

"Oh, I wouldn't miss the Powers' family breakfast for the world," Cory said. Mom laughed and patted him on the shoulder, then walked into the living room where my brother, Wayne, was slumped onto the couch watching the sports channel.

Just then, the doorbell rang again.

"Move it! Moo-ve it!" Molly barked as she ran down the steps. I nearly fell over the pile of shoes lying on the floor as she pushed me out of the way. Luckily, Cory grabbed me and kept me from falling on my ass. I glared at her, but she paid no attention as she quickly opened the door.

Molly let out a high pitched squeal when she saw her new boyfriend standing on the porch.

"Blake must be here," Dad chuckled, walking in from the kitchen. He was wearing his Sunday apron that we all got him for Christmas. It was pink and had a picture of a pig printed on the front along with the words, 'Making Bacon'.

"Good morning, everyone," Blake said as Molly peeled off his coat. Dad patted both of the guys on their shoulders and welcomed them. Having Dad's approval of Cory meant everything to me, especially since I was a Daddy's girl.

Molly was too, but Dad and I always had a special bond. Molly was more a Momma's girl. While Wayne ... well Wayne was just Wayne ... your average typical teenager who cared about nothing except sports, mainly basketball. He paid no more attention to us than the man on the moon, but Mom continued to baby him. I didn't blame her. He's a cute kid with a button nose and blue eyes; however, his rat's nest of hair left something to be desired. He never combed it and every time Mom offered to cut it, he ran in the other direction. We still never figured out where he inherited the afro. Mom always teased Dad, telling him that Wayne belonged to the electric meter man, whom ironically had curly hair. Dad didn't particularly care for the joke.

"Come on, everyone, breakfast is ready," Mom announced as she pushed Wayne into the dining room. The room smelled heavenly of bacon, pancakes, sausage, eggs and toast. I looked down at the table and noticed a helping of my favorite chocolate pancakes loaded with melted butter. I looked up and gave Dad a peculiar look as he laughed. He knew I had been struggling to lose weight, especially since I hooked up with Cory. Cory kept insisting that he didn't care about my weight and that he loved me no matter what. It took me a while, but I finally believed him. However, I still felt self-conscious about myself, especially when we went out together in public. I felt everyone's eyes on us. We were like the odd couple—like Arnold Schwarzenegger dating Rosanne Barr.

I lost thirty pounds since Cory and I started dating and felt good about it, but I needed to lose at least another fifty to be considered just 'overweight' and not obese. Seeing this pile of chocolate pancakes in front of me was definitely not helping my diet.

"Here, babe," Cory said, pulling out a chair for me to sit. I gently set Annie down on the floor beside me, then took my seat. Annie immediately lifted her nose into the air and began sniffing. I think she liked what she was smelling. Cory noticed and laughed.

"Don't worry. I have a special little plate for my grand doggy," Mom said as she came around, picked up Annie and carried her into the kitchen where her special purple bowl set on the floor next to the refrigerator. It was filled with dog food, scrambled eggs and little bits of sausage. Mom knew not to give her too much. With Cory being a fitness buff, he always made sure that Annie ate sensibly, too, but our Sunday breakfast was an exception.

We all took our seats and began filling our plates. I was hesitant to grab a stack of the chocolate pancakes, but I could feel Dad's eyes watching me and I didn't want to hurt his feelings. Out of my peripheral vision I saw a smile form on his lips when I grabbed two chocolate pancakes and slapped them on my plate. We all ate in silence, which was a rarity since Molly usually did most of the talking. She always talked about the current boy she was dating. Blake was the new man of the week and, surprisingly, the first one of her boyfriends to ever come over for our family breakfast. But this didn't mean that he was special. He's obviously either stupid or too smitten with her to say no.

Ever since Cory and I started officially dating, Molly started dating every guy that looked her way. She changed her relationship status on Facebook more often than some people change their underwear. It was sickening.

"So, Cory, where are you two heading off to after breakfast?" Mom asked before shoving a forkful of eggs into her mouth. Mom knew Cory liked to take me out after breakfast. Sometimes it was a surprise like a two hour drive to some flea market or a Sunday matinee. Once, he borrowed a boat from a friend and took me fishing on the dam. That was an experience. We spent more time trying to unsnag our lines then actually fishing. Just when we were about to call it day, I finally got a bite. But as I was reeling in the fish, Annie spotted it and jumped in the water after it. On an impulse Cory jumped in after her and ended up getting tangled in our fishing lines. I laughed so hard, I peed my pants.

"Today is supposed to be a beautiful day, so I have the whole afternoon planned," he replied, then turned and winked at me as my heart fluttered inside my chest. Cory knew from day one I hated surprises, but over time his fun-loving surprises were starting to grow on me. I actually looked forward to them now, but I didn't dare tell him. He would probably stop if I did. I smiled back, then quickly stabbed a piece of pancake and shoved it into my mouth.

"Mom, Blake is taking me miniature golfing this afternoon," Molly quickly added, then turned to Blake who just shoved a whole piece of sausage into his mouth. "Right, Blake?" Molly pressed.

Blake's green eyes grew wide. "Yeah, sure, whatever you want to do." He smiled with his mouth full.

Our family ate at a fast pace, shoving food into our mouths so quickly you would have thought we were having an eating contest. Of course, my brother Wayne would win hands down. He could clean his plate three times over before anyone finished off their first. The kid made me sick. He could eat like a damned pig and not gain a pound. However, if I would so much as glanced at a brownie, I could feel my hips growing wider by the second. While Molly and I cleared the table, Blake, Wayne and Dad headed to the living room to catch whatever game was playing.

"I'm gonna take Annie outside to pee," Cory said as he leaned down to hook the leash to her collar.

"Okay." I smiled, carrying the dirty dishes toward the kitchen. Just as I turned around to walk back into the dining room, Mom whispered into Cory's ear, then followed him outside. They were both laughing as if they had some kind of hidden joke between them.

Molly and I barely spoke a word as we loaded the dishwasher together. It made me sad, really. We used to be the best of friends until Cory came into the picture. I truly wished she believed that I didn't set out to steal him from her. Falling in love with Cory ... well ... it wasn't something that I had planned. It just happened.

After we cleared the table and the dishwasher was running, I quickly ran upstairs to change my clothes and brush my teeth. I never could guess what plans Cory had made, but I always made sure I was prepared. I learned early on to always wear sneakers because whatever he had planned usually involved walking, which was okay with me. I loved holding Cory's hand and walked alongside him. It was the one exercise I could tolerate.

"Kathy, would you mind watching Annie for a while?" Cory asked, turning to my mom just as we were walking out the door.

"Sure. I love watching my grand doggy," she cooed as she leaned down to pick her up.

"What? We always take Annie on our Sunday expeditions," I whined.

Cory laughed and turned around to face me. "Annie, dear, where we're going today, dogs aren't allowed." My cheeks grew warm instantly when he cupped my face in his hands, Mom chuckled behind him. That was odd. Why would she laugh about that?

"Oh ... okay, then," was all I could say as we walked out the door.

It was June 5 and the day was absolutely gorgeous. There were only a few clouds in the sky and the temperature was a cool seventy-six degrees, according to the temperature inside Cory's Mustang. Perfect. My kind of weather.

"Where are we going?" I turned around in the seat so I was facing him. I could feel the blood in my body racing as I stared at his beautiful face. He wore his hair looser these days and not combed to the side. It was my suggestion. I had to, especially when I saw he was wearing the same hair style as my dad. I, on the other hand, still kept my hair short and pixie, but I did add a few blonde highlights. Mom said my hair was perfect for me; it complimented my cheekbones, whatever the hell that meant.

He tanned well over these last few weeks from working outside his house, cleaning the gutters, picking up the broken branches that fell from the trees over the winter and, of course, washing his car. He was anal about his car. If there was a smudge or a teeny tiny speck of mud somewhere on it, he was running it through the carwash. And the inside of the car … he was obsessed with how it smelled. I swear he would change the air freshener at least once a week, sometimes twice, if he didn't like the scent or felt it wasn't strong enough.

I asked Mom once about this ... about Cory's obsession with his car. She laughed and said it was a 'guy thing'. She told me Dad was so obsessed with his first car—a convertible—that he even named it Betty. Honestly, I was surprised that Cory didn't have a name for his car or maybe he just didn't want to tell me.

Cory didn't answer me. He just kept looking straight ahead, smiling.

"Cory, where are we going?" I pressed, starting to get a little agitated. He grabbed my hand and pressed it against his cheek, which felt warm and smooth.

"Did I ever tell you how beautiful you are?" he asked, keeping his eyes on the road as he spoke.

"Yes, a few times, but I don't always believe you," I said honestly. I pulled my hand away and turned in my seat so I could look out the passenger window. Cory slammed on the brakes, causing me to jolt forward, nearly hitting my head on the dashboard. Thank God for seatbelts.

"Annie!" he exclaimed with a sigh. "You don't see yourself as I do and I wish you did. Not only are you beautiful on the outside, but you're beautiful on the inside, too I have to admit, you were a tough nut to crack, but once I got you to open up, I found nothing but joy." He turned in his seat so that he was facing me.

"It sounds like a line in a candy bar commercial," I said, still looking out the window. I could see his reflection in the window and how his facial expressions changed when he spoke.

He laughed. "Yeah, it kind of did, didn't it? I'm sorry. You're far better than a candy bar." Great! Now I'm hungry for an *Almond Joy*.

I felt his hand on my shoulder and slowly turned around. "Please tell me what you're thinking," he said. The smile on his face disappeared as he stared at me with his dark brown eyes. I shook my head no.

"Annie plea ..." Cory stopped when someone began beeping their horn behind us. He quickly looked in the rearview mirror, then shifted the car into drive. We drove in silence for a while longer. I was tempted to turn on the radio, but I didn't want him to see the tears trickling down my cheeks. I didn't know why I was crying. It was stupid really, but I couldn't help it.

We drove to the other side of town where all the farmers and a few of the Amish people lived. I only drove through this part of town a few times, but never in the back roads where the farms were located. Cory kept driving until we crossed a small stone bridge then the road turned into dirt. I rolled down the window and stuck my head out. The cool breeze felt good against my warm, wet cheeks. The air was invigorating; it smelled crisp and fresh and made me smile.

"Where are we going?" I asked again, hoping this time he would answer me.

"We're almost there," he replied with a smile, obviously relieved that I was speaking to him again. On Cory's side of the road was an embankment covered with wild flowers and greenery. On my side was a huge field guarded by a barbed wire fence. Finally, he pulled over to the side of the road next to an old barn that looked to be a hundred years old and ready to collapse at any moment.

"We aren't going inside that barn to make out, are we?"

My eyes grew wide at the thought.

Cory leaned back and laughed so loud that his whole body shook. "No, dear," he said as he pulled the key out of the ignition, then opened the door. I got out at the same time and pulled my jacket from the back seat before closing the door.

"Are you ready to go for a little stroll?" he asked, holding out his hand. I eagerly took it and we walked down a narrow, dirt road. I had no idea where the road would lead us to, but I didn't care. As long as Cory was by my side, I felt safe. We both walked in silence, admiring the beautiful scenery and smelling the fresh outdoors.

"Do you like it back here?" Cory asked.

"Yes, there's something about nature walks that makes you feel all warm and fuzzy inside," I said, smiling. Cory returned the smile and nodded his head.

"Is that an electrical fence?" I asked, pointing at the barb wired fence that blocked us from the wide, open field. I thought it was odd that we hadn't seen a horse or a cow around. Isn't that what a fence is for? To keep the animals in?

"Not sure," he replied, shrugging his shoulders, then he let go of my hand and walked over to the barbed wire fence three layers high.

"Cory! Don't touch that! You might get shocked!" I yelled when I saw him reach out to touch the top wire.

"Oh, it's not like it's going to have a high voltage. It's probably just enough juice to jolt me," he said with a chuckle.

"Yeah, that's the key word … probably," I said sarcastically. He laughed and slowly reached his hand out as my heart raced. Instinctively, I patted my pants pocket, making sure I had my cell phone on me. "Cory, please ... don't touch it." I grabbed his arm, pulling him away from the fence.

"What? You won't give me mouth to mouth if I get the

shit knocked out of me?" He could see the worry in my eyes and yet he was making jokes?

"No, not if you going to be stupid about it." I started to turn around and walk away, but he grabbed my wrist and pulled me into his arms.

"Wow! You really would leave me here fighting for my life if I got shocked?" The smell of his minty breath took my breath away as I stared up into his warm, brown eyes.

"Yes," I breathed, then closed my eyes and leaned in to kiss him. We kissed for a while, until the sound of a crow cawing startled us.

"So are you going to tell me why you chose this particular place to walk?" I asked as we continued walking down the road. Up ahead I noticed an old apple tree in the middle of the field. The tree was beautiful; perfect for lying under and taking a nap or making out. I smiled to myself at the thought.

"Look at that tree. Isn't it beautiful? Too bad we couldn't sit under it." I walked toward the fence to get a better view, but didn't get too close.

"Who says we can't?" There was a mischievous look in his eyes as he asked and I didn't like it.

"Well, the fence is one clue and the "Do not trespass" signs posted every few hundred yards is another clue." He rolled his eyes and stepped closer toward the fence. Before I had a chance to scream, Cory reached out and touched the top wire, but nothing happened.

"See, I told you it wasn't hot." He smiled wide, laughing, as I shook my head and sighed heavily. I needed a minute for my heart to calm down.

"Do you want to go sit under the tree and make out?" He leaned down and breathed in my ear, sending tingles across my face and down my neck.

"Uh huh."

He grabbed my hand and pulled me toward the fence. The top wire was barbed and leveled just below my waist.

There was no way I was going to be able to climb over it without scratching myself all to hell. Cory, on the other hand, carefully jumped over the fence barely touching it, then held out his hand for me.

"I think I'll climb under it," I suggested.

The bottom and third wire was about six inches off the ground. It wasn't barbed so that made it easier for me to climb under it, so I got down on my knees and started crawling. Cory stood by and watched with intense eyes as I blushed from embarrassment. I was sure I looked like a rolley polley crawling on the ground. Just as I got my head half way across the wire, I looked down and saw the weirdest looking bug I ever saw crawling across the grass. I yelled and lifted my head touching the wire. The next thing I knew, everything went black.

"Annie! Annie! Wake up!" Cory's voice was muffled as I slowly opened my eyes to see him kneeling over me. His dark hair was a tousled mess and his face was covered with sweat. My body felt numb and heavy—like something was weighing me down.

"Wha … what happened?" I looked down to see that he was practically lying on top of me. This explained why I felt pinned to the ground.

"Oh Annie, you're okay. You scared the hell out of me." Cory breathed a sigh of relief, then stood up. My eyes immediately spotted the dark red spots on his jeans.

"Cory, what happened?" I reached out and grabbed his hand as he pulled me from the ground. That's when I noticed a funny tingling feeling on the back of my head.

"Is that … blood?" I asked, looking up at him. His dark eyes were wide with fear.

"Yeah," he answered, but didn't seem to be concerned over it. He was too busy looking at the back of my head, pulling my hair from side to side as if he was looking for something.

"What happened?" I asked again, turning around. His usual tanned face was now pale and clammy. Then, panic started setting in. Something was wrong. He sat down on a large rock that was lying on the edge of the road. The dark spots on his jeans were slowly getting bigger.

"You … got shocked climbing under the fence and when you … you passed out, I panicked and jumped over the fence, cutting my leg on the barbed wire."

I gasped, then quickly grabbed his hand and pulled him to his feet. "We need to get you to the hospital. You might need stitches … and a tetanus shot," I ordered as my heart raced. I wanted to run back to the car, but I could see that Cory was having a hard time walking. Every few steps, he cringed, but he never made a sound.

"So much for wanting to be romantic under the apple tree." I said, trying to lighten the mood as we walked as fast as we possibly could toward the car.

"Where does it hurt?" I finally asked, worried that he might have caught his "two little buddies" on the barbed wire fence.

"Mostly my inner thighs. Thank God I didn't hurt my boys. That wouldn't have been good. We both would have been lying on the ground passed out," he replied with a chuckle.

I blew out a sigh of relief and he laughed. I looked up and saw the Mustang a few hundred yards away.

"I'm driving," I said firmly, then opened the passenger side door and motioned for him to get in. Quietly, he did as he was told, which surprised the hell out of me. He really must have been in a lot of pain. I quickly sprinted around to the front of the car and hopped into the driver's side. It felt weird. In the year we had been dating, I'd not once driven his car. I was too scared to ask, knowing how protective he was of it.

We drove most of the way to the hospital in silence, until we got into town, then the lectures started flying. "Annie, please slow down. This is a thirty-five mile an hour speed limit. Annie, watch that pot hole up ahead. Annie, you didn't use your turning signal back there." My blood pressure started rising as each second passed. My knuckles grew white as I held onto the steering wheel in a death grip.

"Do you want to drive?" I asked through clenched teeth.

Cory turned and looked at me, noticing the veins pulsating in my neck. "No."

We drove in silence, which was rather peaceful. It gave my heart enough time to calm down before we got to the hospital. By the time we arrived, the front of his pants were soaked with blood and his face was as pale as a ghost. I quickly pulled up to the emergency doors and got out of the car, leaving the car door open. Then, I ran inside looking for someone to bring out a wheelchair. An older gentleman with grey, curly hair and glasses as thick as an old Coca-Cola bottle followed me out the doors with a wheelchair in tow. He helped Cory out of the car and into the short metal chair.

"I'll be right back. I'm gonna park the car," I told him.

"Make sure you ..." he said, stopping when he saw me roll my eyes. "Okay." He chuckled weakly. As I pulled the car away from the hospital toward the huge parking lot, the old man wheeled Cory into the hospital. For the first time since I laid eyes on him, he looked fragile, not the strong burly man that I was used to seeing. I pulled the car between two SUV's and put it in park. I reached around the back seat of the car and grabbed my jacket, searching my pocket for my cell phone. I speed dialed home and Mom answered on the first ring.

"Mom, we're at the hospital. Can you come?" I tried not to panic, but tears were welling up inside me.

"What? What happened?" she said, sounding panicked.

I chuckled through my tears when I realized she said the exact words I said when I woke up on the ground. "It's a long story. I'll tell you about it when you get here."

"Nobody's dead, are they?" she asked as her voice raised

an octave.

I laughed. "No."

"Okay, I'll be there in ten minutes," she said, then the line disconnected. I looked in the rearview mirror and wiped the wet mascara from under my eyes, but it was useless. The tears kept coming. I shoved my cell phone in my pocket and stepped out of the car. Then, I hit the lock button on Cory's remote and shoved the keys in my other pocket. The air felt heavy, warmer, making it hard for me to breathe as I walked through the parking lot toward the hospital. A few young nurses walked passed me, laughing at something on one of their cell phones. This automatically brought back memories of the day I was in the hospital with me knee and the young, hot nurse who was flirting with Cory—what was her name? Beth!

I suddenly picked up the pace. The thought of Beth undressing Cory to look at his wounds made my stomach queasy as I walked through the emergency doors and looked around. Cory was nowhere in sight. There were a few older heavyweight nurses sitting behind the desk.

"Excuse me, but I just dropped off my boyfriend. Can you tell me where I can find him?" My eyes clouded with tears, but I quickly blinked them back.

"Name?" The nurse's unfriendly voice left something to be desired.

I swallowed the lump in my throat and replied, "Cory Shields."

It felt like minutes passed by as she casually shuffled through her papers, then finally checked the computer. "He's behind curtain number three," she said, pointing down the hall.

"Thank you," I said, then turned ing the direction she pointed. A moment later, I heard Cory talking as I got closer to his curtain.

"Yes, can you please check my girlfriend, too? She got shocked by an electrical fence and passed out." My heart dropped to the pit of my stomach. I snapped opened the curtains to see Cory lying on the bed with his jeans torn open, exposing his bare, bloody legs. Thankfully, his underwear was still intact. There was a male nurse and a female nurse standing over him, examining his wounds.

"I'm fine," I said, glaring.

Cory chuckled, then cringed. He was in more pain than I thought. I looked down and from what I could see, there were at least six puncture wounds. Feeling queasy again, I sat down in the chair next to him and held his hand as the two nurses continued to look over his wounds.

"You're going to need some stitches," the male nurse said, looking too hairy to be a nurse. His hair was brown and curly, reminding me of my brother Wayne, and he had a beard and mustache. He kind of reminded me of Grizzly Adams. Shouldn't there be some kind of hospital rule for doctors and nurses on how hairy they can be?

"Annie, are you alright? You look pale." The small lines on his forehead creased as he stared at me. He was right; I didn't feel well. My stomach was doing flip flops and I could taste my breakfast in the back of my throat.

"Excuse me," I mumbled and ran through the curtain doors. Thank God there was a woman's restroom across the hall.

"Annie! What's wrong?" My mom's voice resonated behind me as I quickly closed the door. I felt bad losing most of the delicious chocolate pancakes Dad made for me. I gargled some water and washed my hands, then stepped out into the hallway. Mom was leaning against the wall talking on her cell phone.

"She's here now, gotta go," she said, then quickly snapped her phone shut. "Annie, are you alright? What happened?" She gently grabbed my arm and walked me out the front door and guided me to an empty bench.

I sat down and felt the queasiness come back. Mom sat beside me in silence, waiting for me to begin. I stared down at her long purple sparkly nails and sighed.

"Cory and I went for a nature walk and spotted an apple tree up on a hill. We … we wanted to …" I stopped, not sure how much to tell my mother. "There was a barbed wire fence and we decided to climb …"

"Annie, those are electric fences!" she yelled. Her dark eyes were as big as quarters.

"Yeah, I found that out when I tried climbing underneath it. Cory said I passed out."

"You passed out!" I turned to watch an ambulance that had pulled up next to the doors.

"Yeah, it scared Cory so bad he jumped back over the fence and ended up cutting himself on the barbed wire."

"Oh my! Is he okay?" Mom grabbed my hands and held them in her lap.

"He needs stitches, but other than that, he seems okay."

The sound of a baby wailing made us both turn toward the ambulance. I gasped when two paramedics pulled out the gurney with a baby strapped to it. A young mother crawled out from the back and followed them inside the hospital.

"I wonder what happened?" I whispered.

"Why did you run to the bathroom? Are you sick?" Mom asked, changing the subject. Suddenly, another wave of nausea come over me.

"I think seeing the blood on Cory made me sick," I said honestly.

"You don't suppose getting shocked by the electrical fence made you sick?" Mom asked, worried.

"I don't think so," I replied, looking at her confused.

"Come on, I want them to check you over, too." She grabbed my arm and pulled me from the bench.

"Oh no ... not you, too," I whined.

"What?" She turned to face me just as we stepped inside the hospital. The room was hectic as doctors, nurses and paramedics hurried around.

"Cory wanted me to get checked over, too."

"Smart boy." Mom turned around to face the same grumpy nurse at the desk. "I want my daughter to get checked over. She got shocked by an electrical fence." I could feel my face growing hot as the woman behind the desk looked me over.

"Well … she's not critical. She may have to wait for a few hours. We have an accident coming involving six people."

"Mom, I'm fine. Please ... don't make me sit here all day and night," I begged, pulling at her arm. "Let's check on Cory and see how much longer he's gonna be," I suggested.

Mom hesitated for a moment, then gave in to my pleas. "Okay, let's go check on Cory." We held hands and walked down the hall to his curtain. My heart fluttered, worrying about what he was going through. I pulled open the curtain and found him sitting on the edge of the bed. He was wearing all his clothes, minus his jeans, and both of his thighs were wrapped with bandages, stopping at the knees.

"Hey love, where have you been? Are you okay?" he asked, concerned.

I looked at him confused, "Okay?"

"Yeah, you ran out of here looking green ... like you were going to puke," he said, chuckling lightly.

"Oh, yeah, I'm okay. I think seeing all that blood made my stomach queasy." Honestly, I wasn't sure what made me queasy. I wasn't usually one of those type of people who got sick at the sight of blood.

"Well, I'm all cleaned up now. They just need to give me a tetanus shot, then we can leave. Good thing it's warm outside because it looks like I'm gonna be leaving here in just my skivvies," he said, laughing, as Mom laughed along with him.

"Do you want me to get you a pair of pants?" I quickly asked.

"No, that's okay. By the time you got back here, I'd already be discharged. I don't mind walking out of here in my boxers. I'm just glad I didn't wear a thong today," he joked, trying to get me to smile. Mom burst out laughing. I couldn't laugh, too, even though I was worried about him and now myself, wondering why I got sick.

"Annie, are you okay?" Cory asked, grabbing my hand into his.

"Yeah, I just want to get out of here. This place …" Suddenly, the nausea came back worse than ever as I quickly ran to the bathroom.

By the time I came out, Cory and Mom were standing in the hallway waiting for me. My face was pale and clammy and my hair was no longer spiked with hairspray; it was just flat and sticky.

"Are you okay?" Mom asked again. I nodded and walked toward the doors with Mom and Cory following close behind. In the parking lot, I immediately spotted Mom's car and walked toward it. The car alarm chirped just as I got to the passenger's side door.

"Do you want me to follow you home?" Cory asked. The deep lines in his forehead creased as he looked down at me with a pitiful look in his eyes.

"I'm just going to go home and take a nap. I think you should do the same. Besides, I think I'm coming down with something and I don't want you getting sick either."

"I don't care if I get sick, Annie. I just want to spend my Sunday with you like I always do."

I reached into my pocket to fetch his keys, then handed them to him.

"Maybe it's best if you both take it easy for the rest of the night, Cory. You can leave little Annie with us tonight. I'll watch her so you can rest," Mom suggested. Cory hesitated for a moment, then nodded in agreement. I quietly opened the door and slid into Mom's car as Cory closed the door.

"I'll call you later to see how you're feeling," he said. I nodded and smiled at him. The stupid tears welled up inside me again as I watched him walk to his car.

The day was going great until I spotted that stupid tree and suggested we sit under it. *Stupid tree! Stupid fence! Stupid me!* I thought, letting out a jagged sigh.

Neither Mom nor I spoke a word on the drive home. I was glad. I didn't feel like talking, but the small dimple above Mom's eyebrows indicated that she had a lot on her mind. We pulled into the driveway and Dad walked out the front door with Annie by his side. Her little butt started shaking vigorously as soon as she spotted me.

"There's my baby girl," I cooed as she ran up to me. I scooped her up in my arms and buried my face into her neck, not wanting Mom and Dad to see my tears. I passed by Dad, into the front door and up the stairs. Then, I quietly closed and locked the door behind me and set Annie on my bed. I peeled off my shoes then climbed into the bed beside her. Within seconds, I fell asleep.

The sound of someone pounding on the door and Annie's barking woke me up from a deep sleep. I quickly jumped from the bed and unlocked the door. Annie ran out of the room and down the stairs.

"Why in hell did you lock the door? Annie has been barking for the last fifteen minutes. Didn't you hear her?" Molly hollered at me.

"I'm sorry. I must have been out of it," I said with a yawn. That's when I realized how dark my room was. I glanced at the clock and it was 11:02 p.m.

"Yeah, I guess. Poor Annie has to pee. She should have peed on your bed. I know I would have." Molly grunted and turned to walk down the stairs, but I grabbed her arm and stopped her.

"Molly, what the hell is your problem? You've been a royal bitch to me ever since the day Cory took me to the hospital for my knee. I'm so sick of you treating me like shit and Cory, too." I clamped my lips together to keep from speaking anymore. Lord only knows, I had a slew of profanities that I wanted to spit at her.

Molly rolled her eyes, which pissed me off even more. "Yeah, whatever."

"Don't 'whatever' me. Grow the hell up! We're nineteen years old now. Don't you think you should start acting like it?" I sighed for brief moment. "It's sad, really. We used to be the best of friends and could tell each other anything. I miss that."

Molly rocked back on her heels, staring at me, but the evil glare in her blue eyes was gone. "I miss that, too," she whispered so softly that I barely heard her. I sighed again, this time with relief.

"But you knew I liked Cory and now you shove him in my face every chance you get," she cried as my mouth dropped open.

"Molly, I'm not shoving him in your face. He's my boyfriend ... and I didn't steal him away. If you remember, I turned him away the first time because I knew you liked him. I tried to help the two of you get together, but he just wasn't interested in ..." I stopped when I saw tears flowing down her cheeks. "Do you know how many times I asked myself why he chose me and not you? You are much prettier than me, and taller ... and slimmer," I added.

"Oh, please. We're twins. How can I be prettier than you?"

"We aren't identical, stupid," I said with a chuckle. "Besides, you inherited Mom's big boobs. Guys love that." The smile on Molly's face grew bigger and so did mine, as the wall between us was slowly crumbling away as we talked. It felt like years since I could laugh and smile at her. It felt good. I really did miss my sister.

"Yeah, I did get her boobs and you got Grandma's child bearing hips," she replied, snickering.

I rolled my eyes. "Please, don't remind me." What she did next totally shocked the hell out of me ... she leaned in and hugged me. We both stood in the hallway, hugging and crying.

"I've missed you," Molly choked, as tears flowed down our cheeks like two blubbering fools. After we let Annie in from outside, we made a huge bowl of popcorn and took it upstairs to my room. We sat up all night talking, eating popcorn and drinking pop, just like old times. We talked about graduation, me going to the local college for nursing and her job as Mom's assistant in the nail salon. Molly's hands were all dolled up like Mom's, except hers were neon green with hot pink crackle. Because of Cory, I decided not to move to Maryland to live with my Aunt Kelly after graduation. I had checked into the nursing program at the local college and it seemed fitting for me.

"Damn, it's after two and I got classes in the morning," I said, yawning.

"You know, Cory's been calling all night," Molly replied, yawning after me.

"Well, I can't call him back now; it's too late," I said, snickering, as Molly lay down next to me in bed and turned off the light. Little Annie was lying between us, already snoring. The room was pitch black except for the soft glow of the moon shining through the window.

"Can I ask you something personal? I promise I won't get mad," Molly whispered.

"Sure," I said with my eyes closed, trying to think about going to sleep.

"Have you and Cory … you know … had sex?" Molly asked, hesitating.

I lay there for a moment, motionless. "Yeah."

"Huh … what's he like?" she asked, giggling quietly. I thought about it for a moment. What was I supposed to tell her? He was my first. It wasn't like I had a ton of guys under my belt to compare him to.

"Promise not to say anything?" I whispered. The bed shifted as she turned to face me. Her eyes glistened in the dark.

"Promise."

"Well, the first time we got intimate, he apologized."

"Apologized for what? Oh, wait a minute, it's true," Molly said.

"What's true?" I asked curiously, turning on my side to face her.

"Guys with big muscles have small penises. They lift weights and bulge out to compensate for their … well … smallness," she said, snickering.

"Oh no, it's nothing like that; he's not small at all. He apologized because he got off without having sex with me," I corrected her.

She sat straight up in bed. "What? He did what?" She busted out laughing hysterically, waking up Annie who started barking. Molly continued to laugh out loud, while I tried to get Annie to quiet down.

Suddenly, we heard footsteps, then my door burst open.

"What the hell is all this ruckus about?" Dad hollered. What hair he had left was standing straight up and he was wearing nothing but his tighty whities.

"Sorry, Dad. Molly and I were just talking. We promise to keep it down."

"You two are talking again? Well … that's nice. Just keep it down. You know how miserable your Mother gets when she doesn't get enough beauty sleep." Molly and I both nodded in agreement.

"Good night, Dad," Molly chimed in.

"Good night, Dad," I repeated, but with less spirit in my voice. My eyes lids were getting heavier and heavier by the second. I lay back down in the bed and closed my eyes. Thankfully, Molly took the hint and did the same. We were both out in seconds.

I woke up the next morning feeling better than I had in weeks, which was odd considering I only got about five hours of sleep. Molly had it made working for Mom; she got to sleep in a little longer.

I tried calling Cory first thing in the morning, but got his voice mail. I left a message telling him that my last class was over at two. I quickly showered, got dressed then ran downstairs to grab a bite to eat before heading off to class. Mom had already put Annie outside and fed her before I was even out of the shower.

"Are you feeling better today? You look better," Mom added with a smile, setting a bowl of Wheaties on the table in front of me.

"Yeah, much better, thanks." I scarfed down the cereal and ate a banana, then grabbed my backpack. I gave Annie a quick kiss on the head and walked toward the front door.

"Annie, wait. I have something to ask you," Mom said in a serious tone. I stopped short at the door and slowly turned around, as my heart beat a little faster. She hesitated for a moment before walking through the dining room. My hands were getting sweaty as I waited for her to speak.

"Are you pregnant?" she finally asked as my jaw dropped and my eyes bulged out of their sockets.

"Wha ... what?" I stammered, floored.

"Well, you seem moody lately and yesterday you were puking ..."

"I must have eaten something bad. I feel fine now," I interrupted her. She stared at me for a moment, trying to read my thoughts.

"Okay. Go on to school." She leaned over and kissed my head, then opened the door for me.

"Thanks, Mom," I said smiling sheepishly, then walked out the door. My legs felt like they weren't moving, but the truck kept getting closer. Numb, I opened the door and threw the backpack on the passenger seat, then climbed into the truck. Even after losing a few pounds, I still had to strain to pull myself into this stupid thing. One of these days, I was going to save my money and get myself a nice, *short* car ... one so low to the ground that I would barely have to lift my legs to get into it. I pulled out of the driveway and saw Mom looking through the dining room window. I quickly turned my head so she wouldn't know I saw her.

Class was unbelievably slow today and I couldn't concentrate on anything. Mom's question kept eating at me all day. Why would she ask such a thing? Ugh! The gall of that woman! When my last class was over, I grabbed my books, shoved them into my backpack and headed toward my truck.

"Looks like you have a visitor," Wanda, one of the other girls in my class said. I looked up to see Cory leaning against my truck. The expression on his face was unreadable, a cross between sorrow and anger.

"Have a great afternoon. See you tomorrow," I told Wanda and waved good-bye as she walked toward the other end of the parking lot.

"Hey," I said, giving him a half a smile.

"Hey, yourself," he said, not looking up at me, keeping his eyes on the pavement.

"How are your legs?"

"Are you trying to avoid me? Are you mad because I took you on the nature walk? Annie, I assure you, I didn't plan on you getting shocked. I didn't plan on my legs looking like I had a fight with a meat cleaver. I just wanted us to spend a nice day together and everything went to hell. I had the whole day planned for us; even your mother knew of my plans. I had reservations and ..."

"What? My mother knew? Knew what?" I interrupted him. He lifted his head up so that our eyes met and sighed.

"I was planning on asking you to marry me, but when you didn't return my calls ... I figured you were pissed at me," he said. My body swayed back and forth and I thought I dropped my backpack, but wasn't sure until I saw Cory bend over to pick it up.

"Did you say marry?" I stammered at the word marry. Suddenly, I felt hot and I couldn't breathe.

"Ann, are you alright?" He grabbed my arm and opened

the door of my truck and set me down on the seat.

"No, I think I'm going to be sick again." As soon as I said the words, I leaned over and puked. Smooshed up Wheaties and banana splattered all over the pavement and Cory's brand new sneakers.

"Oh, my God! I'm so sorry," I said, starting to cry. Cory wrapped his arms around my shoulder and held me tightly until I calmed down.

"Do you want me to drive you home?" he asked, patting my hair.

"No, I can drive, but will you follow me?" I sniffed.

"Sure, love," he replied with a smile and closed the door. I waited until he got into his car and pulled up behind me before I pulled out of the parking lot. Tears fell onto my cheeks at an even pace as my mind raced a mile a minute. Marriage? To Cory? I just couldn't grasp it. Never in a million years did I picture Cory being my husband. Okay, I dreamed of it, but I was so sure that eventually he would leave me for a younger, more attractive girl. I was waiting for the day to come, but this definitely caught me off guard.

The shrill ringing of my cell phone brought me out of my stupor. "Hello?"

"Annie, it's me, Molly. Are you coming home? I thought we could go to the store together. Tonight we're celebrating our new found friendship/sisterhood," she said with a chuckle. "Tonight is Taco night!"

"Sure, that sounds great! We haven't had tacos in like forever," I said, smiling.

"Great! See you in a few."

"Molly, wait!" I quickly hollered.

"Yeah."

"Cory's following me home. I got sick again in the parking lot. I think he proposed," I looked down at the steering and noticed my hand was shaking uncontrollably.

"WHAT?" Molly squealed so loud that I had to pull the phone away from my ear. "Did you say yes?" she asked,

excited. I sighed in relief that she wasn't screaming and calling me names.

"I didn't say anything, just puked."

"What?" She laughed out loud. "That was romantic."

I laughed weakly, "Yeah."

"Well, I think you need to talk to him as soon as you get home. We can go to the store later."

"Okay, sounds good," I said, then hung up the phone as my stomach started getting queasy again. Just thinking about talking to him and answering his proposal … I closed my eyes and covered my mouth to keep from vomiting in the truck. The sound of a horn blasting made me open my eyes. Directly in front of me was another car. I quickly swerved the steering wheel to the right and smacked head-on into tree. The noise was deafening, nothing like anything I ever heard before, as metal crunched and glass shattered. My body jolted forward so hard that I smacked my head on the steering wheel. I sat there for a moment, trying to breathe.

"Annie! Annie!" I heard Cory screaming my name. I tried to turn my head to look at him, but I couldn't move. I was in shock. Suddenly, a cool draft rushed in through the driver's side door as it flew open.

"Annie, are you alright?" There was sheer panic in his voice, which scared me. It must be far worse than I thought.

"Yeah, I'm okay ... I think. I'm afraid to move." Sirens roared in the distance as an ambulance pulled up beside me.

"Did I hit someone? Is anybody else hurt?" I asked, starting to choke. The very thought of hurting or killing another driver made me ill.

"No, just you. You hit a tree," Cory said as I breathed a sigh of relief. His warm hand touched my arm and I slowly lifted my head and turned around to face him. "Oh," he said, shuddering. Then, warm liquid ran down my cheek. I knew it was blood by the horrified look on Cory's face.

"Excuse me, sir," one of the firemen said to Cory.

"Ma'am, are you okay?" the fireman asked.

"I think so." All I remembered was seeing two firemen climbing inside the truck and pulling me out, then everything went black.

I woke up in a dark room with only a glare coming from the small television hanging on the wall. I knew right away I was in the hospital. I gasped as everything started coming back—the talking on my cell, the car in front of me, the tree ... My left leg felt funny and I looked to see Cory's head resting on it. I gently reached out and touched his hair.

"Annie!" His voice was groggy. I gave him a small smile. He stood up from the chair and leaned down so our faces were just inches apart. His hair was a tousled mess and there were dark circles under his eyes. He looked worn.

"How are you feeling?" he asked, as I caught a whiff of his spearmint breath. He was always sucking on spearmint flavored lifesavers. I told him once that his teeth were going to rot sucking on all that sugar, but he just laughed and shrugged it off.

"Like I was run over by a truck ... and hungry," I added weakly. Every muscle in my body ached worse than my last Zumba class experience. I also had a whopper of a headache. Cory smiled and buried his face in my hair with a sigh.

"What time is it? How long have I been in here?"

He lifted his head to look at me. "It's a little after eleven o'clock at night. You've been here since three. Your parents and Molly just left about an hour ago." He sat back down in the chair and held my hand within his.

"Did the doctor say anything? Am I okay?" I asked, worried. I didn't see a cast on any part of my body, so I knew nothing was broken.

"Yeah, the doctor said you are just banged up a little. You're going to be fine. He had to put a few stitches in your head, though."

I released his hand and put my hand on my head. "Ow," I said.

Cory chuckled. "Don't touch it, silly."

"I won't," I promised. There was silence for a moment. I could tell by the way he was looking at me that he had something to say. Then, I remembered the proposal and gasped.

"Ann, is there something you need to tell me?" Cory's voice turned serious as his dark eyes sobered.

I looked at him, confused. "Um … are you talking about our conversation in the parking lot?" Suddenly, my legs started shaking. Cory noticed them shaking, too.

"No, something else."

Again, I was confused. I shook my head, clueless as to what he was talking about. He sighed heavily. "Never mind, then."

"Don't 'never mind' me," I demanded. "What? What're you talking about? What is it that I'm supposed to be telling you?" I was getting mad now. Just then, a young nurse walked in.

"Oh, you're awake. How do you feel, sweetie?" Her voice was like the sound of an angel singing.

"Right now, I'm agitated." I glared at Cory. The nurse turned around to look him. He was now standing near the door.

"Maybe it's best that I go now," he said as despair colored his voice.

"Yes, visiting hours are over. She needs her rest. You can come in after nine tomorrow morning," the nurse said sincerely.

"Okay. Bye, Annie," he said, then left. No hug, no good-bye kiss, no nothing. My heart sank into my chest and tears suddenly clouded my vision.

"Is that your boyfriend?" the nurse asked. I noticed her tag read Kristen Deere.

"Yeah, it is," I said as my voice quivered. Kristen continued to check my vitals, wrapping a cuff around my arm to check my blood pressure.

"How long have you two been dating?" she asked, just trying to have a friendly conversation with me.

"Over a year now." I swallowed the hard lump in my throat. That's when I noticed how dry my mouth was. My stomach started rumbling, too.

"Oh," she said with a chuckle. "I think someone's hungry."

I nodded my head yeah.

"Well, dinner was over hours ago, but I can bring you some snacks. How do graham crackers and pudding sound?" she asked, smiling. Suddenly, the cuff grew tighter and tighter around my arm—until it hurt.

"Can I have some ginger ale or juice, too?" I asked, feeling like a small child asking for permission to have something.

"Sure," she replied. "I'll bring you extra. After all, you're eating for two now." She smiled wide, then ripped the blood pressure cuff off my arm. The Velcro sound ripped through my head like a knife. I hated the sound of Velcro tearing.

"What?" My eyes shot up at her.

She stepped back, stammering a bit. "You don't know? Oh, dear."

"Know what?" I asked, suddenly everything was coming back to me—the vomiting, Mom asking me if I was pregnant ...

"You're pregnant ... about nine weeks," she replied, looking at me with her crystal blue eyes, not knowing whether to smile or not as I stared at her. Shock was too mild of a word to describe how I felt at that moment.

"I'll be right back with your snacks," Kristen stammered as she quickly grabbed the metal clipboard and walked out. I looked around the table beside me for my cell phone and found it in the top drawer, then speed dialed home.

Mom answered the phone. Just the person I wanted to talk to.

"Mom!?" I cried her name as tears streamed down my cheeks. "You know?"

"Annie, are you alright?" There was panic in her voice.

"I'm fine. Do you know?" I asked again, wiping the tears away from my cheeks. Just then, it finally dawned on me what Cory was talking about. He knew. "Oh, God!" I cried louder.

"Annie, I'm coming right now. Stay there," Mom ordered then hung up. I could hear Dad in the background asking what was wrong. This made me cry even harder. Just as I hung up the phone, another nurse came in with my snacks. She quietly laid the tray on top of a small table with wheels and slid it over top of me. I smiled and thanked her, dabbing at my tears.

I stared at the two cups of chocolate pudding, three packs of graham crackers and an apple laying on the tray. There was also a big cup of ginger ale loaded with crushed ice. I grabbed the cup and quickly sucked down half of it, then grabbed my cell phone and pulled up Cory's name. I was just about to text him when Mom came walking through the door, then the water works started again.

"Mom!" She pulled the table away from the bed and sat on the edge and hugged me as I sobbed, soaking her shoulder.

"Shhhh ... everything's going to be okay."

"I'm nineteen and pregnant," my voice quivered through my sobs.

"I know and you have a man who loves you very much. You're not alone; you have Cory and ... us." She pushed me back so that we could look at each other as her dark eyes glistened with tears.

"Cory knows?" I swallowed another hard lump in my throat. Mom nodded her head and smiled. I closed my eyes and leaned against the pillow.

"What did he do or say?" I asked, not opening my eyes.

"Well, he took it a lot better than you did. He genuinely

looked happy. Annie, why didn't you tell him you were pregnant? Were you planning on keeping it a secret?" Mom asked. I opened my eyes and noticed her staring at me with concern.

"Mom, I didn't know. Honestly, when you asked me this morning, it shocked the hell out of me." I hesitated for a moment, "How did you know?" I asked, curious.

Mom let out a hearty laugh. "Let's just say it was Mother's intuition. There was something different about you and when I heard you was sick and was throwing up, that's when I came to the conclusion, but I wasn't sure until the doctor came in this evening and told us." She smiled and took my hand and held it in her lap.

"And Dad? What does he think?" I asked, starting to cry again. I was his baby girl. I didn't ever want to disappoint him and now his baby girl was pregnant.

"Well, at first he was upset. The very thought of his little girl having sex didn't sit well with him, but I explained to him you are no longer a little girl. You have grown into a fine young lady with a bright future ahead of you and a supportive and very handsome young man by your side. That seemed to calm him down. Then, he and Cory went for a long walk and when they came back, your Dad was in the best mood I had seen him in a long time. I don't know what Cory said to him, but whatever it was put him at ease. You have a wonderful man, Annie. Cory absolutely adores you and loves you and wants nothing but the best for you," Mom said, smiling, and I could see in her eyes that she was happy, too.

Mom and I talked for a little while longer. Well ... she did most of the talking while I ate my snacks. After Mom left, I literally passed out. I was emotionally and physically drained.

The next afternoon, the doctor discharged me. I tried all morning to reach Cory, but kept getting his voicemail. After leaving a third message, I finally gave up. Mom and Molly picked me up from the hospital and drove me home. Nobody really had anything to say, except that little Annie was at home waiting for me. She had missed me. This made me smile and I wondered if she was going to be okay with a baby around the house. As we pulled into the driveway, the house looked strange to me. I felt like I was gone for a long time. And I looked like an eighty-year-old woman walking up the walkway to the porch, as every muscle in my body ached. The doctor said I may feel sore for a while and suggested that I take Tylenol for the pain, but I refused. I wasn't taking any pills that might hurt the baby, except for pre-natal vitamins. He also told me to make an appointment with my gynecologist. I followed Mom and Molly into the house and both of them were unusually quiet and had weird expressions on their faces—like deranged looking clowns.

"Where's little Annie?" I asked, disappointed that she didn't greet me at the door.

"She's in your room. She hasn't left your room since you didn't come home yesterday. She only left long enough to go outside and to eat, then back up to your bed she went," Molly said. This brought tears to my eyes as I painstakingly walked up the stairs. Even a turtle would have bypassed me by now.

As I approached my bedroom door, I heard soft music playing from the other side. I opened the door and Annie began barking immediately. Then, there were three things that I noticed at once: Annie, red roses everywhere ... and Cory.

"What?" I asked, befuddled.

Cory rushed quickly to my side and wrapped his arms around my waist. "You're not going to pass out, are you?" He asked as panic flitted across his chocolate eyes. Annie was jumping up and down, scratching at my leg—which hurt. I started to lean down to pet her, but Cory quickly picked her up and held her in his arms. Tears sprung to my eyes as I hugged the two of them. I truly missed them both.

"What's with all the roses? And candles?" I asked

looking around my room. There must have been ten dozen roses all in vases scattered around my room. There were also at least a half dozen long, white tapered candles burning brightly, while Air Supply's *All Out of Love* was playing quietly from my stereo.

"I wanted to tell you how much I've missed you and how much I love you." Cory set little Annie down and opened the door for her to run out.

"Cory … I …"

Cory placed his hand over my mouth and pulled me to the edge of the bed as I slowly sat down. "Please, let me do this before something else happens," he instructed, chuckling nervously as I looked at him, confused. Then, he got down on one knee and I gasped.

"The day I met you at the Civic Center, I knew I had to get to know you. It wasn't easy…considering you kept pushing me away. I've always loved challenges, but my biggest challenge was trying to convince you to give me a chance to love you. I would take that challenge again a thousand times over if I had to." I sucked in a jagged breath. "Annie, you've made me a better person. You made me believe I can accomplish anything I set my mind to. You're proof of that. I know I can be a wonderful and loving husband and father to you and our baby," he said as I gasped. Then, he smiled and took my hand.

"Annie Powers, would you do me the honor of becoming my wife? I promise to make you and our baby the center of my world." Cory then pulled out a small black box from his pants pocket and laid it on my lap. My whole body was shaking. As he opened the box, inside, nestled between the black velvet was the most beautiful diamond ring I had ever seen in my life. It was a heart-shaped diamond with two smaller diamonds nestled on either side of it. When the sunlight from the window hit it just right, it sparkled, leaving tiny crystal lights on the wall.

I let out another jagged sigh as tears streamed down my

cheeks. "I'm sorry," I cried.

The smile on Cory's face disappeared as disappointment slowing grew within his eyes. "Sorry for what?"

"I'm so sorry that I didn't know what you were talking about in the hospital. I honestly didn't know I was pre ... pregnant," I said as my voice quivered. Cory sighed in relief and his shoulders relaxed.

"Annie, please, before I burst here. Yes or no?" Cory pressed.

I chuckled nervously. "Yes!" He jumped to his feet instantly and wrapped his arms around my shoulders. "Ugh," I said.

"Oh, sorry." He gently leaned down and gave me a kiss. I lifted my arms part way and wrapped them around his waist. It hurt my shoulders too badly to wrap them around his shoulders yet. Cory and I turned when we heard the knock on the door.

"Come in," I said as Cory placed the ring on my finger.

"Little Annie wants to know if Mommy and Daddy are getting married?" Molly asked, holding the dog in her arms. Mom was standing next to her smiling.

"Yes, we're getting married," I replied, laughing. Molly and Mom both jumped up and down, but stopped when the candles threatened to tip over.

That evening, we all sat around the table celebrating our engagement with a taco party. It was set. We were going to get married on Valentine's Day.

"Wait a minute," Mom interrupted. We all turned to look at her as she counted on her fingers. "The baby is due in February."

"You might end up having a Valentine's baby instead," Molly cooed as everyone laughed, including little Annie, who let out a bark.

"Well, we're just going to have to change it then. How about a fall wedding? October?" Cory turned to me as I smiled and nodded my head. I liked that idea.

***

Two weeks later ...

Cory and I sat in the doctor's office waiting for the results. The hospital had confirmed my pregnancy weeks ago, but today was the day we would find out my exact due date.

"Sorry to keep you folks waiting. I have babies coming out the ying yang today," Dr. Stone said as he walked through the door, as a middle-age nurse followed behind. He sat down in front of Cory and me, then handed me a small black and white photo. I stared at it in awe, for in the middle of the black mass was a little, grayish-white peanut. I handed the photo to Cory. I could have sworn I saw a tear forming in the corner of his eye. This made me smile.

"Okay, now let's see. You're last period was in April," Dr. Stone began, humming as he stared at then little circular chart in his hand, twisting and turning it. My heart raced and I think Cory's did, too, as he reached over to hold my hand. "Doo doo doo, hum hum hum," he continued to sing. He was a goofy looking thing with gray, balding hair and big green eyes, but I liked him and he made me comfortable. "Okay, it looks to me like you might have to postpone your Valentine's Day dinner. You're due February 14," he said, laughing.

"Oh, my God! Mom was right!" I shook my head, astonished as Cory laughed. We both shook hands with and thanked Dr. Stone, then left.

That evening at Cory's house, we sat on the couch planning our wedding and the arrival of our baby, while little Annie sat at Cory's feet snoring. Life was bliss.

***

Look for Remembering Zane, The Unfaithful Widow, *and* My Haunting Love, *also by J.S. Wilsoncroft, published by Write More Publications.*

Crazy Love
By: Molly Bryant

The characters in this story are based on the book

Immortal Souls

By: Molly Bryant

Published by Tate Publishing

"Happy Valentine's Day!" Tatum, my gorgeous wife chirped excitedly. The light from the window shone through my eyelids as she opened the curtains. I smiled, imagining her face lit up with excitement.

"Happy Valentine's Day," I mumbled, stretching out my legs. Still with my eyes closed, I heard the patter of little feet trailing behind, padding down the hallway toward us.

"Daddy," Madeline and Tane said as the bed suddenly moved. I opened my eyes to see my two beautiful, blonde twins smiling brightly at me. As they were ready to pounce on me, I laughed as anticipation sparked within their eyes. Madeline had the brightest Indigo colored eyes—my eyes—and Tane had his Uncle Seth's emerald green eyes.

"Good morning," I said, smiling widely. The muscles in my body tensed as they jumped. I huffed as they landed on top of me, rolled over and started tickling them. They laughed hysterically.

"Daddy!" they said, laughing.

"Okay, okay, kids … let's give your dad a few minutes to wake up." Tatum stood at the foot of the bed with her arms crossed, smiling.

Madeline and Tane groaned as they hopped off of the bed and made their way out the door. "Otay," They said in unison.

"Love you," I said to the children.

"Wuv you too, Daddy," I heard them say in unison from the hallway.

"So ..." Tatum said sweetly, lying on the bed beside me. I leaned back against the pillows, waiting for her to reach me, then wrapped my arm around her shoulder as she lay next to me in the crook of my arm. "We get to be alone tonight," she said, raising an eyebrow at me before trailing kisses down my chest.

"We do," I said, running my hands through her hair, feeling the burn her soft lips left behind upon my skin.

Tonight, I planned to take Tatum to a bed and breakfast with palm trees, a private beach, massages, facials and the greatest breakfast served in all of Hawaii, although I would be happy eating here at home. When I told Tatum where we were going, it was the only thing that she and her friends could talk about. Her best friend, Lainey, insisted on watching Madeline and Tane for us tonight so we could go. I trust her, but I was anxious about it. I mean, honestly, who could blame me after what happened with my brother Seth? Madeline and Tane are nearly three years old we've never spent the night away from them.

"Why did you say it like that, Lance?" Tatum asked, stopping her kisses as she lay on top of me, looking into my eyes.

"Like what?" I asked as I looked at her.

"Like you aren't excited about going away with me tonight," she said, frowning.

I touched her cheek and sighed. "I am, honey. I'm just nervous about leaving the kids all night."

"Really? Lainey is good with kids and she loves Madeline and Tane. It'll be fine," she reassured me.

"It's not about Lainey," I replied, as my eyebrows pulled together in concern.

"Then, what is it?" she asked sullenly.

"I'm just worried that something's going to happen and …"

"Lance, we go through this all the time," she said, getting out of bed and heading toward the door. "Nothing's going to happen! It was three years ago. You need to relax."

"I'm sorry," I replied, sitting up on the edge of the bed. "I don't want to ruin your Valentine's Day." Then, I rose from the bed and walked across the room to Tatum, who looked extremely sexy in her black leggings and T-shirt hanging off of her right shoulder. I wrapped my arms around her waist and kissed her lightly on the lips.

"Will you try to relax? For me? All I'm asking is for you to try," she whispered against my lips.

I leaned my forehead against hers. "Yes, I'll try," I promised reluctantly, kissing her nose. Then, I opened the bedroom door and hollered down the hallway, "Okay, who's helping Daddy make Momma breakfast?"

Both children ran toward me as I made my way down the stairs to the kitchen. "Me! Me!" the twins yelled in unison, jumping up and down excitedly.

I shook my head, smiling, knowing this was going to be the longest Valentine's Day of my life.

***

"Daddy?" Madeline asked, pretending to help as she fiddled with a dish towel, pretending to wipe down the countertop.

"Yes, honey?" I said, handing Tane a plate. He turned to place it into the dishwasher.

"Auntie Waney is coming over," Madeline sang as she wiped. The twins have problems saying their L's.

I groaned. "Yes, she is," I replied nervously. I took it out on the next plate, scrubbing it vigorously.

"We wike her," Tane added.

"She likes you guys, too," I said as Tatum entered the kitchen.

"Okay, we're all packed up," she mumbled, writing things down onto a pad next to the phone.

The twins ran into the living room to watch cartoons. I sigh, closing the dishwasher door and leaned back against the counter, watching Tatum concentrate on what she was writing down. She had changed her clothes and was ready to go, which made me even more nervous. I wanted to say something … to tell her that I just wanted to stay home and have Valentine's Day here with her and the kids, but I didn't say anything.

"What are you writing?" I asked, trying to look over her shoulder.

She looked up at me for a moment. "Oh, I'm writing numbers down just in case … Dr. Anahua, the police station, the fire station, Poison Control, my parent's number. Wait … she should know that number." She laughed, shaking her head.

Dr. Anahua, the fire station, and the police? Oh … and Poison Control? My heart pounded within my chest and my palms are sweating. "Why all of those numbers?"

"Just in case Lainey needs it for anything, Lance," she replied, matter of fact. "That's all."

That's all? I couldn't take it. I pushed off the counter with my hip and walked toward the living room where I could have a heart attack in peace.

"It's the best day ever …" SpongeBob's voice resounded from the television. I smiled standing behind the white leather couch, watching the twins swing their arms happily and stomp their feet along with SpongeBob, dancing around on the flat screen. A pang pulled at my heart. Ignoring the suitcases setting by the front door, I danced along with the kids, spending what few minutes I had left with them before

we had to leave. They laughed hysterically as they watch me.

"Daddy is funny," Madeline said, laughing.

"Spin, Daddy, spin!" Tane yelled, watching me intently. I spun quickly around as they laughed.

A moment later, Tatum cleared her throat behind me. I turned around to see that she was watching us, trying not to laugh."Cute," she said, giving me a sexy smile.

"I try," I shrugged, then resumed dancing with the kids again.

"Lance, go get dressed. Lainey should be here any minute," she said, then, as if on cue, the door opened.

"Auntie Lainey is in the house!" she announced, strutting through the entry way. "Hey, kids!"

"Auntie Waney!" the children yelled happily, running to her and clinging to her legs.

"Are we going to have fun or what?" she asked, hugging them both.

"Yes! Yes!" they yelled in unison, jumping up and down. Then, they noticed that she was carrying a bag and tried to look in it.

"Auntie Waney, what did you bring us?" Tane asked.

"What makes you think I brought candy, popcorn, and all the SpongeBob movies we can handle?" she asked, hugging the bag to her chest.

"Yay!" the twins shrieked together, following Lainey into the kitchen.

I looked over at Tatum, who was smiling from ear to ear. "They love her," she replied.

"Yup, they sure do," I answered, staring at her.

"Lance, please … go get dressed while I go over things with Lainey," she insisted, placing a kiss on my cheek. I watched her retreating back as she walked toward the kitchen.

As I walked up the stairs headed for the bathroom to take a shower, I looked at all of our family pictures hanging along the stairwell and hallway. *Am I overreacting? Possibly,* I thought with a sigh.

***

I quickly slid on my faded blue jeans on along with a light blue polo shirt. Then, I threw some pomade into my hair. I exhaled nervously, trying to relax a little bit. I didn't want to ruin this for Tatum, but I was having a really hard time.

I walked out of the bathroom then stepped into our huge walk-in closet. The chocolate brown teddy bears I bought for the twins a few days ago were still sitting on the top shelf. I reached up and grabbed them down, then stared into their coal black eyes and red velvet noses.

Now, these aren't your ordinary teddy bears. These little guys had cameras in them. *Oh, yes ...* I thought, smiling. I took them out of their cozy boxes and threw away all evidence before I brought them into the house, not wanting Tatum to know the extremes I had stooped to. I grabbed my laptop, then downloaded the software for the teddy bears into it. Then, I crept down the stairs and secretly placed the laptop into my suitcase. Ah, technology nowadays, I love it.

"It's about time, princess," Lainey said, looking at me from the back of the couch.

"Hey, Lainey," I said, leaning down to give her a hug.

"Relax, everything's going to be fine," she reassured me confidently, smiling.

"Daddy, what are those?" Madeline asked, eying the teddy bears. Tane snapped his head up from his doodle-pad when he heard.

"These ..." I said, kneeling down next to them, "are a present from Daddy."

"Teddy bears!" Tane shrieked. He grabbed one of the bears and squeezed it tightly to his chest.

"I wuv it, Daddy," Madeline said as she squeezed the life out of hers.

I smiled, watching them admire their new gifts, then stood up when I heard Tatum's heels hitting the floor, coming from the kitchen.

"Are you ready?" she asked excitedly.

"Yeah," I said, still watching the kids.

"Lance," Lainey said to get my attention. "Say goodbye and go."

Tatum laughed. "Okay, babies. Come walk Mommy and Daddy to the door," Tatum said, taking their hands.

"You two have fun. Go be teenagers again," Lainey said with a wink.

Tatum gave her a look of disbelief, then gave the kids a hug and a kiss. "Now, you guys make sure you listen to Auntie Lainey. Don't cause any problems for her."

"We won't, Mommy," they promised together.

"I love you both," I said, pulling them into a tight hug.

"Wuv you, too, Daddy," they groaned. "Too tight."

"Okay, Lance," Lainey said, patting me on the back.

"Babe," Tatum said, pulling on my arm.

"Behave yourselves," I finally said to the kids, kissing them both on the cheek.

"Don't worry. If anything happens, I'll call the National Guard," Lainey joked.

"Seriously, not funny," I said, staring down at her as she laughed.

"That's it, I'm not going," I said, throwing my arms up into the air.

"Yes, you are," Tatum replied, watching me, then she turned to Lainey, "and you … stop making him more anxious then he already is!" Lainey smirked in reply, clearly enjoying my discomfort about leaving the kids. "Now, let's go," Tatum ordered. Then, she grabbed my shirt and pulled me toward the door.

I picked up the suitcases and followed Tatum out to the truck. As we pull away from the house, Lainey and the twins were standing by the door waving goodbye.

***

I smiled, watching Tatum stare at the map with her brow furrowed. "I know where I'm going, honey. We don't need the map," I said.

She gently folded up the map and shoved it back into the glove box. She sighed as she laid her head back against the headrest. "I can't wait until we get there. It's going to be so much fun," she said, closing her eyes.

"I think we'll have a great time," I replied. And to be honest, I was starting to calm down. Tatum's mother watched the kids for us a few times when we ran errands or went shopping for the twin's birthdays or Christmas shopping. I was used to being away for a few hours, but nothing more than that.

Four hours later, I was sitting on the bed in our room, watching Tatum as she admired the sexy ambiance of the room. She picked up each candle and smelled it, taking her time, letting the aroma soothe her. Me? I stared at my suitcase, wanting so badly to turn the laptop on to see what the twins are up to.

"This is so perfect! I'm in heaven," Tatum squealed as she plopped down onto the bed next to me. "What do you want to do first? Spa, swim, have lunch?" she asked, rubbing her hands together vigorously.

Go back home? Yeah, not an option. I smiled and leaned over to kiss her tenderly until our kisses grew more passionate. She got the hint. After all, what better way was there to release anxiety? She shrieked and laughed out loud as I jumped on her.

Afterward, I lay beside my wife breathing heavily, wrapped only in the white-cotton sheets, staring up at the ceiling with Tatum in my arms … and all I could think about were the kids at home.

~ 235 ~

"That was truly amazing," she said, kissing my chest, breathing heavily, too. "Just the way you jumped on me and … and wow!"

Yeah, pent up anxiety will do that to you. I laughed. "Well, thank you."

"Mmmm, no thank you," she said, kissing my cheek. "I'm going to take a quick shower, then we can go to dinner."

I rolled over on my side as she hopped out of bed humming. I watched her perfect body move across the room with pure grace as she made her way to the bathroom. Then, the door closed. When I heard the shower start, I hopped out of bed, threw on my boxers and ran to my suitcase to grab my laptop. I sat on the bed and quickly turned it on, then clicked the teddy bear icon on my desktop. Within seconds, the screen popped up and I had a view of the flat screen. *SpongeBob,* I thought, laughing. I can't see which twin was which. All I can see was a split screen and both views were the same. In the background, I could hear them eating popcorn and laughing.

"Patrick Star is my favorite, what about you guys?" Lainey asked them.

"I wike Sandy." Ah, that would be Madeline.

"I wike Pwancton." And that was Tane.

"Plankton? That's nice," Lainey added.

"Yeah," Tane said as his hand reached for more popcorn.

In our hotel room, I heard the shower stop, so I quickly clicked out of the window and slammed my laptop shut. Then, I slid it under the bed and I lay back against the headboard, then crossed my arms just as the bathroom door opened.

"Get up, lazy butt!" Tatum said, laughing as she grabbed a sundress from her suitcase.

After seeing that the kids were doing exactly what we would be doing if we were home, I relaxed a bit … for the moment, anyway.

***

"This pasta is super good! How is your steak?" Tatum asked, eyeing my barely eaten plate of food.

My nervousness returned, as I couldn't help but wonder what the children were doing now. After all, a lot could change in an hour's time. "It's good," I said with a shrug.

"Lance, you've barely touched your food. What's wrong?" she asked as she took a sip of water.

I frowned, jabbing a fork into my baked potato. "Do you think we should call and check on the kids?" I asked.

"Babe, they're fine," she said. She gave my hand a gentle squeeze, noticing that I wasn't feeling any better. "Okay, you start eating and I'll step outside and call them." Then, she took her cell phone out of her purse.

"Okay," I agreed, sitting up straight.

"I'll be right back, now eat," she ordered, smiling, then rose from the table. I watched her as she walked out the door with her cell phone in hand. I dug into my food, knowing that everything would be alright in just a few minutes. And yes, my steak was amazing. A few minutes later and with half the steak gone, Tatum came back to the table a few minutes later, smiling. "Everything's just fine," she announced, sliding her phone back ino her purse.

"Good. What're they doing?" I asked, taking a drink of my tea.

"They're playing hide and seek and we both know they're having a blast. There's so many places that they can hide in our house. It's huge!" she said, giggling.

Hide? Oh, my gosh ... what if Lainey can't find them? What if she doesn't find them all night? I know what it's like playing hide and seek with twins. They won't say one word the entire time you search for them. I refused to play the game with them anymore. The last time, I found Madeline almost instantly, as she hides in the same place every time, but Tane ... it took me four and a half hours to find him. I freaked out after hearing what they were playing, then rose to my feet as if my seat was on fire. "I'll be right back," I said, walking quickly away from the table.

"Lance, where are you going?" Tatum hollered from the table.

"I'll be right back!"

After I was away from the restaurant, I ran as quickly as I could to our room. Out of breath, I reached under the bed and grabbed my laptop. Then, I flung it open and clicked on the teddy bear icon. Instantly, the split screen popped open. I could see that one of them left their teddy bear lying on the couch, as there was a sideways view of the flat screen—SpongeBob was in Jellyfish Fields swatting his jelly fishing net crazily. I looked at the other screen to see that one of the twins was hiding in one of the closets on the third floor. That had to be Tane. It's not Madeline's favorite spot.

"I found you!" I heard Lainey say and Madeline's laugh echoed throughout the house.

"Tane … where are you?" I hear Lainey sing out.

Come on Lainey, third floor, third floor.

"Tane …" she sang out again. This time her voice was a little closer to him. *Oh, thank you, God!*

"Gotcha'!" She says as she opened the door. Tane screamed and ran out of the closet. Lainey was laughing so hard that I couldn't help but laugh, too. I took a deep breath and sighed, feeling a bit better … for now.

Suddenly, the doorknob of the hotel door jiggled. *Shit!* I click out of the screens and threw the laptop back under the bed. I spun around in circles then stopped, wondering what I should do. *The bathroom!* I thought to myself as I quickly darted in.

"Lance?" Tatum's voice echoed into the room as I stood in the bathroom. "What are you doing?" she asked on the other side of the closed bathroom door. "Are you okay?"

I looked around the bathroom quickly, then flushed the

toilet. "Oh … uh … yeah," I said, turning on the water to fake washing my hands. Then, I opened the door barely enough to slide out and closed it behind me. "The peppers I put in my eggs this morning made my stomach upset, that's all," I lied.

"Aw," she said, touching my cheek as she frowned. "Why didn't you use the bathroom at the restaurant?"

"I don't know," I shrugged. "I didn't know how bad it was going to be."

She raised her brows. "Oh …" she replied, laughing, with a disgusted look on her face. "Okay, then." That was close.

***

I stood in my white terrycloth robe and slippers as the tall-lanky masseuse walked around the room preparing her table with warm oil, hot towels and hot rocks, as the serene sound of a waterfall resounded from the speakers. I really had no interest in this, but I was doing my best to make Tatum happy. She insisted that I needed to relax, and that was exactly what I intended to do.

"Okay, Mr. Mitchell, hop up there, face down," she ordered, smiling.

Here goes nothing, I thought. Taking a deep breath, I hopped onto the table keeping a towel wrapped around my waist. Then, I placed my head on the headrest, looking through the giant hole, but I still felt tense.

"Just close your eyes, Mr. Mitchell … relax," she said soothingly, as she poured warm oil onto my back and started to massage my shoulders. My entire body melted into the padding as I closed my eyes. That's what I'm talking about.

Later in the day, I was sitting in the indoor pool at the spa with Tatum, enjoying a cocktail, when an employee from the front desk approached. "Mr. and Mrs. Mitchell?" he asked as he bowed.

"Yes?" Tatum answered. Uncertainty colored her voice, making me uneasy.

"You have a phone call at the front desk," he replied, then turned and pointed to the pool bar. "I had it transferred here."

"Thank you," I said, then quickly hopped out of the pool and grabbed a towel to dry myself off. Then, I rushed to the bar and leaned on the counter. "Hi, I'm Lance Mitchell. I have a phone call?"

"Absolutely, Mr. Mitchell," the young bartender said, handing me the phone. I held the phone up to my ear and nodded. He pushed the blinking red button on the base.

"Hello?" I asked into the receiver.

"Lance? It's Lainey," she said, crying.

"Lainey, what's wrong?" I asked, as my heart raced.

"I don't know what happened ..." she yelled into the phone, sobbing. "... I put the twins to bed and lay down on the couch, then five minutes later I heard them screaming from upstairs."

Breathe, Lance, breathe. Tatum came up behind me, placing her hand on my shoulder.

"Is everything okay?" she asked from behind me. I shook my head. "What?" Tatum asked as her voice shook.

"Lainey ..." I said frantically.

"I ran to their room and they were gone. I don't know where they went, Lance! I'm so sorry!" she said, sobbing into the phone. "The police are here and there was no sign of a break in or anything ... they just vanished."

Vanished? Immediately, I thought of my brother. "Seth ..." I whispered.

My eyes flew open wide, staring at the ground through the hole in the table, as the masseuse's hands kneaded away at my back. Thank God it was just a dream. My heart pounded within my chest. I got up so quickly that I knocked her table over, spilling the massage oil all over the stone tiles and the hot rocks were strewn into every corner of the tiny room.

"I'm so sorry," I said, running out of the room.

In nothing but my towel, I ran to our hotel room. People pointed and stared as I ran through the Inn, but I didn't care. After a dream like that, I had to make sure the twins were okay. I reach my room and realized that the key to the room was in my jeans back at the spa. *Damn it!* Then, I remembered that Tatum left the sliding door open to the private beach. Our room was on the first floor, so I ran down the hallway, out to the side door around to the back of the building. Sand flung up from the ground, sticking to the oil on my back. I stopped, spotting our little balcony, knowing I could clear it easily. So, I placed my hand on the railing and threw my legs over it as my towel went flying, landing in the sand. Behind me, I heard a few gasps and whistles. I turned around to see a few ladies standing there. One of them was in her sixties and her face was bright red. She smiled, then waved at me as I smirked.

I quickly went inside and grabbed a pair of boxers out of my suitcase, threw them on and retrieved my laptop from under the bed. I open it up, clicked the teddy bear icon and finally relaxed when I saw on the split screen that the twins were lying on either side of Lainey. I had two views of their ceilings. *Nap time,* I thought to myself, smiling.

"So, Goldilocks ate the Momma Bear's porridge and it …"

"Auntie Wainey, what is porridge?" Madeline asked. She always asked questions when you tell them stories. My curious Maddie.

"Oh, I meant oatmeal … she ate Momma Bear's oatmeal."

"Otay … what kind of oatmeaw?" Tane asked.

"Oh, I don't know. What kind is you're favorite?" she asked them.

I tried not to laugh as I awaited their answer, already knowing what they were going to say.

"The dirty kind," Tane said, laughing aloud.

"With worms," Madeline added and they both cracked up.

I started laughing and my stomach muscles started burning. About a week ago, Tatum was shopping and we experimented with the nasty, plain oatmeal she wanted them to eat by adding crushed up Oreo's and Gummy Worms. It's our 'dirty oatmeal.' If Tatum found out about that she would kick my ass. All three of us were sworn to secrecy.

"Dirt and worms! Gross!" Lainey said as the twins laughed.

Outside the hotel room, someone sneezed as they walked by. It made me jump, catching my attention. *Oh no ... Tatum.* Then, I remembered that she was still at the spa, but I closed the laptop and slid it back under the bed just in case. Next, I wrapped a white towel around myself again. I couldn't put on another change of clothes, as Tatum would see that it wasn't the same clothes I wore earlier to the spa. I was so tired and it wasn't even evening yet. This was one of the longest Valentine's Days I'd ever had.

I walked into the spa to see that Tatum wasn't done yet, *oh thank you, God.* I rushed into the room I was in to see my masseuse mopping up the oil from the floor. She looked at me with wide eyes as I walked in.

"I am so sorry," I said quietly, grabbing my clothes. I threw the boxers I wore earlier in the trash, since I have a different pair on now. The lady just stared at me as if I was crazy, and I was beginning to feel like I was.

"You didn't see anything ... nothing," I said, looking at her sternly.

She just shook her head with both hands up.

"Thank you," I said as I slid into my jeans. After I finished dressing, I walked into the lobby at the same time

Tatum did. She had the biggest grin on her face.

"Now, that was fabulous," she said, smiling.

"Yup, it sure was," I replied, swinging my arms. "I feel great!" *I am such a poor excuse for a husband ... ugh!* I groaned.

***

Later that day, we are lying out in the sand. It was about a quarter after three in the afternoon. I tried to relax, knowing the children were taking a nap.

Tatum sighed. "I wonder what the twins are doing?" she asked softly.

"They should be down for a nap," I said with my eyes closed, absorbing the sun.

"Yeah, you're right. It's nap time," she agreed. I could hear the smile in her voice.

Nap time ... wait ... why didn't I think of it earlier? During my dream the twins were asleep when they disappeared. *Oh no ... here I go again,* I thought to myself as I rose to my feet.

"What are you doing?" she asked, sitting up on her elbows.

"I feel like I am burning, I need some sunscreen," I said with a smile.

She stared at me for a moment and I could only imagine her facial expression under those sunglasses. "Uh ... okay ... but we don't have any." We only buy it for the kids as Tatum and I never burn.

"Oh ... uh ... babe, you just relax. I'll run to the store a few miles down the road." *Yeah, that's it. We're only about thirty minutes away. I'll rush home real quick and check on the kids.* I felt elated at the thought ... screw the teddy bears and all of their fuzziness.

"Ummmm," she said, looking around. "Uh ... okay ... are you alright?"

"I'm good! That massage worked great! Totally relaxed," I said, giving her my famous half smile she loved so much, making her blush. It worked like a charm every time. "I want to layout and maybe even take a nap, I just don't want to burn," I said with a shrug.

"Well, I love you, honey," she said, lying back down.

"I love you, too," I said, then turned and ran toward the valet.

"Last name?" a short black-haired man with a perfectly trimmed mustache asked.

"Mitchell, Lance Mitchell," I said quickly. Just come on already, I'm on a serious time crunch here. Within two minutes, they pulled my truck around and I hopped in and peeled out of the parking lot. Everyone stared as my tires smoked.

***

I made record time, making it home in about twenty-two minutes. I parked down the street of our cul-de-sac, out of sight. As I ran around the yard and was nearly to the back of the house, I heard a growl. I turned around to see that the neighbor's dog had gotten loose … again.

"Hi, Buster … that's a good doggy," I said quietly, as the giant, fluffy, brown and white Saint Bernard barked.

"Shh, Buster," I said as he barked again and ran toward me.

"No, Buster," I said, holding my hands out. He picked up speed so I turned and ran as fast as I could into my back yard with Buster hot on my heels. His slimy slobber landed on my bare calves as I looked up at the second-story windows. I spotted the twins' window and started scaling up the tree next to the side of the house as Buster barked below me.

Jumping from a tree limb, my fingertips gripped the white trim of the twins' bedroom window. With every ounce of strength I had, I pulled myself up onto the window sill and

~ 244 ~

smiled. Lainey had fallen asleep with the children on either side of her with her arms wrapped around them. Madeline had her bear hugged tightly against her and Tane had his arm dangling off the bed, clinging onto his teddy bear for dear life. Suddenly, my hands grew sweaty and I started to slip. *Oh shit ....* I fell right into the bushes below.

"Ouch," I said in a monotone voice as I lay there, as Buster licked my face.

***

Driving back to the Inn, my forehead was stinging, so I adjusted the rearview mirror to take a quick look at myself. "Of course," I said with a sigh. I cut my forehead. How the hell was I going to hide this from Tatum?

Tatum ... I looked down at the clock on my stereo. I'd been gone for over an hour. I started to panic at the vision of her alone on the beach, wondering where in the world I was. I frantically looked around at all of the small businesses as I drove slowly back and spotted a little jewelry store ... *a present. You, Lance Mitchell, are an absolute mastermind.*

I parked in the nearest spot, hopped out of the truck and ran inside.

"Hello, sir, how can we ... ummm ..." the proper woman dressed in a suit gave me a look of fear, noticing that I was bleeding. "... help you?"

"Oh," I touched my forehead. "It's nothing. I just tripped over the curb."

"Oh," She said, smiling. "Well, what can I do for you?"

"Give me the most expensive item of jewelry you think my wife would love," I smirked. She nodded, then walked around for a moment before pulling a diamond tennis bracelet out of a special case behind the counter. She held it up. It glistened under the florescent lights. "Will this be cash or charge?"

So, $4,500.00 and a bouquet of red roses later, I pulled into the parking lot of the Inn and hopped out of the truck. I walked around the building to the private beach and Tatum was still lying where I left her. It was dinner time now, a little after five in the evening. *Here goes nothing ...*

I stood above her and saw that her chest was rising and falling; she had fallen asleep. Then, I had another idea. Taking my tank top off, I lay down next to her, faking sleep as I heard her groan. Everything was falling perfectly into place.

"Lance?" she mumbled.

"Yeah, babe?" I asked groggily.

"I fell asleep," she said with a giggle, putting her arm around my waist. "I must have been tired. I didn't hear you come back."

I turned toward her and she gasped. "What?" I asked frantically.

"You're forehead! What happened to you?" she asked as she took her bottled water, poured some on a towel and wiped the blood away from my scratches.

"That ... oh ... I ... uh ..." I thought for a second. "It was so lame. I tripped over the sidewalk in the parking lot."

"Oh, my gosh. They didn't even offer you something to clean up with? I should complain, Lance. That's seriously not cool," she said angrily.

"No, no ... they did," I replied, smiling at her. "It must have just bled more, it's been a while."

"Oh, yeah ... we fell asleep. Did you get your sunscreen, honey?" she asked as she sat up, stretching. "And is that ... slobber?" she stuttered, staring at my hair. She reached up and wiped it away, making a disgusted face as she studied it on her fingers.

"Nope, didn't get the sunscreen," I said, smiling, avoiding her question.

"Well, why were you gone so long?" she asked sullenly.

"Because of this," I said as I reached under our blanket.

Then, I pulled out the bouquet of red roses with a white velvet box that contained her bracelet nestled within them. Did I mention it was $4,500.00? "Happy Valentine's Day, Tatum. I love you."

"Oh, wow," she said, starting to cry. "You are so sweet! Flowers!" She pulled her sunglasses off and set them on top of her head. Then, she put her nose to the roses and inhaled deeply. I watched her face as she noticed something else. I smiled as she hesitantly reached in and pulled out the box.

"I hope you like it," I said as she opened the box. Like it? She loved it, I could tell because she pretty much screamed when the sun hit the diamonds.

"Ah, Lance! It is beautiful!" she gasped in a shrill voice.

I couldn't help but laugh. It was one of those moments that I should have recorded. It would have gotten millions of hits on You Tube. I laughed.

She jumped on me, kissing me passionately.

That was close … and all thoughts of the slobber were gone.

***

After going back to the room, I hopped into the shower quickly, hoping to get out before Tatum got in with me. I wanted to check on the twins just once more before we went down for dinner, drinks, and dancing. As I hopped out of the shower, Tatum was standing there, disappointed, with her robe half off.

"Aw, you were going to get in with me," I said sadly as I dried off and threw on my boxers.

"Well, yeah, this is our time to be alone, Lance. I want to take every advantage of it that I can," she said, taking her robe off to hang it upon the back of the bathroom door.

I walked up to her as my eyes rake over her amazing body. "No worries, we have all night," I said, kissing her softy as she moaned against my lips. When I pulled away, she groaned, disappointed.

"Fine," she huffed and stepped into the shower, roughly closing the curtain.

After a second passed, I ran to the bed and pulled the laptop out from its hiding place. I smiled when I saw that they are coloring. Well, one bear had a view of the living room ceiling, and the other was sideways, facing the coffee table.

"That's very nice, Madeline. What is it?" Lainey asked.

"It's Mommy and Daddy," she said, vigorously coloring the paper.

"And what are you making, Tane?" she asked, leaning over to look at his paper.

"It's my teddy bear that Daddy gave me," he said thoughtfully.

I felt sad, as I bought the bears so I could watch them. He really thought that I gave them something special. But I *did* give the bears to them as a special gift, didn't I? Or was it for me, just being a paranoid father?

"So, babe, I was thinking. I want to try the Halibut tonight," Tatum said from the bathroom.

Feeling bad about the bears, I failed to realize that she was already out of the shower. With no time to spare, I tossed the laptop under the bed.

"Yeah, whatever you decide, honey," I said at the exact moment she walked out in her robe.

Oh, wow! That was close, I thought, smiling.

"You'd better hurry and get dressed. I'm starving." Then, she pulled on her tight fitting black dress before walking back to the bathroom to finish getting ready.

***

Dinner went by in a blur. I felt guilty about those damned teddy bears. I was suddenly finding a lack of love toward technology. It wasn't so great anymore.

"Want to dance?" Tatum asked, moving in her seat to the sound of the band playing.

"I thought you'd never ask, sexy," I smirked.

She held out her hand for me to take, and I raised it to my lips, kissing her finely manicured fingers up past the bracelet I bought her up to her elbow.

"You look absolutely gorgeous, honey," I said, smiling thoughtfully at her.

"Thank you," she said, leading me to the dance floor.

After a few drinks, and dancing I started to relax, knowing the twins should be in bed. I had a feeling that I should let this whole thing go and enjoy the rest of my Valentine's night with my beautiful wife. I'll see Madeline and Tane in the morning. Everything is just fine.

Tatum swung her hips, rubbing against me in all of the right places, causing me to groan in her ear. She spun around and continued to dance against me, trailing kisses down my neck.

"I love you," I whispered against her lips.

"I love you, too," she whispered back, pressing her body tightly against mine.

I let my lips lightly trace her jaw, then kissed her softly down to her collarbone. It must have sent her body into overdrive because the next thing I knew, her lips came to my ear.

"I want you," she purred.

That did it … I picked her up and carried her as swiftly as I could out of the restaurant without dropping her. When we got to the hallway by our room, I set her down on her feet, searching in my pockets for the room key as she kissed me fervidly. I was just as anxious as she was to get into the room and do things to her that you could only imagine.

"I found it," I said, smiling.

"Uh, huh," she said, breathing heavily as she jumped on me, wrapping her legs around my waist.

Heat radiated from her body as I unlocked the door, not

breaking our kiss. After we entered the room, she let her legs drop and I set her down gently on her feet. She ripped open the buttons from my shirt, sending them flying to the floor. Reaching down, I pulled her dress up to her thighs as she unbuckled my belt. I pick her up and once again with all of her strength, she wrapped her perfect legs around my hips holding me tightly against her. As we kissed, I held her up with my right hand underneath her thighs while knocking everything off of the table with my left. We laughed against each other's lips as we heard the very expensive crystal fruit bowl crash to the floor. She started to undo my jeans, but I pulled away to look into her eyes. I held her face in my hands, caressing her cheeks with my thumbs. "You know, I love you more than anything in this world."

"I love you, too," she said with a smile. Moments later, one long Valentine's Day morning and afternoon turned out to be the best Valentine's Day night I ever had.

***

"Owd McDonawd had a farm, ee-I, ee-I, oh..." One of the twins sang quietly as I rolled over. *"And the farm had a wamb, ee-I, ee-I, oh..."* the twins laughed. *"With a baa here, and baa there ..."*

"No, Madewine, that's not how it goes," Tane argued.

"Yes, huh, it is, too," Madeline insisted.

"No, I'll ask Mommy when she comes."

"No, don't say it to Mommy," Madeline said, starting to cry.

"I'll go see what's going on," Tatum groaned as she staggered out of bed.

"Okay, babe," I mumbled.

"Uh, Lance?"

"Hmmm," I say as I flip over onto my stomach.

"Were not at home, what is that? Where is it coming from?" she asked wearily.

~ *250* ~

My eyes sprang open with a start as I stared at the knocked over lamp on the bedside table. *Oh, no ... the laptop. I didn't close out of the teddy-cams! Oh, this is not happening, say this isn't happening!*

"Oh, no, no... don't fight, you two," Lainey said, in a sleepy voice.

"Madewine singing the Owd McDonawd song wrong …" he complains.

"No, I am not, Tane," Madeline replied, defending herself.

"Okay, okay … now shh …" Lainey said, trying to stop their fighting. "You know what Auntie Lainey says?"

"What?" they said in sync.

"The song goes however you sing it, just go with it. Now, let's make some breakfast. Who wants pancakes?" she asked cheerfully. I could hear them laughing and running down the hallway following Lainey.

"Wait, Autnie Wainey … my teddy bear," one of the twins said. I could hear the ruffle of the bedding as Mr. Fuzzy Wuzzy Was a Bear slid roughly across the bed. When I look at Tatum, I guaranteed they'll disappear when we get home.

"Okay, kids, who wants to help Auntie Lainey?" she asked loudly.

"I do, I do!" they both yelled, making the speakers on the laptop roar.

"What the hell is that, Lance?" Tatum asked me again as she searched around the room. "Where is it coming from?"

I bury my head into the pillow as the air from her swiftly walking by the bed rushed past. She looked under her side. *Warm ...* she walked around to my side, *warmer ...* I peeked to see her kneeling on my side of the bed, *red hot ... Ah, I am so screwed!* I groan into the pillow.

"Lance, what is this?" she gasped. "Teddy Cams?"

"I'm sorry, I couldn't help it, babe," I said, rolling over onto my side to sit up.

"You couldn't help what? Giving our children a toy that

they obviously love and are guaranteed to carry around ... just so you could spy on them?" she yelled, her voice raising an octave.

"I know you're upset, but honestly, Tatum, I didn't do it to spy on them." I ran my hands through my hair as I got to my feet. "I did it because I was worried about them. Any time I had any doubt, I looked and saw that everything was okay. Please ... I'm really sorry."

The look on her face scared me. "Anytime you had doubt? Lance, how many times did you look?" she asked curiously. "Wait, no ..." She shook her finger and started pacing. I knew I was in so much trouble. "The shower ... you wouldn't shower with me ... and the beach ... you left me at the beach ... alone! Oh, and when you ran to the bathroom because of your 'eggs'?!" she asked, plopping into the chair at the table to look at me. "Really, Lance?"

"Look, I never meant to keep it from you. I just thought you'd be upset if you knew I bought those," I said, kneeling in front of her. "I can't help but be anxious being away from them ... please try to understand."

"Oh, Lance, I understand perfectly that you've been lying to me! You totally sabotaged our Valentine's Day so that you could spy on my best friend and our children because you were worried about being honest with me? Nice!" She nodded as she stared at the bracelet on the table. She picked it up. "So, let me guess ... this is yourself pity present to me? For lying?"

"No, no... babe, it truly was a gift from me to you. I mean ... yeah, I felt bad about everything when I bought it, but, I didn't do it out of guilt." I just contradicted myself, didn't I? Then, she stared at the scratches on my forehead, pointing.

"That scratch, you didn't get it from tripping in the valet, did you?" she asked. "Did you Lance?" She asked louder this time as she stood up.

I was honest. "No," I said in defeat.

"How did you get it?" she asked quietly. Was this the calm before the storm? It had to be because when I tell her how I got it, she is going to hit the roof.

"I … uh …" I stuttered as I sat down in the chair in front of me, looking into her eyes. "I ran home to check on them when you were at the beach and I fell, landed in a bush, and Buster was there, it was a wet mess and I …" I stopped talking instantly when I saw her face change. Shutting up would be the best thing for me to do at this very moment.

Her eyes got so wide that I thought they were going to pop out of their sockets. Not one word came out of her mouth except for a loud growl as she threw her arms in the air. Then, she walked into the bathroom and slammed the door behind her.

I sat on the edge of the bed, sulking a few minutes, reflecting on my actions when the bathroom door opened. Tatum came stomping out, fully dressed. "I want to go home. This trip, is seriously over, Lance," she grumbled as she started packing her suitcase.

"Babe, please, let's have breakfast and try to talk this out," I begged, grabbing her elbow.

She stood up straight and wriggled her arm out of my grip. "Don't touch me right now," she said with her eyes closed, highly irritated. "I've tried and tried to be patient with your anxiety over the children. I really have. But you need to understand that I am not mad that you bought those Teddy Cam's, Lance. I'm livid because you felt that you had to hide it from me and lied for our entire trip." She zipped her suitcase. "I am going down to get a muffin and some juice. Pack your things and let's just go home." She stopped as she placed her hand on the door. "I'll be waiting in the lobby for you." With that, she walked out with her suitcase, slamming the door as I jumped.

***

I got dressed, put everything in my suitcase and headed to the lobby. Tatum was sitting in one of the white chairs in front of the fireplace, staring at nothing as she ate her muffin.

"Are you ready?" I asked, standing behind the chair with my suitcase in hand.

She only responded to me through her actions. She got up and walked out the door as I followed.

"Please, don't shut me out, Tatum. I'm seriously very sorry," I pleaded, looking over at the valet. "Mitchell, Lance Mitchell," I said to him before turning back to Tatum. "I know that keeping it from you was wrong, but I didn't know what you would say." I stared at her, but there was no response. What can I say? I really messed up and I deserved the silent treatment.

The valet pulled up with the truck a moment later and before I could open the door for her like I always do, she grabbed the handle, swung the door open, hopped in and slammed the door. It made my heart ache as we headed home.

We were about ten minutes away from home when I tried again. "So ... what about last night, right?" I asked, smiling at her before looking back to the road. "We rocked that room," I said, dancing a little in my seat. I watched her, but she didn't smile, smirk, eye twitch ... nothing. I sighed.

"Look, when we get home, we act as though nothing happened, understand?" she ordered, looking me in the eye. I nodded. "If Lainey found out that those teddy bears have cameras in them, her feelings will seriously be hurt, Lance."

"Okay," I said quietly. I didn't even think about how all of this would make Lainey feel. I felt horribly guilty. She loves us ... our kids ... and would do anything for us if we needed her to.

I pulled up to the house and parked in the driveway next to Lainey's Accord. Guilt grew like a demon shadow coming for my soul within me. I look over at Tatum and she hopped out of the truck. I jump out to get the suitcases and followed her inside.

"Hey, kids," I yelled.

"Where are you guys?" Tatum hollered toward the stairs.

Just then, I heard their little feet running toward the entry way. As they bounded toward us, flour covered their faces and pajamas.

"Mommy, Daddy!" they both said, taking turns hugging our legs.

"What's all over your faces?" Tatum asked as she places a hand on each of their backs guiding them into the kitchen.

"We made pancakes with Auntie Wainey, Momma," Madeline said.

Tane turned toward me. "You want some, Daddy?" he asked.

I wiped the flour off of his nose gently. "You bet I want pancakes," I said as his little face lit up, then followed him into the kitchen.

"Hi, Lance!" Lainey greeted me as I entered the kitchen. "I hear you both had a fabulous time! That's awesome." Then, she looked from me back to Tatum, who was biting her lip.

"Oh ... uh ... yeah ... it was really relaxing," I said, smiling.

"Here, Daddy! Try it," Madeline said, handing me a cold pancake. I took the biggest bite I could and was shocked that it was actually pretty good. I kept eating it, making Tatum and Lainey laugh at my chipmunk cheeks.

"What do think, Daddy?" Tane asked.

"Well, I don't know ..." I say as I think about it.

"Here, Daddy! Eat this one," Tane said, handing me another pancake. I shoved the entire thing into my mouth. Good thing they weren't large pancakes.

"Oh, yeah ..." I say as I rub my belly. "These are the best pancakes ever!" The kids burst out laughing, falling to the ground.

"Daddy, you funny," Madeline said between laughs.

***

I spent the rest of the day trying my hardest to apologize to Tatum, but she refused to talk to me. Like earlier when I came out of the bathroom, there was a pillow and a blanket on the couch waiting for me as my heart sank. Is this really how she feels? I tried to apologize several times, in fact. I even made her dinner and picked some flowers out of the flower bed, but she ate her dinner silently, not giving me so much as a thank you … nothing. I just didn't know how to fix the Valentine's Day that I ruined for her. What was I supposed to do?

I sighed as I lay upon the couch. Trying to get comfortable, I rolled over and over until I finally throw the damned pillow onto the floor. "Jeez," I mumbled, annoyed.

"Daddy, why are you on the couch?"

I jumped and sat up as fast as I could to see Tane standing at the bottom of the stairs with a curious look on his face.

"Hey, buddy! You're supposed to be in bed?"

He ignored me. "Why are you not with Mommy? Are you mad at her?" he asked sullenly.

"Oh, no! Not at all … come here," I said, patting the cushion next to me for him to climb up. "I'm not mad at Mommy. Why do you think that?"

"I heard you say sorry a wot today," he replied with a shrug.

I nodded, Okay, so he watches everything. It is very easy to take for granted, the little ones. You would think after having kids that I would know better, but I don't. Each one is a challenge with their own ideas and personalities.

"Hey, this isn't something you need to worry about, Tane," I remark, pulling him onto my lap. "It's just that Daddy did something to upset Mommy, but it will be alright. She's not that mad." That was the understatement of the century.

"Are you sure?" he asked.

I laughed. "Yes, buddy, I'm sure."

"Young man, you're supposed to be in bed. Let's go," Tatum said sternly. She is so sexy when she tries to be tough.

"Otay, Mommy," he replied, hugging me tightly and whispered into my ear, "She's mad. I wuv you Daddy," He hopped off the couch and ran off to bed.

"Love you!" I said as he climbed up the stairs. "Goodnight."

Tatum turned to run up the stairs after him, but I hopped quickly off the couch and caught her. "Hey … wait … can we talk?"

"About what, Lance? I'm mad, okay? Can't I be mad that you lied?" she asked with a sigh.

"Yes, you have every right to be mad, just …" I said, shrugging. "Just tell me what to do to fix this … please."

"Ever since you found out that we were going on this trip you've been acting weird," she said, placing one foot on the first step and her hand on the rail as she turned to face me. "I miss you, Lance. When you find you … let me know. You're the only one that can fix it." She shrugged. "Goodnight."

"Wait, I *am* me. I've just been nervous about leaving the kids," I said as she kept walking up the stairs. "Tatum, wait," I called after her, but she disappeared into the dark hallway.

"Mommy!" I hear Tane yell excitedly in the distance as I plop back down onto the couch.

***

I spent the rest of the night laying on the couch thinking about everything. I didn't quite understand what in the world she meant by finding myself. I ran through all of my actions in the last few weeks and okay, yeah, I could see where things have been a little crazy. I've been a little distant with so much on my mind while worrying about this whole trip, but I've always been me, haven't I?

Not being able to sleep, I turned the flat screen on and stared at the commercial break. I got up to get a beer out of the fridge, hoping that after one or two I could get to sleep. I twisted off the top and threw the bottle cap into the trash can, then make my way into the living room. I sat down, got comfortable and started flipping through the channels. After looking for a while, I finally gave up, tossing the remote onto the cushions. I took a sip of my beer as I watched a scene of a Hawaiian beach come on.

"Do you need time away from everyday life and stress? A weekend of pampering, exquisite dining, and a day of soaking up the sun ..."

I huff, taking another sip of my beer as I continued to watch. I recognized the room, the beach, the spa and I couldn't stop thinking about Tatum and everything that happened yesterday and how I've been behaving lately. I was feeling really low about ruining our Valentine's Day trip. I shouldn't have behaved in such a manner; it was immature and totally ... well ... not me.

I smiled at the thought of Tatum being right. I mean, was me taking her there in my nature in the first place? No, it wasn't. I'm very old fashioned and like to do special things for her, I always have. But, to me it's the things I do for her from the heart that makes her happy and, in return, it makes me happy. That's why we've always gotten along so well from the first day I met her. She appreciates the small things I do for her instead of some posh Inn like the one we went to yesterday. I remember when I told her I reserved a room at the Inn, I was so excited to tell her, thinking it was what she really wanted, but was it? I looked back now to the day I told her.

I came home from taking a tour of the Inn after I made reservations, scheduled our massages at the spa and couldn't wait to tell her. I saw that the twins were down for a nap and Tatum was cleaning the kitchen from lunch, singing to the music playing in the background. I snuck up behind her and snaked my arms around her waist. She jumped, dropping a plastic sippy cup into the sink.

"Oh, Lance, you scared me!" she exclaimed, laughing, then continued cleaning the dishes.

"Sorry," I said, kissing her cheek. Then, I backed away and leaned on the counter.

"So, guess what I did this morning?" I asked impatiently.

"Hmmm ..." She thought about it for a second before closing the dishwasher. Then, she turned around to face me. "You got the screen to repair the back door that the twins stuck their fingers through?" she smirked.

I laughed. "Yes, babe, I got the screen," I agreed, "but, I also did something else." I winked.

"What?" she asked, drying her hands off with the dishtowel.

"Mrs. Mitchell," I said as seductively as I could, slowly walking up to her. "I just so happened to check out that Inn you and your friends talk about so much."

"You did?" she asked, shocked.

"Yup," I said, smiling, "and I made reservations for us for Valentine's Day!" I fist pumped the air.

"Oh wow! You did?" she asked. "How exciting is that?"

"Right?" I smiled.

Apparently, I was so excited thinking that's what she truly wanted I didn't pay attention to her tone. She was happy, but her eyes didn't sparkle, and well, she didn't do what most women do—shriek, bounce up and down, etc.

I continued to think about that day and the following few weeks up until Valentine's Day. As the days passed, and the more I thought about leaving Madeline and Tane, the more nervous and distant I became. I could also remember Tatum not really saying much about going, except to her friends when they came over the following day to visit. The girls freaked with envy, and ... well ... Tatum was just said, "Yeah, I can't wait."

I don't think she truly wanted to go. I think she wanted something that I planned, something that I truly wanted to do for her. Lavishing gifts and surprises on her are nice as long as they come along with a lavished plan of your own.

"I got it," I said to myself. Why was I so blind to all of this after so many years with her? She didn't want me to take her to the Inn, she wanted me to bring the Inn … to her. *Hell, yes!*

***

I was up pretty much all night coming up with an elaborate plan to give Tatum the Valentine's Day she always wanted. Before Tatum and the twins came down, I was already at work, preparing for that night, for in the Mitchell household, it was going to be Valentine's Day.

I went to a chic place that sells smelly good things like candles, oils, lotions … things of that nature. I purchase some oil for her massage, candles for not only the Mitchell Spa, but for the heart I am going to light in the sand behind our home. It may not be a private beach, but tonight, it will be.

I ran to the grocery store and bought the groceries I needed for dinner and breakfast in the morning. I picked out her favorite wine—Pinot Noir—and five dozen red roses.

I made it home in time to see that Tatum was backing out of the driveway. I stopped next to her and rolled down my window.

"Daddy!" the twins say.

"Hey, babies, where are you going?" Yes! She was leaving! Perfect!

"Were going to meet Lainey at the mall," she said, smiling.

"Well, I'll see you when you get home, have fun," I replied, smiling back.

I mouthed "I love you" as I rolled up the window and she mouthed "I love you" back. She didn't seem so mad at me anymore. She probably just needed a night to cool off, but it didn't matter, as this was something I needed to do for her ... and for me.

I stayed in the car until I saw her disappear out of sight. Then, I quickly hopped out of the truck and got everything out of the backseat. If I was lucky, I had a few hours until she and the kids got home. I excitedly let myself in and turned on the music. Cleaning time ... I roll up the sleeves of my plaid shirt and got to work.

I was running through the house like a chicken with my head cut of, cleaning like a maniac. I found half-eaten cookies under the couch, dirty socks in random corners of rooms and empty toilet paper rolls in every bathroom. I am such a pig! I can't believe I do this to her and not think twice about it. I grab the glass cleaner and go to town squirting and wiping every surface I can see has a fingerprint, a smudge, a ... what is that? Ugh, I scrub harder. Then, I ran into the laundry room and saw a heap of clothes in the laundry basket. I reached in, grabbing everything I could get my hands on, then ran to the washer and shoved it in. The load was so big that it got stuck at the top. I yanked, trying to get it out when the clothes give and someone's wet pajamas smacked me in the face.

"Ah, God! Come on now!" I cried out, wiping my face with the bottom of my shirt.

A little over an hour of vacuuming and mopping later, I'm done with the house work. I stood with my hands on my hips, spinning around in circles, admiring my ability to clean up. Then, I looked down at my watch. I had less than an hour to go before they get home, so I hustled and started dinner. I add water to a large pan and turned up the heat before adding spaghetti sauce to another. I buttered the French bread, then added a dash of garlic and parmesan cheese. I quickly spread the red roses all over the dining room, which I made into an official spa. I threw a sheet over the dining room table and voila! Who knew? I set the oils out and lit the candles on the table, then dimmed the lights and turned the satellite radio to a soothing station. I closed my eyes and felt the spa I was in yesterday ... perfect.

I ran back to the stove and added spaghetti to the boiling water and stirred the sauce a few times and threw the French bread into the oven. Then, I covered the sauce and quickly ran out back to set the table up on the patio. I placed a silk table cloth over the table, then candles, our china out of the cupboard and crystal wine glasses. With the added touch of the plastic plates, and sippy cups, I smiled. Next, I grabbed the silver bowl Tatum's mother had given us on our wedding day and filled it with ice and shoved the bottle of wine inside and set it on top of the table. I took a step back, admiring my handiwork. Perfect!

Hurrying as fast as I could, I quickly drained the noodles, turned the sauce down low and pulled the French bread from the oven and set it onto the counter. Dinner was done. I grabbed the bag off of the counter that had about fifty tea lite candles in it and ran toward the sandy shore and placed each one deeply into the sand, forming a heart. I stood up and licked my thumb, holding it out to the air ... no wind. *Alright!*

With the weather cooperating, I lit them and saw that I made a perfect, blazing heart. I stared at it for a moment; the flickering flames are hypnotizing. I think back to the first day I saw Tatum in the diner—biting her lip, her eyes sparkling— and smiled. I couldn't help but be nervous about everything that happened with my brother three years ago. The thought of losing her or the twins makes me go mad. I would walk to the ends of the Earth for them if I had to, but for right now, I settled with being over anxious.

The crashing of the waves against the shore snapped me out of my thoughts. I looked down at my watch again and could see that I was cutting it close ... too close. Running toward the house, I tripped through the sand and fell flat on my face. I lifted my head and open my mouth, letting sand fall from my mouth. I coughed and spit several times, but to no avail. I stood and dusted myself off, and ran into the house. Swiftly, I took a red rose from one of the many vases around the house along with a few tea lites I had left and headed up the stairs toward our bedroom. I burst through the door and pulled the petals off, then scattered them all over the bed and onto the floor. Next, I ran to the bathroom and shoved the empty stem into the trash, poking myself with a thorn.

"Ah, jeez," I said under my breath, shaking my hand.

I suck on my finger as I started the shower and quickly stepped in, letting the spray of water blast into my mouth to try and get rid of the rest of the sand. I jumped when I heard Buster bark outside over the noise of my shower and gasped, sending water down into my lungs ... choking. Then, I bent over to cough and smacked my forehead right onto the knob of the shower.

"Ah, God! Why?!" I say aloud, holding my forehead. I could still hear Buster barking outside. "Stupid dog," I mumble to myself as I stepped out of the shower. My forehead was still throbbing as I threw on a nice pair of jeans and a white button down shirt, then I rolled up the sleeves, and ran my fingers roughly through my hair ... done. I. Am. Done.

Now, I wait ...

***

I sat on the couch for a good twenty to twenty-five minutes, flipping through the channels with the sound on mute, listening to the serene sounds of the rainforest humming through the speakers. I suppose I underestimated the amount of time, as they had been gone for three hours now. My eyes fluttered, starting to close. Now, I could see why they play this stuff in spas.

Then, the car doors closed and I jumped and my eyes flew open wide, quickly turning off the flat-screen television. I rushed to wait in the dining room. I couldn't wait, eager to see Tatum's surprised face. I knew her, and I could honestly say that she would love this.

"Hello?" I heard her say as the front door opened, then bags dropped in the entry way.

"Daddy!" Madeline yelled. "Mommy, I hear birds."

"I'm in here," I hollered back, trying not to laugh. Within seconds, the twins ran into the dining room, finding me first. They stop dead in their tracks when they see the spa—candles, and roses.

"Whoa, Daddy!" Tane said, jumping up and down with excitement.

"Pretty, Daddy!" Madeline said, looking around. "Did we get a bird?"

"Sorry we were gone so long. Lainey found a cute ..." She stopped dead in her tracks when she took in the scene around her and entered the dining room.

"Lance ..." she said, overwhelmed. "This is amazing!"

"Happy Valentine's Day, Tatum," I said, smiling.

"You understood what I meant last night," she said, starting to cry. "This is you, this was all I ever wanted." Then, she walked up and kissed me softly.

"So, Mrs. Mitchell, what shall we do first? Dinner or spa?" I whispered against her lips. *Or possibly some ibuprofen and an ice pack?*

She looked up at my forehead. "Babe, your head! The knot is huge!" She tried to touch it and I winced.

"I hit my head in the shower. I'm fine," I reassured her.

"Seriously, why don't you go lay down and I'll get you some ice," she said, starting to walk away, but I grabbed her and spun her around.

"Babe, I'm fine, I promise ..." I said, kissing her gently. "Now, what should we do first?"

She looks down at the kids hugging our legs. "What do

you think, guys? What should we do first?"

"Spa, spa!" Madeline said, jumping up and down.

"Mommy, what is a spa?" Tane asked, confused.

***

An hour later after I started the massage, the kids fell asleep at the table. Their cheeks were pressed firmly onto the sheet. Both of them were drooling, with oil in their hair and all over their clothes as they insisted on helping with Tatum's massage. We wouldn't have it any other way.

"Babe," I whispered into her ear, rubbing my thumbs up the length of her spine.

"Hmmm," she mumbled.

"They fell asleep," I said, leaning down to kiss her softly on the exposed skin of her neck. "Let's have some dinner."

I carried the kids to the couch and laid them down, careful not to wake them up while Tatum cleaned herself up. I turned to head back to the kitchen, when I saw Tatum staring at me with a huge grin on her face.

"I'm in love with you, ya' know," she whispered.

"I know," I said softly, wrapping my arms around her waist. "Actually, dinner can wait … I have something I want to show you while the twins are sleeping."

"Wait … you mean there's more than this?" she asked. I give her a look as though she should know better and she did. "Of course there is," she answered herself, laughing. I smiled, took her hand into my own and pulled her toward the back door.

I open the sliding glass door and led her out back.

"Lance," she gasped, taking in the restaurant ambiance I put together. "I can't believe you did all of this in such a short time."

"I was actually nervous that I wasn't going to get it all done," I said, clenching my jaw, biting down on a piece of sand.

"This isn't what I wanted to show you … yet," I smirked, watching her beautiful smile grow even bigger.

"First thing's first, though," I said, then leaned over and grabbed a long piece of fabric that lay on the table. "A blindfold," I said, laughing, spinning her around.

I found it very sexy that she didn't object. She didn't sigh … she just kept smiling … a smile that took my breath away … a smile that I hadn't seen in weeks since I told her we were going to the Inn. I was so wrapped up in my anxiousness about leaving the twins that I hadn't even noticed. I carefully led her onto the sand behind our house. We laughed, tripping through the sand, as her fragile hands held onto me tightly until I stop.

"Okay, Tatum, ready?" I asked, holding onto the knot of the blindfold. She nodded, biting her lip, nervous. I quickly undid the knot.

She stared toward the ocean, blinking rapidly for a moment before the flickering of candles caught her eye. She looked down toward the ground. I watched her expression as she stared at the glowing heart in the sand. Her skin radiates under the candlelight as she smiled, but I could also see that she was starting to cry.

"Do you like it?" I asked, almost a whisper.

She looked at me as a tear escaped, slowly rolling down her flushed cheek. "Lance," she sniffed, wiping the tear away. She took a step closer to me until her chest was against mine. "I love it," she said, standing on her tiptoes to plant a soft, sweet kiss on my lips. She turned and took a few steps down the beach to look at the heart one more time.

"I am so sorry that I behaved the way that I did yesterday. I ruined everything," I said, walking up to her slowly, pressing my chest against her back and whispered into her ear, "Please, forgive me."

She turned to face me. "Lance, of course I forgive you. I wanted to go more than you know, but the truth is, I don't want elaborate getaways, spa treatments or private beaches. All I want is you … and this, Lance …" Then, she gestured toward the heart in the sand and toward the house. "What you did for me tonight is you. This is why I love you so much."

I smile. "Really?"

"Do you remember the time you made me my necklace?" she asked, smiling as she touched the Ivory Pikake around her neck.

I laughed. "Yeah, I do." I smiled, remembering how frustrated I had gotten chipping away at the ivory stone, trying to make flowers out of it.

"Right? You worked on this thing for weeks past my birthday," she said, smiling at the memory. "I love you for making things special in your own way and I love you for making me feel special. Expensive things don't make me feel the way you do. You and the twins are all I need."

I sigh. "You know, I would never forgive myself if anything happened to you guys. Because of my brother, I almost lost you when you were pregnant with them. I can't live without you, and I want you to understand why I get so upset about leaving Tane and Madeline, especially overnight. I'm just so sorry that I went to such extremes."

She smiled, placing her soft hand against my cheek. I leaned into her touch and closed my eyes for a moment. "I do understand, Lance. That's half the reason why I was so upset when I found the laptop. I was ignorant to your feelings about leaving the kids," she said, looking at me with sincerity. "I'm so sorry. I love you and I shouldn't have pushed you to go."

"Tatum, don't apologize. You have nothing to be sorry for …"

"Yes, I do," she said, cutting me off, "and I'll never push you to be away from them again, until you're ready. To me, your happiness is far more important than going anywhere without the kids."

"You're amazing, Tatum. You know that?" I asked,

smiling widely.

"I try," she said with a shrug.

I looked toward the house then back at her. "Are you ready for dinner?"

"No, not yet," she said quietly as she looked into my eyes. I get elated staring at the intensity her sparkling eyes. "I think we have a few more minutes."

She took a step closer and wrapped her arms gently around my neck. I wrap my arms around her lower back, letting my fingers caress the warm skin underneath her shirt. Goosebumps rose on her skin as I let my fingers explore the softness of her back. Then, I kissed her for a moment and wrapped my arms around her, pulling her tightly to my chest. Not saying a word to one another, we were just enjoying having each other in our arms. We stayed like this for a moment, watching the sunset.

"I could stay like this forever," she whispered.

"Me too," I said, content.

"Why in the three and a half years that we've lived here together have we never watched the sunset?" she asked curiously.

"I guess we never took the time," I replied with a sigh.

"Can we start making time?" she asked, laying her head on my shoulder.

I rested my cheek on the top of her head. "All we have is time."

***

"Mmmm, this is far better than the restaurant, Lance," Tatum said with a mouthful of pasta.

I gave her a look as I took another sip of my wine. "You're just being modest," I said, smiling, sliding another piece of bread onto her plate.

"It's good, Daddy," Madeline said as she shoves a forkful into her mouth. Hungry, they both woke up after we went inside.

I looked over at Tane to see him just going to town, not taking a second to breathe. In repetition—noodles, bread, sippy ... noodles, bread, sippy.

"See?" Tatum laughed.

"Want some wine, babe?" I asked as I poured more into my crystal glass.

"Ah ... no, thank you. I'm seriously full," she said, leaning back against her chair, groaning.

"Okay," I replied, smiling at her before digging into my dinner.

"Daddy?" Tane asked.

"Yeah?" I said, taking another bite of my pasta.

"What is Vawentine's?" he asked, his mouth full of garlic bread.

"It's the day that you show someone how much you love and appreciate them," I answered, squeezing Tatum's hand.

"Is that why you had us color?" Madeline asked, ripping her bread apart.

"Absolutely! Why don't you kids go and get your pictures you made?" I asked them.

I watched as they hopped off the chairs and disappeared into the house.

"They made me something?" Tatum asked, ready to cry.

"Of course they did," I replied, leaning in to kiss her cheek.

"Here, Mommy!" they yelled in unison as they ran out of the back door nudging each other with their elbows.

"Mine first, Madewine," Tane whined.

"She wikes mine better!" she argued, knocking him with her hip.

"Now, now, I love them both," Tatum said, smiling with her hands outstretched. "On the count of three, you both put you're pictures in my hands and I'll look at them both at the exact same time."

They nod. "Otay," I just sat back, smiling as I watched

Tatum take control. I could never have asked for a better wife or mother for my children. She amazed me every single day.

"Okay, ready?" she asked as the twins nodded expectantly. "One ... two ... three." Then, they quickly placed the papers in each of her hands.

"Thank you," she said, kissing them both on the cheeks.

"You're wewcome, Mommy," they replied.

Tatum held the pictures out in front of her, admiring their glued on hearts, glitter and scribbles.

"These are fantastic! I love them both," she said, smiling at Tane and Madeline.

***

After cleaning off the table out back, blowing out all of the candles and putting away all traces of the Mitchell Spa, I loaded the dishwasher while Tatum gave the kids a bath, getting them ready for bed. I insisted on cleaning everything up for her so she could relax.

"I should pay you," Tatum said, laughing behind me. I stopped cleaning and turned around to look at her.

"What?" I ask, laughing.

"You're seriously spoiling me tonight," she said, bending over to pick up the sippy cup off the floor. Then, she set it in the sink and grabbed the broom and started sweeping. "Thank you, Lance."

"You're welcome, babe," I said. I rinsed out the cup and placed it into the dishwasher, then turned it on. I watched as she dumped the dustpan into the trash and placed the broom back into the closet by the fridge.

"Did the oil come off easily?" I joked.

"Yup, it sure did," she said, smiling, "although I'd have to say that it made for an awesome Slip-N-Slide for the twins in the bottom of the tub after the water drained."

I laughed. "Seriously?"

She nodded. "Oh yes ... *wee!*" She sang, imitating the

twins as we both laugh.

"Oh, wow …" I said, composing myself. "I love you, Tatum." I said thoughtfully.

"I love you, too," she replied, leaning against the closet door.

"Are you ready for the rest of your Valentine's Day?" I asked, taking her hand into mine, leading her to the bedroom.

"Is there a time when my Valentine's Day ends so you can have yours?" she asked sweetly, halfway up the stairs.

"What … you got me something?" I asked, feigning shock, but I wasn't really surprised. She always gets me little surprises here and there.

She laughs. "Shut up! You know I have something for you," she said as I laugh with her.

Then, we stop at the bedroom door. "You didn't go into our room while you were up here earlier, did you?" I asked, searching her eyes.

She shook her head and smiled. "Nope," she laughed. "Although I was very tempted to."

I grinned, sweeping her off her feet, then carried her into our bedroom as Tatum laughed the entire time.

I laid her onto the bed as she slowly released her hands from around the back of my neck and looked around the room. Her eyes lit up as she took in the red rose petals and candles.

"I would hate to ravish this amazing set up you have got going on here, but I have to say, Mr. Lance Mitchell, that you are looking seriously sexy," she said, rolling her tongue across her upper lip while throwing a few red rose petals at me. I couldn't help but laugh. She was never like this. I was blushing. "Do you think it's funny?" she asked me seductively, leaning over to trace her finger along the rim of one of the many lit candles I had around our room. Then, she sat up straight, took off her shirt and let it fall to the floor. "Why, I do believe you're blushin'," she said in a thick, country accent.

I looked at her intensely. Utter pleasure coursed through my veins as I watched her. "No, I don't find it funny."

"I didn't think so," she said and stood up to takes her jeans off, then kicked them at me. She sat back down onto the bed and scooted back against the pillows gracefully. Anything this girl does is always satisfying to watch.

I watched her with my mouth hanging open, smiling at her seductively while I undid the buttons of my shirt. I let it fall to the floor exposing my chest and stomach. Her lust-filled eyes trace every inch of my tanned skin as I knelt on the bed and crawled toward her. But before I reached her, she sat up again and took off her bra. She screamed as I pounced on her, laughing hysterically. She was just too sexy for her own good.

***

I washed the oil off her back with a sponge and kissed trails across the top of her shoulders, as she leaned her head back into my chest and groaned.

"You are too good to me," she said softly.

"I'd have to say you treat me fairly well yourself," I replied, smiling.

"So, is my Valentine's Day over with yet?" she asked, sitting up to look at me.

"It doesn't have to be," I smirk. "Nope."

"Well, then you're just going to have to wait," she said, matter of fact. "I'm enjoying this way too much." Then, she turned around and pointed to her back. "Wash," she demanded.

"Oh, really?" I laughed, raising an eyebrow. "You're demanding me to wash your back?" I laughed out loud again.

"Yes," she said sweetly. "I am."

I kept sponging her back as I watched her head slowly tilt to the side. "What's up?" I ask her.

"Babe, do we have strawberries?"

I placed a strawberry in her mouth and she took a bite.

"Aw, so good," she mumbled with a mouthful of juicy strawberries. She held one up to my mouth and I ate the entire thing, green leafy top and all.

"Oh, ewe!" she said, laughing. "Gross!"

"I got a reaction out of you though, didn't I?" I smirked. "You're turn. Eat it." I try to take on the demanding roll, but it didn't turn out the way I hoped. I laughed, pressing the leafy green part to her mouth. She couldn't help but shriek, laughing. Then, she ducked, trying to get away from the strawberry.

"It's good, just try it!" I insisted, but she was still laughing as I pressed it to her lips again. Then, she started tickling me.

"Oh, yeah?" I asked, completely unphased by her wriggling fingers wedged into my armpit as I hover above her. "You want to be tickled then?" Without waiting for an answer I tickle her neck, ribs, inner thighs and feet.

"Please ... stop," she yelled, laughing uncontrollably.

"What's that?" I ask as I tickled her feet.

"I can't take it, stop!" Then, she sat up and grabbed me by my bicep. I turned to her and purposely made a funny face. She just smiled and kissed me passionately. I let my tongue taste the sweet strawberry she ate just moments before our tickling war.

"Do you think this is what Lainey meant by being teenagers again?" she asked against my lips.

"Absolutely," I said with a smile.

***

I woke up as Tatum rolled over and laid her head upon my chest. I looked down at her and saw that she had strawberries on her face, in her hair ... and it was all over our sheets. It's all I could smell.

"Good morning, babe," I said quietly, as the twins were

still asleep.

"Mmmm, morning," she said, smiling. "My face is sticky," she said, giggling with her eyes still closed.

"So is your hair," I giggle, trying to run my fingers through it.

"Ouch," she whined, then smacked my chest lightly with her hand.

"Sorry," I replied, smiling. I was staring at her face when it hit me. "You seriously devoured those strawberries last night."

"I did. They were so yummy," she said in a baby voice and snuggled up tighter against me.

The last time I saw her go to town on fruit like that was when she was pregnant with the twins. Then, it was apples and bananas.

"If I didn't know any better, I'd say you have one cookin'," I said again. That was the first thing I said to her when I noticed her eating habits when she was first pregnant. I was right, too. She was nearly six weeks along.

She laughed and sat up, blinking her eyes open. "You still need your Valentine's Day present," she said, watching me thoughtfully.

I reached up and rubbed her cheek softly with my thumb, trying to wipe away a strawberry seed. "Oh, that's right … well, let's have it," I said, sitting up, rubbing my hands together excitedly.

"I'm pregnant," she said, smiling broadly. "Happy Valentine's Day!"

***

Look for Impassioned *also by Molly Bryant, published by Write More Publications.*

Acknowledgements

A special thank you to the authors
featured within this anthology, and who
came up with this idea!
Kudos, everyone!

Rebecca Boucher
Molly Bryant
Stephanie Greenhalgh
Theresa Oliver
Jennifer Paquette
Amber White,
Elaine White
J.S. Wilsoncroft

It was a pleasure to work on this project
with you all!
Looking forward for more to come!